"Miss Parker, do y...

"I can think of better use... than talking."

Eden blinked, and the mouth... dropped open. "Ex-excuse me?"

"I said, there are other things to do with your mouth than talking."

"Oh. I see." She was staring at *his* mouth, which, strangely, seemed almost soft, tempting. "Other things," she echoed idiotically.

"You want me to show you?"

Did she nod? She wasn't sure. If she did, she shouldn't have. Yet if she didn't, she wanted to. But whether she nodded or not, it happened anyway.

Jared's mouth descended on hers.

Eden gasped. Then sighed. It was wonderful. It was heaven. It was the kind of thing that only happened in sexy novels...and it was happening to her.

Dear Reader,

Welcome to Silhouette Special Edition...welcome to romance. We've got six wonderful books for you this month—a true bouquet of spring flowers!

Just Hold On Tight! by Andrea Edwards is our THAT SPECIAL WOMAN! selection for this month. This warm, poignant story features a heroine who longs for love—and the wonderful man who convinces her to take what she needs!

And that's not all! *Dangerous Alliance,* the next installment in Lindsay McKenna's thrilling new series MEN OF COURAGE, is available this month, as well as Christine Rimmer's *Man of the Mountain,* the first story in the family-oriented series THE JONES GANG. Sherryl Woods keeps us up-to-date on the Halloran clan in *A Vow To Love,* and *Wild Is the Wind,* by Laurie Paige, brings us back to "Wild River" territory for an exciting new tale of love.

May also welcomes Noreen Brownlie to Silhouette Special Edition with her book, *That Outlaw Attitude.*

I hope that you enjoy this book and all of the stories to come.

Happy Spring!

Sincerely,

Tara Gavin
Senior Editor

Please address questions and book requests to:
Reader Service
U.S.: P.O. Box 1325, Buffalo, NY 14269
Canadian: P.O. Box 1050, Niagara Falls, Ont. L2E 7G7

CHRISTINE RIMMER

MAN OF THE MOUNTAIN

Silhouette®

SPECIAL EDITION®

Published by Silhouette Books
America's Publisher of Contemporary Romance

For my dear cousin, Gail Clemo,
who looked out for me when I started out—
and when I started over

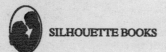 SILHOUETTE BOOKS

ISBN 0-373-09886-3

MAN OF THE MOUNTAIN

Copyright © 1994 by Christine Rimmer

This edition published by arrangement with Harlequin Enterprises B. V.

® and TM are trademarks of Harlequin Enterprises B. V., used under
license. Trademarks indicated with ® are registered in the United States
Patent and Trademark Office, the Canadian Trade Marks Office and in
other countries.

Printed in U.S.A.

CHRISTINE RIMMER

is a third-generation Californian who came to her profession the long way around. Before settling down to write about the magic of romance, she'd been an actress, a salesclerk, a janitor, a model, a phone sales representative, a teacher, a waitress, a playwright and an office manager. Now that she's finally found work that suits her perfectly, she insists she never had a problem keeping a job—she was merely gaining "life experience" for her future as a novelist. Those who know her best withhold comment when she makes such claims; they are grateful that she's at last found steady work. Christine is grateful, too—not only for the joy she finds in writing, but for what waits when the day's work is through: a man she loves, who loves her right back, and the privilege of watching their children grow and change day to day.

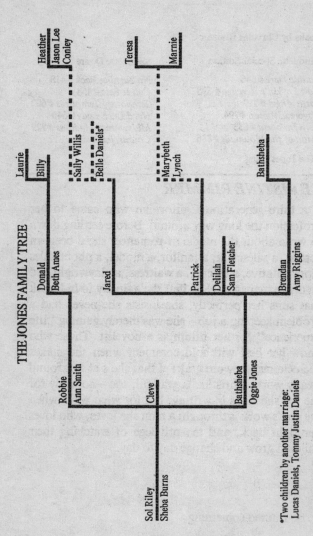

THE JONES FAMILY TREE

*Two children by another marriage:
Lucas Daniels, Tommy Justin Daniels

Note: Broken lines indicate previous marriage(s).

Chapter One

Eden had no idea what woke her. Perhaps a strange sound. Or maybe just a feeling that something wasn't right.

She stirred and turned over, then fitfully turned over again. But changing positions did no good. Sleep had fled. With a little moan, she rolled to her back and slowly opened her eyes.

A man stood at the foot of her bed.

Eden gasped.

And then she realized what must be happening. She must still be asleep. She *thought* she saw a man. But it was only the shadows, only the last after-image of an already forgotten dream.

She closed her eyes again, sure that the man would be gone on a second look.

When she opened her eyes the man was still there.

He murmured something.

Eden made no sense of his words. Her heart had just kicked into overdrive. It seemed to expand in her chest. Her mouth tasted like old pennies. Her blood roared in her ears.

She sat up, rubbed her eyes, looked again.

He was still there. Oh God, still there...

This couldn't be happening. Not here, not in her darling little cabin by the river in lovely, safe North Magdalene.

Disoriented, terrified, Eden glanced down and beheld her own long legs gleaming palely in the darkness. It had been a hot night, and she'd drifted off without pulling up the sheet. Now her legs were visible all the way to the hip because her sleep shirt had ridden up. And *he* could see exactly what she could see—which was way too much.

Yanking down the hem of her shirt, Eden scuttled back against the headboard, tucking her legs up under her, trying vainly to hide them from his view.

Cowering there among the pillows, shaking all over, she demanded, "Wh-who are you? What do you want?"

"An answer." He stepped around the end of the bed.

"Don't you come any closer!"

He swore softly. "What the hell's your problem? Settle down." He took another step toward her.

Frantic, she stuck out a hand for the night table, groping for something—anything—to use in her own defense. Her fingers found the hard, firm shape of her old-fashioned windup alarm clock. She grabbed it and raised it high.

"You get back from me. Don't come any closer. I mean it!"

"Put that damn thing down."

Her heart was pounding way too fast. Adrenaline slammed through her system, beckoning her to give in to pure hysteria. She was trying desperately to keep her head, not to let herself admit how far away she was from the next house and how unlikely the chance that her cries for help might be heard.

The intruder gave a low, disgusted grunt. "Put it down, I'm warning you." He took another step.

That did it. For Eden, it was either take action, or start shrieking like some helpless victim in a bad horror film. Eden was no victim. She hurled the clock.

And then, not pausing to see if she'd actually hit her target, she shot off the bed on the other side and headed for the door.

She didn't make it.

She heard the clock bounce on the little throw rug by the bed and then something snared her sleep shirt. The shirt stretched like a huge rubber band. She prayed it would tear. It didn't.

Grunting, the intruder hauled her in with a jerk, wrapping an arm that felt like a steel band around her the minute he had her close enough. She spun and found herself plastered against a hard, broad chest.

"Why you little—"

"Let me go, you creep! Let go!" She pounded his chest and kicked at his shins.

"What the hell is the matter with you? You're crazy—oof!"

There. She'd done it, kneed him close enough to his privates that he flinched. She tore backward.

But the man was an octopus. He held on. They toppled to the floor in a tangle of arms and legs. Her sleep shirt slithered up. She could feel the hard length of him, all along every inch of her struggling body. Once or twice, she felt the harsh scrape of his boot. She fought on and she fought hard, scratching and punching and squirming with all her might.

But the intruder was as hard as tempered steel, as lean and sinuous as a snake. And Eden Parker, slim and strong as she was, was simply no match for him.

With unfailing, unswerving determination, he subdued her. He redirected her. He slithered out of her way. And yet somehow he managed never to let go of her.

How long she fought him, Eden didn't know. Time lost all meaning in the battle for survival, for self-protection.

But eventually, she felt herself weakening. Her blows had less and less effect. He managed to capture both her wrists, forcing them over her head and pinning them to the floor.

His body was like a lead weight on top of hers, pressing her down. Exhausted, she panted and squirmed, hating her own lesser strength. She knew she had to keep her mind clear. She had to be ready for any slightest chance he might give her to get free.

Her cruel captor panted, too, his hard chest moving in and out against her own. "Are you done?" he muttered in a harsh growl.

"I'll never be done. Never," she managed to say between painful gulps for air.

Then, unable to look at the shadow of him, her unknown attacker, so close above her, she turned her head so her cheek touched the floor. She shut her eyes. She wasn't giving up, oh no. All she needed was a few more good breaths and she'd be ready to fight again.

But then, just as she closed her eyes to concentrate on regrouping, she felt it. She felt *him* down there, where the placket of his jeans was pressed so unmercifully against her womanhood. He was growing hard....

"Oh, no," she moaned in desperation.

He swore, crudely and succinctly.

And then he reared back on his knees.

Eden blinked, not understanding his withdrawal when she had feared the worst. And then she realized that right now was the chance she'd hoped for.

She rolled, then scrambled to her knees.

"Oh, no, you don't," he muttered grimly. He grabbed her arm and yanked her to her feet. Then he groped with his free arm for a moment, until he found her brass-backed vanity chair. He spun it around and shoved her down in it, flicking on the vanity table light at the same time.

For a moment, now that they could both see more than mere shadows and shapes, they stared at each other. To Eden, he looked just as she'd expected him to look: hard and mean and dangerous. His grim slash of a mouth was set in an ungiving line. His steel gray eyes were slits.

She saw with bleak satisfaction that her makeshift weapon had actually hit its mark. A trickle of blood dripped down above his left eye. As she watched, he swiped the blood away with a forearm. She stared at that arm, noticing the ropy tendons in it, the complete lack of any softness to it.

She thought how lean he was, too lean. There wasn't an ounce of fat on him. He was all tendon and muscle and bone. Like a wolf or a junkyard dog, he looked hungry, ready for anything—and not an animal that should be let in the house.

He muttered another invective, then demanded, "Don't you have a robe or something?"

The question totally bewildered her. "Huh?"

"A robe." He looked at her as if he wondered what she used for brains. "Do you have a robe?"

"Yes, I...on the back of the door."

He whirled and saw it. Then he strode to it, grabbed it off the hook behind the door and tossed it at her. "Now for godsakes, cover yourself."

Eden just gaped at him for a moment. If he intended to rape her, then why would he—?

"Do what I said. Put on that robe."

"O-okay. I will. Sure." Swiftly, gratefully, she stuck her hands into the sleeves of the robe and gathered it close about her.

"Now talk," he demanded in that low, sibilant voice of his.

"A-about what?"

"Answer the questions I asked you before."

"Y-you didn't ask me any questions."

He drew in a long breath and then he spoke very slowly, very patiently, the way a man does when he's trying to hold himself back from doing something he'll regret. "Yes, I did. I asked you two questions when you first woke up. Before you attacked me with that damn clock."

Eden frowned. "What questions?"

"I asked who you are—and what the hell you're doing in my house."

Chapter Two

"**Y**our house?"

Eden's dazed mind struggled to comprehend what he was telling her. That he was no rapist, that he wasn't even really an intruder. That he *owned* the cabin.

She stammered out, "But if this is your house, then you must be..."

She peered at him more closely. Yes, she could see it. A little of sweet old Oggie around the mouth and something of Heather, who had rented Eden the cabin, in the determined set of the jaw. She swallowed.

"Er... Mr. Jones?"

His gunmetal eyes stayed narrowed. His mouth remained grim. But he did grant her a slow nod. "Right."

"You're... Heather's dad, Jared Jones?"

He grunted in acknowledgment.

Eden just couldn't believe it. Relief that he was not what she'd feared, coupled with embarrassment at what had just happened between them, loosened her tongue.

"But you live out in the woods. By yourself. You hardly ever come to town. You're a *hermit* . . . "

As soon as the word was out, Eden regretted her own tactlessness. It seemed rude to call a man a hermit to his face, even if it was the truth.

She felt her cheeks flushing, looked away and then added defensively, "Heather said the last time you came to North Magdalene was four months ago. When your sister, Delilah, married Sam Fletcher."

"So?"

She faced him again. "So what in the world are you doing here now?"

He gave another grunt. "You ask too many damn questions." Then he was the one looking away.

"I think I have a right to ask some questions. After all, you broke into my house—"

"*My* house."

"—in the middle of the night. And you—"

"Look. Could you just put a lid on it for a few minutes here?" He rubbed the back of his neck. "Give a man a chance to think."

She stared at him, frustrated and bewildered. "Think. You want to *think*. . . . "

"Yeah."

"Great. Fine." She raked her hair back from her face. "You just think."

He made another of those grunting sounds and sank to the edge of the bed. Wincing, he prodded the tender spot over his eye.

She watched him, feeling a slight twinge of guilt and hoping she hadn't hurt him too badly. Reluctantly she decided she probably should apologize for smacking him with the clock, though there was no doubt that what had happened was more his fault than hers.

She offered, "I'm sorry that I hit you."

He granted her a doubting glance. "You still haven't told me who the hell you are."

She tucked her robe more closely around her and made herself sit straighter. "I'm Eden Parker, a friend of Laurie's."

He said nothing, but just looked at her with that strange flat expression.

She heard herself reminding him, "You know, your second cousin, Laurie Riley?"

"I know who Laurie is. Where do you come in?"

"I told you. I'm Laurie's friend."

"I mean, how do you know her?"

"Laurie and I met in Sacramento, where she goes to college." He went on staring. She elaborated, "You did know Laurie's going to college in Sacramento?"

He nodded. He was peering at her mouth. One corner of *his* mouth was lifted just slightly, in a sort of wary, silent snarl. She thought again of hungry wolves and wild dogs.

Though she was no longer exactly afraid of him, the way he kept watching her made her nervous.

"Look. It's very simple, really. We met because Laurie needed a part-time job." Eden found that the sound of her own voice soothed her nervousness a little, made this whole bizarre situation seem a little less strange. She prattled on. "I'm sure you know how expensive college is in California these days. Even though her folks are paying the tuition and basic expenses, Laurie couldn't get by on that alone. So she applied at La Cantina. That's a Mexican restaurant on Howe Avenue."

"So?"

"So that's where we met. I was the manager there and I hired her. And we just hit it off from the very beginning. Right away, we became best friends." She forced what she hoped was a cheerful smile.

"So you're just visiting here, then?"

"No, I live here."

"Since when?"

"A few months ago. Laurie brought me up here for a visit. And I just...fell in love with this place. And with your family, too. You really do have a terrific family. And I was looking for a change in my life. So I decided to leave my job in Sacramento and move up here. I needed a place to stay and Laurie said you told Heather to rent this cabin if she could find a trustworthy tenant. So I met with Heather and—"

"That was two years ago."

"Excuse me?"

"It was two years ago, when I told Heather to rent this place."

"Well, I know but—"

"I've been back half a dozen times since then and my place is always right here, waiting for me. Until now."

Eden looked at him sideways. It was becoming painfully clear that Jared Jones was not happy with the news that he had a tenant.

Well, if he didn't like it, then *he* had a problem. She had a signed agreement that said she had every right to be here.

Eden drew herself up. "Mr. Jones. From what I understand, most of the time you're not an easy man to find. I'm sure Heather intended to tell you that she'd found you a tenant as soon as you gave her the chance."

"Yeah, great. But that doesn't do me a hell of a lot of good right now."

"What do you mean?"

He gave her another of those brooding, snarly looks of his.

She prompted, "Well?"

Instead of answering, he looked away.

Eden had the impression he was deciding how to proceed from here, and that until he *had* decided what he was going to do, she'd be lucky to get even one more surly grunt out of him.

"Oh, never mind," she supplied unnecessarily.

Then *she* fell silent. And since Jared Jones wasn't much of a talker, the room was suddenly deathly quiet.

In the soft light from her vanity table lamp, Eden stared at his rugged profile. As she stared she realized she still had no idea what this man had thought he was doing, appearing at the foot of her bed in the middle of the night, scaring several years off her life.

She said pointedly, "So now you know all about what *I'm* doing here. But you haven't said a word about what you thought *you* were doing, a total stranger to me, appearing at the foot of my bed in the middle of the night. I have to tell you, I've never been so terrified in my life. What was going through your mind? You must have realized that when I woke up I would be frightened out of my wits, but still you—"

He pinned her with those piercing eyes again and waved a hand for silence.

Generously Eden held her tongue for a moment, waiting for him to explain himself. But he didn't explain a thing. He just sat there on the bed, glaring at her as if *she* were the intruder instead of him. Then he poked at the cut over his eye again.

Right then, it occurred to her that after bopping her landlord on the head, she probably ought to patch him up. Even if she had only thrown the clock in what she'd honestly believed was self-defense.

"You should put some ice on that," she suggested, trying for a sympathetic tone and somehow ending up sounding abrasively cheerful.

He shot her a pained look. "Never mind. It's fine."

She said nothing for a moment. And then she made up her mind to do what *she* thought was best, not what *he* told her to do.

"I'll get the ice." She stood up.

"I said forget it."

It was a simple thing to pretend she hadn't heard him, since she was already out of the chair and halfway to the door. She marched through the big living area, around the end of the stairs that led up to an open sleeping loft and straight to the kitchen. There, she flipped on the light and set right to work knocking ice cubes from a tray to wrap in a hand towel. As she was arranging the ice on the towel, she noticed a flicker of movement out of the corner of her eye. It was him.

She glanced his way, thinking that it was the next thing to creepy, how quietly he could move around. She hadn't *heard* him follow her at all. She'd simply happened to turn her head when he came in the room.

Small surprise, after all, that he had been able to enter the cabin, find his way to her bedroom and stand at the foot of her bed for heaven knew how long without her even knowing it. And actually, the more she thought about it, the way he'd entered the house *and* her bedroom without her knowledge really did aggravate her.

She spoke a bit harshly. "Sit down at the table. I'll be right back."

"Look, I said I—"

"Sit down," she told him and swept past him, not deigning to check to see if he did as she ordered. She strode to the cabin's one bathroom and found the first-aid kit she kept in the medicine cabinet. Then she returned to the kitchen.

He'd done as she'd told him and was sitting at the end of the table. His expression was no longer quite so stony as before. Now, if she had to define his look, she'd probably call it glum.

Well, she decided, it didn't matter how he looked. She was going to patch him up and find out what, precisely, he was doing here and then send him on his way. To that end, she set down the first-aid kit on the table and then crossed to the sink to collect her makeshift ice pack.

"What did you do with my stuff?" he said in a flat voice as she returned to him.

Eden was instantly defensive. "What stuff?"

"You know, my furniture. The clothes in the closets. My pots and pans."

"*I* didn't do anything with it. Oggie took care of all that before I moved in. I understood he was going to store everything for you." She held out the ice pack.

He ignored it. "You're on a first-name basis with my dad?" He looked up at her, both eyes slitted and one of them swelling perceptibly because of the injury she'd inflicted.

Eden's irritation with him increased, partly because he wouldn't take the darn ice pack. And partly because he was right. She most definitely was on a first-name basis with Oggie Jones. And she suspected that Jared Jones was not going to be pleased to hear the exact nature of her relationship with his father.

"Your dad is my friend. He's about the sweetest old guy I've ever met."

Jared Jones snorted in response to that, then looked away. Her irritation at him increasing, Eden slapped the ice pack down on the table. He glanced at her again, a very superior glance.

Eden seriously considered turning on her heel, striding to her bedroom and locking herself in for the rest of the night. But that would solve nothing. Judging by his behavior so far, Jared Jones would probably still be here at dawn if she did something like that. She'd emerge from the bedroom to find him snoring on the couch. After all, he'd entered without even bothering to knock. And even when he'd found out who she was and that she was a legal tenant, he still hadn't left. It was going to take more than walking away from him, she feared, to get him out of the cabin so she could get back to sleep.

But before she got rid of him, she was going to disinfect that wound. She'd caused it and she would treat it, whether he welcomed her efforts at nursing or not.

Resolutely she opened the first-aid kit and took out a sterile pad. She doused the pad with hydrogen peroxide.

He was slouched in the chair, his legs aggressively spread. She pointedly slid around him, moved to his left side and nudged his thigh with her knee. He had the grace to pull his legs together so she could get near without stepping between his thighs.

She began swabbing the wound. Up close, she could see that the cut was only minor. The bleeding had almost stopped. But he was going to have a real shiner by tomorrow. Already, the swelling flesh was turning the color of a ripe plum.

"There. All clean," she murmured.

He gave a small shrug. "Fine." He started to duck away from her.

She caught his shoulder. "Wait."

He looked up at her. All at once, she was acutely aware of the feel of his shoulder beneath her hand: lean, sharply contoured, as strong as tempered steel. She picked up the scent of him, an outdoorsy scent, like evergreen and leather and dust.

His expression was very strange. She couldn't read it at all, but suddenly she was pondering things that, until that moment, she'd been very careful not to consider in any depth.

This man had watched her as she slept. He had wrestled her to the floor of her bedroom and subdued her. He had been pressed against her intimately. And he had become physically aroused.

She let go of his shoulder as if the heat of it burned her.

He was still looking in her eyes. "What?" he asked.

She frowned at him, feeling a slow warmth creeping up over her cheeks. She hadn't the faintest idea what he was asking her.

He reminded her. "You said to wait. What for?"

"Oh. Right." She glanced away, then back, hoping he hadn't noticed her blush. She made her tone very business-like. "Because I have some antibiotic ointment. I'll put a little on the scratch."

"Not necessary. It's fine."

"It'll only take a second." She edged around his knees and took a little foil pouch from the kit. Then she moved back into place at his side and squeezed the contents of the pouch onto the cut.

In spite of his protests, he allowed this final ministration, remaining very still and seeming to look off toward a far corner of the room as she bent over him. One of her fingers touched his cheekbone. His skin there had a rough, new-beard feel. Her knee accidentally brushed his thigh. It was as solid as granite. She felt bewildered suddenly, to be so very conscious of this rough stranger, of the scent of him, of his hardness and his strength.

"All right. Is that it?"

She stepped back, conflicting emotions playing leapfrog inside her. "Unless you'd like a bandage."

"No."

"Well, okay then. that's all." She swiftly gathered up the contents of the first-aid kit and took it back to the bath-room, where she put it away.

When she returned, he was still sitting in the kitchen chair where she'd left him.

She stood in the doorway and sighed. What to do now? The clock on the kitchen wall said it was 2:15 a.m. She wanted to return to her bed. Yet Jared Jones was infuriat-ingly unforthcoming about what he was doing here. And he was showing no inclination whatsoever to be on his way.

Eden decided to take one more crack at polite inquiry. "Does . . . anyone else know you're in town, Mr. Jones?"

He tore his gaze away from the far wall to give her another of those expressionless stares of his. "You talk a lot."

She took a deep breath, released it slowly and kept her voice calm and unchallenging. "Yes, I do talk a lot when I'm nervous, Mr. Jones. And, in this situation, you really can't blame me for being nervous. After all, you—"

He waved a preemptive hand. "Look. Let's cut through the chitchat here. I don't know any other way around this situation but to tell it to you straight. It's like this. Things have changed. I don't want to rent this place after all. You'll have to move out."

Chapter Three

Eden rubbed her eyes. She'd suspected this was coming, when he'd seemed so annoyed at the news that he had a tenant. But still, to hear him actually say the words made her very, very tired.

She slumped against the doorjamb, feeling put-upon. First, he'd terrified her half to death, then he'd wrestled her into exhausted submission, and now he was telling her that she was evicted.

Well, he had another thing coming, and that was all there was to it.

She was the soul of reason when she spoke. "I'm sorry, Mr. Jones. But you can't just order me to leave."

"What do you mean? I'm doing it, aren't I?"

"I have a signed rental agreement."

"So?"

"So you are required by the terms of that agreement to give me sixty days notice to vacate the premises."

"Lady, it's only a piece of paper."

"It has your own signature on it, as well as mine. Heather said you gave it to her when you told her to look for a tenant."

"That was then. I've changed my mind since then."

"Well, apparently you never bothered to inform your daughter."

"Look. I need a place to live."

Eden blinked, confused by what his words implied. Was this more than a visit? Did he actually plan to live here? Jared Jones was supposed to be through with towns and people, from what everyone in his family said. But he was talking as if he intended to return here to stay.

Well, if he is moving back to town, Eden thought, he'll have to find another house. She remained firm. "I need a place to live, too."

He stood up. "You can move out tomorrow."

"How generous of you." She folded her arms across her breasts. "Forget it. I'm staying. I get sixty days notice to vacate, and I intend to use them to find another place."

He took a step toward her, his lip curling in that mean-dog snarl again. "You keep jabbering about that damn contract. What do you think you are, a lawyer?"

Eden eyed him warily, but refused to back down. "No, I'm no lawyer. But I do have a legal right to be here. For at least another two months."

"I want my house back."

"Well, that's just too bad."

"I oughtta . . ."

"You ought to what?" she challenged, keeping her chin up and her shoulders back. "Spy on me in the middle of the night? Terrify me out of my mind? Tackle me and knock me down and . . . sit on me and fight with me until I'm too tired to fight anymore?"

"I did not sit on you."

"Right. But you did everything else. We both know what you did. And you *still* haven't said why you came in my room and just stood there. And I'd also like to know, exactly how long *were* you standing there?"

"Not long. A minute or two. Hardly any time at all."

"Right. I'll bet."

"You are a damned irritating woman."

"Fine. So answer my questions. Or get out of my house."

"*My* house."

"Okay, *your* house that *I'm* renting. *Your* house that I don't have to leave until sixty—count 'em—*six-o* days after you serve me formal, written notice to vacate."

He was less than two feet from her now, glaring and snarling and looking like he could snap her neck with his bare hands and not think twice about it. For several seconds, they stared each other down.

And then, with a low, enraged growl, he whirled around and stomped out the kitchen door.

Eden stood where she was and stared at the place where he had been and didn't know whether she felt shaken or triumphant.

Jared Jones had a reputation as a hot-tempered man. It was said of him that he never came to town without getting in at least one good fistfight—and more likely than not, precipitating a brawl. Of course, it was also said that he would never hit a child or a woman and that he was as protective of women as he was distrustful of them. So it was probably unlikely that he would have actually hurt Eden, no matter how much she had goaded him. Still, after witnessing the seething rage in those pewter eyes, she knew she'd been taking a chance to taunt him like that.

But it had been worth it, she told herself. Because she had made him so mad, he left. Now she could go back to her bedroom, crawl beneath the covers and get what was left of a decent night's sleep. Outside, Eden heard a vehicle door slam.

Over on the table, her homemade ice pack had begun to drip. She went and got it and emptied the melting ice cubes in the sink, then she wrung out the towel and laid it over the counter rim to dry. While she did all this, she was listening, waiting to hear the engine start up and the crunching of tires on gravel that would mean Jared Jones was driving away.

Those sounds never came.

Instead, moments later, the kitchen door was thrown back and he strode in once again. This time, he was carrying a backpack in one hand and a sleeping bag slung over his shoulder.

Eden longed to scream. But she didn't. She asked, "Just what do you think you're doing?"

"I'm beat. I'll sleep in the loft."

"But you can't just—"

"I won't bother you at all. Go back to bed."

He brushed past her and headed through the door that went to the living area and the stairs that led up to the loft. Eden stared after him with her mouth hanging open, thinking she ought to chase after him and *demand* he leave the cabin this instant.

But then she reconsidered. It *was* late. And it wouldn't really put her out at all for him to roll out his sleeping bag on the guest bed in the loft. Beyond that, this *was* his house, even if she had a legal claim to stay in it. And he *had* returned here thinking he would find it vacant. And he was Laurie's second cousin. And Oggie's son . . .

He had already disappeared in the shadows overhead before she collected herself enough to march to the foot of the stairs and call up to him, "All right! But just for tonight!" He didn't bother to answer. She had no idea what he was doing up there. Perhaps laying out his sleeping bag—or peering down at her from the shadows with a smug grin on his face. She added, "And if you want to use the bathroom, please do so right now!"

That got a response. "Fine, I will!"

"Well, good night, then!"

"Good night!"

Not knowing what else to do, Eden returned to her room. She was careful to engage the privacy locks on both the door to the hall and the one to the bathroom. She found her alarm clock on the floor and checked it for dents. There were none. Then she reset it for an hour later than usual and put it back on the little table by her bed. She took off her robe and climbed in beneath the covers.

A few minutes later, she heard water running in the bathroom, which had another entrance in the main part of the cabin. She also heard the toilet flush.

And then there was silence.

A pair of squirrels jabbering and chasing each other up and down the big fir tree outside her open window woke Eden the next morning. Then the alarm chimed in.

Eden reached out and silenced the clock. After that, she got up on her knees at the head of the bed and leaned on her brass headboard to watch the squirrels for a while. The squirrels scampered like furry trapeze artists, following each other from limb to limb, letting out their urgent, breathy squirrel noises, sounds that made Eden smile.

Overhead, the sky was pale blue and clear. And though it was only nine o'clock, the air was already warm. Today would be another scorcher, by North Magdalene standards. It might even hit a hundred at the height of the afternoon.

But Eden wouldn't suffer from the heat, nor would her customers over at The Hole in the Wall Saloon. Since June, thanks to Eden, The Hole in the Wall had boasted air-conditioning.

She'd been insistent about putting in central air, explaining to her new partner, "Oggie, it's an important investment. People have to be comfortable. Especially if we want to draw in a wider range of clientele."

Oggie had let out one of his cackling laughs. "You mean less lowlifes, more regular folks."

"Well, Oggie. I mean, since we're the only game in town, if we spiff things up a little, appeal to the ladies as well as the gentlemen—"

"Gentlemen?" Oggie cackled again. "What gentlemen? We ain't never had no gentlemen around this joint."

Eden grinned to herself, thinking of Oggie. The cagey old charmer was just such a sweetheart. He was crotchety and crude and full of naughty jokes. Yet his heart was as big as the whole Sierra Nevada mountain range. Eden had adored him from the first.

"Hell," Oggie had said. "It's your money, gal. If you wanna spend it on air-conditioning, then you go right ahead."

Eden had begun collecting estimates that very day. And now, when the mercury got near the triple figures, people in town often came into the tavern just to cool off a little from the heat of the day.

Yes, The Hole In The Wall was a lot different than it used to be. Eden was proud of the improvements she'd made there. She'd done a lot in a very short time.

Outside, the squirrels dashed out of sight. From the bathroom Eden heard water running, the shower this time.

With a sigh, she fell back on the bed and closed her eyes.

For a few moments, she'd succeeded in forgetting about Jared Jones. But the respite was over.

This morning, one way or another, she had to deal with him. She had to get his agreement that he'd let her have the cabin for sixty days. Or at least until she could find somewhere else to live.

She also knew she should break the news to him about her partnership with his father. But that was something she wasn't looking forward to at all. In fact, it got her heart going a little too fast just thinking about telling him.

She'd been informed by more than one person in town that Oggie had promised to leave The Hole in the Wall to Jared when he died. Of course, she'd gone right to Oggie when she heard about that. And Oggie had given her several reasons why she shouldn't worry about Jared. So she *hadn't* worried about Jared.

Until now.

"Relax, Parker," she muttered to herself. She reminded herself firmly that she had no reason to feel guilty. She had done nothing wrong.

"So why do I feel so... reprehensible?" Eden asked her own reflection in her vanity table mirror.

She had no answer for herself. So she pulled on her robe and went out to turn on the coffeemaker, so the coffee would be ready whenever her uninvited visitor wanted a cup.

Eden took a quick shower after Jared left the bathroom. She dressed swiftly for work in black slacks, a man-tailored white shirt with a string tie and a black vest. She slid her feet into low-heeled black shoes. Then she pinned up her chin-length strawberry-blond hair. For work, she wore it off her neck, but loose and curly around her face.

After that, she went out to the kitchen and set about making breakfast. She fried bacon and toasted bread. She set the table for two and mixed up a can of frozen orange juice. Judging by the level of the coffee in the pot, Jared had already been into the kitchen once or twice. She was counting on the smell of frying bacon to bring him downstairs again.

He came just as she began cracking the eggs in the pan. Again, she caught a glimpse of him coming through the door before she heard a sound. It was really amazing how silently he could move around.

She beamed him a smile. Today was a new day, after all. Maybe they could start it off by being pleasant with each other.

"How do you like your eggs?"

He didn't smile back. "Cooked."

She refused to be less than cheerful. "Over easy is fine, then?"

He grunted.

She decided that would have to do for a yes. "How many would you like?"

He went to the coffeemaker and refilled his cup. Then he turned and leaned against the counter with a kind of rangy, ready grace that made her distinctly uncomfortable. The eye she'd smacked with the clock was swollen shut and the color of burgundy wine. His good eye, though, could see just fine. It made a slow, roving pass from the top of her curly head to her trim black flats and then back up again. "What kind of getup is that?"

"I'm dressed for work."

"What kind of work?"

As soon as she told him, she'd have to explain about the partnership. She evaded his query. "Do you want eggs or not?"

"Yeah."

"How many, three? Four?"

He sipped from his coffee again. "Sure. Four." She set about frying the eggs, all the while waiting grimly for him to quiz her more about the work she did. But he seemed to have become more interested in the meal she'd prepared than in her job.

He looked at the table, at the two place settings, the carafe of orange juice, the tall stack of toast and the bacon, crisp and brown on a serving plate. "What are you up to?"

"Look." She pointed her spatula at him. "Do you want these eggs I'm cooking or not?" This time, she didn't bother to keep the edge from her voice.

He considered. Then he shrugged. "Yeah, sure. I want those eggs."

"Fine, then." She gestured at the chair across from the one where she liked to sit. "Sit down there."

He slid in where she'd told him to and got right to work pouring himself a big glass of juice and piling bacon slices on his plate. Then he grabbed the jam and slathered some on a slice of toast. He shoved the toast into his mouth and stuck a couple of slices of bacon in right after it. Then he grunted in satisfied pleasure as he chewed with stolid concentration, grabbing more toast to pile with jam at the same time.

To Eden, he looked just like what she knew he was: a logger who'd been out in the woods too long, a man who ate most of his meals off of a tin plate with a bunch of other snorting, grunting loggers for company.

She wrapped the pot holder around the handle of the frying pan and carried the pan to the table, where she dished up her single egg first. Then she moved around to his side of the table.

"Excuse me," she said.

He looked up at her in midchew, his mouth so full he looked like an huge, greedy chipmunk—with a black eye. "Ungh?"

Eden sighed and shook her head. "Mr. Jones, what would your mama say?"

The effect of her words was immediate. Jared swallowed, wiped his mouth and hands on his napkin and then smoothed his napkin over his lap. Then he sat up very straight.

"Uh, pardon me," he said sheepishly.

Eden smiled sweetly down at him. "That's quite all right."

It was amazing, really, what mentioning his mother could accomplish. It was that way with the other two Jones boys, Patrick and Brendan, too. Oggie and the boys had worshiped Bathsheba Riley Jones and though she'd been dead for almost a quarter of a century now, one still had only to refer to her in passing to elicit mannerly behavior from any one of her rowdy sons—or her widowed husband, for that matter.

Carefully, Eden slid Jared's four eggs onto his plate.

"Thank you," he said, when she was done.

"You're very welcome."

Eden carried the pan back to the stove and then, after pouring herself a fresh cup of coffee, joined Jared at the table. They ate in silence for a few minutes. And then Eden decided to make another attempt at reaching some sort of understanding with him.

"Jared?"

"Yeah?" He was spreading more jam on yet another piece of toast. He did it slowly and with great care.

"You know, you really did, um, surprise me last night."

"Yeah."

"And, I really would appreciate knowing . . ."

"What?"

"Well, for one thing, why, exactly, did you arrive so late?"

Jared bit into the toast and chewed with extreme conscientiousness. Then he swallowed. Then he answered, "Decompression time," before he took another careful bite.

"What do you mean?"

Jared shot her an impatient scowl. But as soon as he finished chewing, he explained, "I wanted to get in and get settled before I had to deal with any people. And the only way to do that in North Magdalene is to sneak in after midnight with your headlights off." He put the last of the toast into his mouth and patiently began chewing again.

Eden watched him for a moment. Truth to tell, she was longing to remind him of how frightening it had been for her to wake to the sight of him looming over her bed. However, she wanted him to be reasonable about the cabin.

And she wanted him to be in a good mood when she told him about her business arrangement with his father. So as far as last night went, she'd probably better let bygones be bygones.

She continued with her tactful inquiry. "So then, you're planning to move back to North Magdalene?"

Jared narrowed his good eye at her. "Haven't we already been through this?"

"Well, yes. But I'm still trying to understand. Why would someone like you suddenly decide to live in town again?"

Jared shook his head and wiped his mouth with his napkin. Then he stood. "Lady, there's a question mark coming at me every time you open your mouth." He picked up his plate and carried it to the sink.

Eden turned in her chair. "I just feel it would be good for us to come to some sort of agreement about—"

His dish and juice glass clattered into the sink. He turned on her. "Get this straight. It's my business why I do things. What matters to you is I'm back and I'm staying. Here. In *my* house."

Eden sighed. So much for trying to get along with him. She took her napkin from her lap and tucked it beneath the rim of her plate. Then she pushed back her chair and stood.

"Where the hell do you think you're going?" Jared Jones demanded.

Eden said nothing. She calmly strode from the room and straight to her little desk by the big window in the living area. From the desk, she took her copy of the rental agreement. Then she returned to the kitchen, where Jared Jones stood, glowering hatefully, by the sink.

She marched right up to him and waved the agreement under his nose. "Not until my sixty days are up, you're not," she said.

"I could rip that thing to pieces right now."

"But you won't. I know you Joneses. You can be mean and rough, but you're not cheats." She gave the agreement another taunting wave in front of his face.

He grabbed her wrist. "You *think* you know us Joneses."

Eden blinked. His grip seemed to burn her. His palm was rough, scratchy against the tender flesh of her wrist. One side of his mouth had lifted, in that half snarl of his.

"L-let me go," she said, the command sounding shaky and breathy and not convincing at all.

He exerted a little more pressure on her captured wrist, enough to bring her up closer, so he could warn in a too-soft hiss, "You oughtta watch yourself, Miss Parker. You wave a red cape in front of an angry bull, you just might get gored."

She could smell the coffee on his breath, and the soap he must have used when he showered. His face was smoother than last night. He must have shaved. . . .

"You listening to me?"

"Y-yes." She swallowed. "I heard every word you said."

"Good." He breathed the word almost tenderly.

His mouth was very close. She had no idea where the thought came from, but it was there: just the slightest lift of her chin, and their lips would meet. . . .

She asked, "Jared?"

And he blinked. Then he seemed to shake himself. He let go of her wrist. That broke the spell. She was able to step back.

They regarded each other. Eden was trembling. She wanted to order him out. She wanted to throw herself against him.

Again, she recalled the way he had lain on top of her last night. This time, it was more than a recollection of her own terror and, later, her embarrassment, more than the knowledge that he had physically responded to her. This time, she pinpointed her own reaction.

She could desire this man.

Could desire him? Sweet Lord. She *did* desire him, right now.

And it was crazy. It was totally inappropriate. Completely out of line.

He said, in that voice of his that was as soft and deadly as the hiss of a rattlesnake, "I don't like this. I don't like it one damn bit."

She didn't need to ask him what he meant. She knew exactly what he meant. He didn't like this . . . magnetism between them any more than she did.

She said, "I agree. Look. Forget the rental contract." She crumpled it into a ball and tossed it in the sink. "Give me the rest of the month, okay? Two and a half weeks. I'll find another place and be out by September first."

He measured her with his undamaged eye, as if trying to decide whether he should trust her. "Let me think about it."

Then, without another word, he turned for the door.

Eden stared after him for a moment, as her baffled mind registered the fact that he was walking out, just like he had last night, abruptly and without so much as a "See you around."

"Hey, wait! Where are you going?"

He opened the door and went through it.

"Take your things with you!"

He didn't even pause. Instead, he closed the door behind him. Outside, she heard the slamming of a vehicle door. Shortly after that, she heard the vehicle start up and drive away.

Chapter Four

Fifteen minutes after he walked out on Eden, Jared Jones shoved back the door of Lily's Café. He was looking for his daughter, who had worked the morning shift at the café five days a week for the past year and half.

Heather was there, all right, standing over by the cook's window, buttering toast fresh from the toaster. Jared's heart swelled a little at the sight of her. More and more every time he saw her, she resembled her mother, Sally, who had been dead for seven years now.

Right then, as he was thinking how much his daughter looked like her mother, Heather turned with a plate of toast in her hand and saw him. Her hazel eyes—Sally's eyes—lit up. Her smile was Sally's smile.

"Dad!" She tossed the toast on the counter in front of Rocky Collins. Rocky, who spent most of his waking hours at The Hole in the Wall, gasped in pain at the slight clattering sound that the dish made. Jared guessed he was nursing a hangover, as usual.

Heather bounced around the end of the counter, arms outstretched. "Dad, this is great. It's been too darn long."

Jared hugged his daughter, moved as he always was each time he saw her. She had turned out to be such a nice, warm, open person.

Heather was twenty-one now. She was married to Jason Lee Conley, her high school sweetheart, and she was about the happiest person Jared had ever know. Around town people called her Sunshine, because she always had a smile on her face. Jared knew lots of people marveled that a kind, sweet young woman like Heather could have had a malcontent like himself for her dad. After Sally died, he'd finished raising her himself. And the way she had turned out was about the only thing in his life of which he was truly proud.

Jared pulled back enough to look down at Heather. "Got a minute?"

"For you, anything." She was still smiling, but the smile wavered now. She was getting a good look at what Eden Parker had done to his eye. She called over her shoulder, "Lily, I'm going outside! I'll only be a moment!"

From beyond the cook's window, Lily shouted, "Don't be all day!"

"Five minutes, max, I promise!" And then Heather was grabbing his hand and towing him through the swinging doors that led to the kitchen and the rear entrance.

There was a bench right outside the back door, in the bright morning sun. Heather sat down on it and pulled coaxingly on Jared's hand so he would join her. He dropped down beside her.

Right next door to the café was Santino's BBV—Barber, Beauty and Variety. Jared said nothing for a moment as he watched Maria Santino, who ran both the *Beauty* and the *Variety* parts of the store, lean out an upstairs window and shake the dust from a throw rug. The Santino family lived on the upper floor. Mrs. Santino spotted Jared and Heather and gave them a wave. Jared nodded.

Heather called, "Hi!" and then tactfully waited until Mrs. Santino had disappeared inside. Then she asked quietly, "Dad, are you okay?"

"Fine."

"But you've... had a fight, right?"

He gave his eye a careful tap. "You mean this?"

She nodded, looking subdued and concerned.

"No, not a fight. Not exactly, anyway."

"Then what?"

"Look. It wasn't a fight. And no one else was hurt, so you don't need to worry."

"You mean you don't want to talk about it?"

"You got it."

"Okay, Dad." Heather closed her eyes, turned her face up to the sun and waited. She was a hell of a girl, his Heather. She knew when to keep her mouth shut—unlike some people he could think of.

Jared remembered she had to return to work in a few minutes, so he went straight to the point. "I hear you rented my cabin."

Heather's eyes popped open and she looked at him. "Did I do wrong?"

"Well..."

Heather was all contrition. "Oh, I *knew* I should have waited to talk to you first."

"Then why didn't you?"

"Oh, Dad. A lot of reasons. I never know when you'll show up, for one thing. And Eden's such a terrific lady. And Grandpa and Laurie—heck, everyone in the family, really—thought it was a great idea. And Grandpa made it so easy. He stored your things. He also insisted that there's no reason you can't stay with him whenever you come to town. And also, I thought you'd like the extra money."

Heather sighed. "But I should have waited, I can see that now."

Awkwardly Jared patted her hand. "It's okay, honey. You only did what you thought I wanted. Don't worry. I'll work it out."

"Dad?" Heather peered at him anxiously. "You didn't...scare Eden, did you? You didn't show up at the cabin in the middle of the night and order her out or anything...did you?"

He coughed. "What do you mean, *scare*?"

Heather looked at him for a moment more, then shook her head. "Oh, Dad. Is she okay?"

Jared snorted. "More okay than I am."

He watched Heather's face and saw understanding dawn. "Oh, my goodness. *She* punched you in the eye?"

"Not really. She threw a clock at me."

Heather clucked her tongue. "That Eden. She's something."

Jared leaned his head back against the wall of the café and wondered why he couldn't get more sympathy from his own flesh and blood.

Heather asked, "Dad, I know this is a crazy notion. But since you aren't happy about having a tenant at the cabin, is it possible that you're thinking of moving back to town?"

He took a minute before he answered. "Yeah."

She stared at him. "Really? You're moving back to town?"

"Right."

"Oh," his daughter said.

That *oh* told Jared everything. When he'd left for the woods two years ago, he'd sworn it was for good. He'd vowed he was through with towns and people, that an occasional visit to civilization was about all that he could take. Judging by his daughter's shock at the news that he was coming home to stay, he realized he must have been very convincing back then.

But that had been a rough time for him. It was right after Belle, his second wife, had taken her two sons and returned to her first husband. He'd had to get away from people then, because he'd been as sensitive as a skinned rattler and every bit as mean. It had gotten so he could hardly walk down the street without ending up in a fight. And he'd been tempted—God, how he'd been tempted—to go back on the booze again.

But things were different now. He was ready now to try once more to get along with the rest of the world.

Beside him, Heather slowly smiled. "Well, okay. Now that I've had a minute to consider the idea, I think it's great, Dad. I'm glad. I've missed not having you around."

Jared squeezed her shoulder. "I've missed you, too. And besides, I've been thinking a lot about your grandpa lately. The past few times I've been to town, he's done nothing but complain that he's overworked running The Hole in the Wall alone. I think it's about time I helped him out a little. After all, the tavern will be mine someday. And he needs to start taking it easy. He's not getting any younger, you know."

Heather was looking at him strangely. "But Dad, I..." She seemed to run out of words.

"What?"

"Er... nobody's told you yet?"

"Told me what?"

Lily chose that moment to stick her head out the back door. "Heather, are you here to work or yak?"

"Be right in." Heather stood up. "Look, Dad, I—"

"I mean it, Heather," Lily insisted. "You got two new couples in the booths and three singles at the counter. They're all gettin' seriously irritated that they ain't even got coffee yet."

"But I—"

Jared took his daughter by the shoulders and turned her toward the door. "Don't be losing you job over me, Sunshine. We can talk later."

"Yeah," Lily said. "Like after her shift's over."

"Okay, Lil," Heather said just a tad curtly, "I will be there in one minute."

"You better," Lily growled, but she did leave them alone.

Heather turned back to Jared. "Dad, I—"

He cut her off. "It's okay. Whatever it is, it can wait a few hours."

"Sure. I guess so." Heather looked doubtful. "Just... um, stay calm, okay."

"Yeah. No problem."

She was smiling again, somewhat ruefully. And then she was going up on tiptoe to kiss his cheek. "Love you. Come for dinner tonight. Six sharp. I'll get Jason Lee to barbecue us some ribs."

"Sounds like a great idea."

"Does that mean yes?"

"You bet."

Jared watched as Heather disappeared through the door into the café, wondering what it could have been that she thought he should know yet was nervous about telling him.

Well, whatever she was afraid to tell him, he'd find out soon enough. This was North Magdalene, after all. And in North Magdalene, secrets lasted about as long as an ice cube in a forest fire.

Jared lifted his wrist to find out what time it was and realized he'd run off without his watch, an oversight he blamed on the redhead who'd stolen his house. Because of her, he'd been in a hell of hurry to get out of there. Grabbing his watch had been the last thing on his mind.

He shaded his eyes and checked the position of the sun: around ten. His father, still a night owl even now in his seventies, would be unlikely to show up at The Hole in the

Wall until at least noon. Ten to one, the old coot was still sprawled on his bed, snoring away.

Jared decided it was time Oggie woke up. So he walked around the side of the café, climbed into his pickup and headed down Main Street.

He had to pass The Hole in the Wall before he made the turn that would take him to his father's house. One look at the bar his father had owned since before Jared was born, and Jared knew something really strange was going on.

The tavern was transformed. There was a fancy sign out front that announced The Hole in the Wall in lariat script. Red café curtains hung in the spic-and-span windows. And the several layers of paint that had been peeling off the exterior of the building the last time Jared had seen it were now completely camouflaged by new wood shingles.

Jared swore roundly under his breath and managed to swerve just in time to avoid hitting the fire hydrant on the corner. He was damned anxious to have a few words with the old man now. Something was definitely going on. More and more, it looked as if Oggie would be the one who could tell him just what it was.

When he pulled up in front of the house where he'd grown up, he wasted no time. He jumped out of the pickup and marched up to the door, which he banged on for a good minute to give the old man a chance to get his butt out of bed. Then he waited, expecting a rumpled, grouchy Oggie to fling back the door and swear at him for disturbing an old man's slumber. But that didn't happen.

He tried the door. It was open so he went on in.

A quick pass through all the rooms proved that Oggie wasn't there. So Jared went out back to check the garage. Not counting the usual clutter, he found it empty. Oggie's ancient Eldorado was nowhere to be seen.

Jared stood in the driveway and rubbed his chin. Then he climbed back in his pickup and headed for Main Street once more.

* * *

At exactly ten-thirty, Eden parked her car in the small lot behind The Hole in the Wall. She got out of the car and did *not* lock it behind her. That was another thing she loved about North Magdalene. You never had to lock up anything. No one ever stole anything here. It simply was not done. She let herself in the back way with her own key and set about getting ready to open up at eleven.

Inside, the tavern was as dim and shadowy as most bars, but much cleaner and more welcoming than it had been before Eden became Oggie's partner. Eden smiled to herself in satisfaction at the scrubbed-clean bar and tables and the deep shine she herself had waxed into the hardwood floor. She glanced up in approval at the new molded ceiling. She'd paid for it and had it installed not too long ago. The old one had been riddled with bullet holes. Oggie used to be forever shooting holes in it with his .38 special, trying to get his customers' attention long enough that they'd break up whatever brawl happened to be going on at the time.

Since Eden had become Oggie's partner, there had been no brawls.

Yes, Eden had done a heck of a job with the place. And next spring, when she opened up The Mercantile Grill in the vacant landmark building next door, people would be coming from the small towns all around the area to enjoy an evening of good food and good times in the charming gold rush town of North Magdalene. Feeling quite satisfied with herself and her plans, Eden went about counting the take from last night and setting up the cash drawer for the day and evening ahead. She had the drawer in order and was sliding it back into the register, when she thought she heard the back door squeak.

She turned around and peered into the shadows of the hall that led to the door. But she saw no one, so she shrugged and went out to the main floor to take the chairs off the tables, where Oggie left them each night after mopping up.

A moment later, she turned around again and came face-to-face with Jared Jones.

Eden gasped in frightened surprise. And then she realized who it was.

"What is the matter with you?" She exerted great effort to keep her voice calm. "Can't you enter a room like a normal human being?"

"Sorry." He didn't look sorry at all. He immediately demanded, "And just what the hell are you doing here?"

Eden glared at him. She was getting tired of the way he kept popping up out of nowhere every time she turned around. Also, she was not looking forward to his reaction when she told him why she was here. She wished she had told him earlier, as she'd meant to, right after he'd finished that nice breakfast she'd cooked for him. Now, in the dimness of the deserted tavern, with him scowling and fuming at her, seemed altogether a bad time.

Well, to be honest, anytime was probably a bad time.

She decided to put off answering him, though she knew that in the end there was no escaping his finding out. She turned her back on him again and continued taking down the chairs.

Jared wasn't about to be stalled. He grabbed her elbow. "Answer me, damn it." He whirled her around to face him.

And their eyes met.

And it was happening again. The exact same way it had happened this morning, only more intense. As sudden as a flash fire and every bit as hot, it arced between them. A searing burst of sexual heat.

"Damn," he muttered darkly. He tugged her up closer, so her breasts just grazed his hard chest.

Eden felt her nipples tightening, a sweetly agonizing sensation that set off an answering awareness in her most private place.

"Oh, no," she whispered on a breath.

"Damn," he said again.

Then, heaven knew how, she found the strength to pull away. He didn't try to stop her. In fact, he let go and quickly stepped back from her.

Shaken, weak-kneed, she patted her hair, which he'd never even touched. Then she pulled herself together and forced herself to take down the last of chairs.

She was careful, as she did this, not to look at him. And anyway, she didn't *need* to look at him. She knew exactly what he was doing. It was just what she was doing. He was trying to put that instant of hunger and desire they'd just shared completely out of his mind.

At last he demanded, "Where's my father?"

Lord, she thought, this is an effort. This man is rude and crude. He doesn't even have a good sense of humor. And still I wish he'd grab me and hold me close and put his lips on mine and . . . oh, I can't let myself even *think* what else.

She wanted to tell him to take a hike—almost as much as she longed to move closer to him and see if he'd grab more than her arm this time.

Somehow, she kept her distance and spoke civilly. "If he's not at his house, he's probably fishing. But I don't really know. He's not due in here until seven tonight."

He scanned the large, shadowy room, obviously ticking off the changes she'd made. "How long have you been working for my father?"

"Three months." Eden drew herself up. Then she said the words that she regretted almost before they were fully out of her mouth. "And I don't work *for* him, I work *with* him. We're partners."

The pause that ensued lasted a very long time. Eden stared at his stunned face and accepted the grim fact that she'd really put her foot in it. She truly had meant to tell him about the partnership in a more tactful manner. But a woman would have to be a saint to stay diplomatic around this barbarian.

"*Partners?*" Jared's dismay was painful to look at.

"Yes." From the way he was looking at her, Eden decided maybe she'd be better off to put a little distance between them. She trotted purposefully to the end of the bar. The flap there was up, so she darted through the opening, flipping it shut behind her.

Once she had the bar between them, she dared to face him. He was watching her the way a cat looks at a canary. If he'd had a tail, it would have been twitching. She was acutely aware that the bar would be no barrier at all if he really wanted to get to her.

Jared spoke, his voice low and icy cold. "I suppose you have some damn piece of paper that says you own half this place, just like you've got one that says you can stay in my house."

She knew it would do no good to hedge. She looked him square in the eye. "I've spent most of my savings, between what I paid your father outright to become his partner and the improvements I've made since then. You can be sure I have a contract that says what I *get* in return for what I've spent." Then she added without pausing to consider what the words would imply. "I am not a fool."

Jared leapt over the bar. He did it so swiftly and gracefully that, to Eden, it was as if he never moved, as if he dematerialized in one place and reappeared right in front of her.

"Oh!" she managed to murmur in surprise, before he grabbed her by the arms and yanked her up against his chest. "Are you calling *me* a fool, Miss Parker?" His voice was soft—too soft.

And all those awful, wonderful feelings that seemed to occur whenever he touched her were occurring again.

Eden's last trace of reckless bravado fled. She gaped at him. "No. No, I'm not. I swear to you..."

He breathed the next words into her upturned face. "But you know damn well this place is supposed to be mine someday. You know that it's promised to me when my old man dies, don't you?"

Eden blinked. She was totally disoriented. First, there was the feel of him, so close, his hard chest against her breasts. And then there was his claim about The Hole in the Wall, a claim that she knew had at least some validity to it.

"B-but I was told you never cared about the place..."

"By who?"

"By Laurie. And your father. By your brothers and your sister Delilah. By everybody. They all said you would never come back to live in town and if you did, the last thing you'd want to do was run the bar. After all, you're an..." Eden gulped as the sentence trailed off unfinished.

Talk about tactless! What she had been about to say was way out of line. It was not something any considerate person would throw in a man's face after having known him less than twenty-four hours. Somehow, Jared Jones brought out her most insensitive side.

"I'm what?"

"Jared, look..."

He released her then, setting her away from him carefully—as if she were some sort of human detonating device, dangerous to touch, to be handled with extreme caution.

He stepped back. "No. Say what you were about to say."

"Jared—"

"All right. *I'll* say it." He spoke with great precision. "I am an alcoholic. That is why I do not drink. I haven't had a drink in over fifteen years now. And I have no trouble at all being in a bar for long periods of time without *taking* a drink. In fact, that's exactly what I do every time I come to town. I come here, where most of the bad actors like me hang out. I drink cola. And I manage, in my own low-class way, to have a helluva time."

"Jared, I—"

"I'm not through talking yet."

"O-okay."

"So, my point is, my being an alcoholic wouldn't stop me from running this place. And my old man knows it, too."

"I see. I—"

"And as for that other feeble excuse you just threw at me, that I don't *care* about this bar. Well, Miss Parker, get this. Whether I care or not doesn't matter a damn. What matters is that my father had three sons and one daughter, and he made a promise to each one of us. He promised that when he dies, his house goes to Brendan, the house our mother got from *her* father to Delilah, The Mercantile building next door to Patrick and *this bar to me.*"

Eden swallowed hard and then forced what she hoped was a coaxing smile. "B-but you'll still get *half* of it someday." As she said that, she silently prayed that Oggie would live a long, long time. Being partners with Jared Jones was not her idea of something to look forward to. Jared continued to scowl at her. She babbled on, "I swear, Oggie said it would be okay with you, that you'd be glad to hear he found himself some help."

"And naturally you just took his word for it."

Eden did feel awful. And she knew her guilt could be heard in her voice as she trotted out more justifications. "Your father said you'd understand. I guess I really wanted to believe him. And since there was no trust agreement involved, I didn't question him too much about it. And everybody really did say you wouldn't mind, that as soon as you saw what a good thing this was for Oggie, you'd go along..."

"They all said I'd go along." He repeated her words as if testing their veracity.

"Yes." She lifted her chin. "They did."

Jared peered at her. She felt that he was trying to see into her mind, to ferret out whether she was telling him anything close to the truth.

At last he said, "All right. That makes sense."

"You believe me?" She tried not to sound as amazed as she felt.

"I said it makes sense. And I can see you're not at fault here."

Eden released a long sigh of relief.

But she realized she'd sighed too soon when Jared added, "My father's the one to blame. That old coot, I'll wrap his damn fishing pole around his neck."

Visions of poor Oggie, strangled to death by his own son, flashed through her mind. "Oh, you wouldn't. Not really."

Jared didn't answer. Instead, he jumped over the bar again and headed out the way he'd come in.

"Wait! He's an old man. You won't really hurt him, will you?"

But all she got in reply was the squeak of the back door as it swung shut behind him.

Chapter Five

At the end of Bullfinch Lane, right where he thought it might be, Jared found his father's Cadillac. He pulled in beside the dusty old boat of a car. Then he got out of his pickup and started down the steep path that led to the river below.

When he reached the river's edge he didn't have to look far. To the right of the trail, where the rocks petered out to dirt ground, a big, gnarled oak grew close to the stream. There Oggie sat, his back propped against the oak, his fishing line bobbing on the current a few yards away. The old cheat appeared to be sound asleep.

"Dad?"

Oggie snorted a little at the sound of his son's voice, but he didn't wake up.

"Dad?"

In his sleep, Oggie turned his head away from Jared and his fishing pole sank a little closer to the surface of the stream. Jared started to shake him, but then something made him hesitate.

Jared gazed down at the top of his father's head. He couldn't help noticing that what was left of the old scoundrel's hair was all white now. The wispy strands framed a bald crown dusted with age spots. Oggie's chin drooped on his chest, the loose skin of his neck hanging wattles. His hands, folded on his slightly protruding belly, looked as wrinkled and gnarled as the aged oak he was leaning against, now Jared could see them in repose. Strange, for all of Jared's life, his father's hands had always seemed so swift and sure. No one could mix a drink with the style and grace of Oggie Jones....

"What the hell you gawkin' at, boy?" Oggie turned his head and winked at him. His face was a road map of a long, hard-lived life.

Jared shook himself. He'd almost started to feel sorry for his father. And the last thing a swindler deserved was sympathy.

"You old bastard," Jared accused. "You were awake the whole time."

Oggie chortled. "Ah son, it's good to see your ugly mug. Whoa. That's quite a shiner you got there."

Jared didn't want to talk about the black eye Eden had given him. "I ran into a door."

"Yeah. Right. Where you been keepin' yourself, anyway?" Oggie patted the ground beside him.

But Jared wasn't about to sit down. He wanted the truth. "Why'd you screw me over, Dad?"

"Screw you over?" Oggie yanked his line out of the water and set his pole on the ground. He sat up straighter and assumed an expression of outraged dignity. "Who says I screwed you over? You give it to me straight. I'll beat the livin' daylights out of whoever thought he could—"

"Cut the malarkey, Dad. You took on a partner over at The Hole in the Wall. I know it. You know it. Everybody knows it. You also pushed Heather into renting out my place."

"Now you listen here, Jared Jones, *you're* the one who told Heather to find a tenant and—"

"She wouldn't have done it without you pushing her into it. She would have waited to talk to me."

"Yeah. Sure. And when exactly would that have been? We never know when the hell you'll show up anymore. If we waited to do what needs doin' until after consultin' you, nothin'd get done around here, and that's a plain fact."

"You always promised that bar to me, old man."

"And you'll still get half of it."

Jared snorted. "Half. Thanks a lot. What you did wasn't right."

"I did what I had to do."

"Yeah. What you had to do. Sure. Without even a word to me. When we both know I've got rights to that place, that I've put my own good money in on that place—from the card room at the back to the plumbing to the wiring to that new pool table you just had to have last summer."

Oggie sniffed. "Well, it's right you should put in on what will someday be yours."

"Exactly. Mine. *All* mine." Jared turned from his father, looked out over the river and concentrated hard on staying calm. Right then, his hands were just itching to close around the old fraud's neck.

Behind him, he heard Oggie haul himself, grunting, to his feet. Then he felt his father's hand on his shoulder. "Okay, son. I admit. I acted out of line. I oughtta be gutted and skinned and hung up for quartering."

Jared pulled away from his father's touch. "Damn you, old man. You could have at least let me know what you were planning. You didn't have to let me find it out like this."

"Now listen to yourself, will you?" Oggie pulled a stubby cigar from his shirt pocket. He studied the cigar for a moment, then bit off the end and spit it into the river. "Just think about what you're asking here. How exactly was I to let you know? When you disappear into the woods, no one can find you for months." Oggie gestured grandly with the cigar as he pulled out a book of matches. "You're with a crew up by Tahoe, then you're over near Hayfork. The only way we know you're alive is when a check comes for Heather in the mail. I knew you'd find out when you finally showed up. It's all worked out fine." Oggie stuck the cigar in his mouth and put a match to it. Then he puffed until the end of it glowed red.

Jared stuck his hands into his pockets—to keep from picking up his father and tossing him into the river in front of them. "If you weren't my father, I'd—"

Oggie blew a cloud of smoke and let loose with that watery cackle of his. "Settle down, boy. I always take care of my own, and you know it. You're still gonna get half of that bar. And that little gal I partnered up with has got one fine head for business. By the time I go to be with your mama, the half you get will be worth twice what the whole shebang was before Eden Parker came along. I'm gettin' old, and I'm gettin' tired. I needed a little help around that place. And then Eden showed up. It was like the answer to a prayer."

Now that he had his cigar going, Oggie clamped it between his teeth, picked up his fishing pole and reeled in his line. Then he set about gathering up his gear, pausing only to glance at his son and explain, "You know, this year is the first year since I was knee-high to a horsefly that I've gone fishing. I never had the time before. And I'd like to try to get me a buck this deer season. Truth is, I'm headin' home right now to get down my old huntin' rifle and clean it up nice."

"Damn it, Dad . . ."

"C'mon boy, what's done is done. And maybe it'll turn out just fine in the end anyway. In any case, you'll know your old man's gettin' a little time to himself in his wanin' years."

Hearing his father put it that way, Jared felt all the fight go out of him. Hell, the old man was right. Oggie had needed someone to work with him. He'd said so more than once. Jared had never been quite willing to provide that help. And then Eden Parker had come along.

The simple fact was, Jared had returned too late.

Slowly Jared sank to the ground in the space his father had left and leaned his back against the old tree. He closed his eyes. For a few minutes, there was only the sighing of the wind in the pines and the soft rush of the river flowing past.

Then Oggie asked, "What's happened, son?"

Jared didn't even open his eyes. "The company's shutting down. I've been laid off. I'm through running logging crews. The damn spotted owls are getting their revenge."

Oggie heard his father huffing as he sank beside him. "Hell, son. Tough break."

"Yeah."

"So what'll you do?"

"I'll get by."

"You bet you will."

"And besides . . ."

"Yeah, son?"

Jared picked up a flat rock and skipped it across the river. "Well, just lately I've been thinking it's time I got over what happened with Belle. Time I stopped hiding out and feeling sorry for myself."

Oggie lit up like a light bulb. "Are you sayin' what I hope you're sayin'?"

Jared looked at his father sideways. "What's that?"

"That you're ready to try again at findin' the right woman for you?"

Jared stood up. "Stop it, old man. Stop it before you even get started. Two out of four of your kids are happily married. Be satisfied with that. I'm back because I think it's time I learned to get along with people, in general. But I'm through with *women*. And that means love and marriage and all that bunk. I'm just no good at that stuff, and that's a proven fact.''

"You worked things out with Sally in the end, didn't you?''

"Yeah. I did. But we had a damn rough time doing it.''

"But the point is, you *did* do it.''

"Look, Dad. Let's drop this subject, okay?''

"I'm only saying that you've married two women and you did okay with one of 'em, when all was said and done. In this day and age, one out of two ain't half-bad. And, if you ask me—''

"I'm *not* asking you, Dad.''

"Don't interrupt. If you ask me, the problem with Belle was that you jumped right to the wedding, without stopping to, um, smell the flowers first.''

"Dad. Drop it.''

"No, it's time you thought about this. Maybe part of your problem is you always thought you should be married to a woman before you—''

Jared picked up his father's tackle box and the wicker basket in which the old man's catch was stored and started for the trail to the road.

Oggie, grabbing up his pole, hustled after him. "Wait up. And I don't see why we can't talk about this. I'm only sayin' that if you'd a slept with Belle first, you might have found out—''

Jared turned on his father. "Did *you* sleep with Ma before you married her?''

Oggie's beady black eyes went wide. He stopped on the trail. "What's got into you son, askin' questions like that about your sainted mother?''

"Just giving you a taste of what it feels like to have another man pry into your private life.''

"All right, all right." Oggie puffed on his cigar and waved at Jared to move on up the trail. They walked the rest of the way to the Cadillac without speaking.

Then Oggie went to the trunk and opened it. "You're home to stay, then?"

Jared tossed the tackle box and the basket of fish into the trunk. "I thought so. But I also thought I'd go in with you at the bar. Now, I don't know. Maybe I'll head down to Sacramento, see if I can find something there."

Oggie took his pole apart and tucked the two sections in next to the tackle box. "The hell you will. You'll stay right here." He closed the trunk. "You'll take over your half of The Hole in the Wall now. I got my nest egg put aside. I'm more than ready to retire."

Jared shook his head. "Thanks, Dad. But it would never work."

"Why not?"

"You've got a partner. You don't need me."

"Hell yes, I need you. I'm seventy-five. I need all the help I can get. You got a problem with Eden, is that what we're talkin' about here?"

"No," Jared muttered. "She's fine. I've got no problem with her." He leaned against the dusty back door of the Cadillac and looked away toward the trail they'd just come up.

"Good," Oggie said. " 'Cause truth to tell, son, I got a soft spot for Eden. That sweet little gal kinda reminds me of your mother."

Jared's head snapped around. "My God, Dad. What are you talking about? She's nothing like Ma. Ma didn't have orange hair."

Oggie actually looked kind of dreamy. "That hair of hers is strawberry-blond, boy. Strawberry-blond. And I was talkin' more about her smile, that wide, sweet mouth she's got. And those legs. Why, that gal's got legs longer than—"

Jared wasn't about to hear any more of this. He'd seen Eden's legs. He gave his father a stern look. "For god-sakes, Dad. You're old enough to be her *grandfather.* Hell, you could be her *great*-grandfather. You have to be aware of that!"

Oggie let out one of his raspy cackles. "You always was a bit of a prude, boy. A hell of a temper and a mean man to cross. But more scruples than an old maid, yessiree."

Jared knew he shouldn't ask, but somehow the words were out of his mouth all by themselves. "Have you got something . . . going with her? Is that what you're telling me?"

Oggie looked wounded. "You know me better than that, son. If I had something going with a woman, you wouldn't need to ask me about it. Everyone in town would know it. I'm a Jones, after all."

Jared clamped his mouth shut. He wanted to demand the truth of his father. He wanted to know for certain if Oggie was more than a business partner to Eden Parker. But that was none of his concern and Jared knew it damned well.

And then Oggie volunteered, "Naw, there's nothin' be-tween her and me, son. She thinks of me as a second fa-ther. But an old man can dream, can't he?"

Jared sighed. He felt relief, and he had no intention whatsoever of examining why. He clapped his father on the shoulder. "Hell, Dad. Sure. Why not?"

Oggie got into his car and then rolled down the window. "Look. Give yourself a few days before you head out of town. Think it over, 'cause I really am ready to retire."

"I've made up my mind, Dad."

Oggie started up the car. "We'll see. Tell you what. Fol-low me home. I'll fry you up some fresh trout."

Jared was halfway to his father's house, tagging obedi-ently along behind the Cadillac, before he realized that he didn't trust the way his father had given in so easily, or the sound of the old rascal's voice when he had said, "We'll see..."

But then he shrugged. It really didn't matter what Oggie Jones had up his sleeve. Jared had made up his mind. Miss Eden Parker could have his house after all. He'd be moving on.

Chapter Six

It was well past midnight when Eden arrived back at the cabin. Friday nights were always busy at The Hole in the Wall. Eden always stayed as late as Oggie needed her. She did the same on Saturday nights and any other night when things were jumping. It didn't bother her in the least that she occasionally worked as many as sixteen hours in a day. Eden liked to work, especially since she'd joined forces with Oggie and she was working for herself. Usually a mere thirteen or fourteen hours on her feet didn't daunt her in the least.

But tonight Eden felt distinctly droopy as she got out of her car and trudged toward the natural stone steps that led up to the kitchen door. The events of late Thursday night and Friday morning had gotten to her. And realizing that she was going to have to find another place to live, even though she loved it right here, only increased her weariness.

Her mood was not improved when she saw the pickup truck that was parked, as if it belonged there, beneath a fir tree that grew right by the front deck. It didn't take any serious mental gymnastics to guess whose pickup truck it might be. Eden dropped her key into her purse, since she was sure she was going to find her door unlocked.

But she was wrong. The door *was* locked, just as she'd left it when she went out the previous morning. She'd been careful, as she rarely was anymore, to lock it behind her. Which, now that she thought about it, was pretty silly. After all, the only person who would want to break in had a key of his own. Judging by the pickup under the tree, he'd used it, too. And then added insult to injury by locking Eden out.

All the lights inside seemed to be off. The rat was probably asleep up in the loft. She considered pounding on the door until he answered. But after measuring the paltry satisfaction of disturbing his slumber against the real trial it was to deal with him, Eden decided to let him sleep.

She had to fumble in her bag to retrieve the key. And then, since he hadn't bothered to leave on the light by the kitchen door, she had to fumble some more to get the key into the lock.

Once inside, she half expected him to leap on her from the shadows, demanding to know what the hell she thought she was doing in *his* house. But that didn't happen. She flipped on the kitchen light and saw that everything was pretty much as she'd left it, except for the single glass on the drainboard. Apparently Jared Jones had helped himself to a drink of water before turning in for the night.

Eden turned off the kitchen light behind her and went out into the main room. She started to flick on the wall switch to light her way to her room, but then she hesitated. If he really was asleep up there, which it seemed all but certain that he was, then the light might wake him. And if he woke, they'd only end up in another unpleasant scene.

They could have one of those in the morning, after she'd had a good night's sleep. She turned from the stairs and started to make her way to her room in the dark.

But then she hesitated. She just plain wasn't comfortable with the idea of going off to her room not even knowing for sure whether there was someone else in the house. She'd never get to sleep, wondering if he was there, or if he wasn't there.

Better, she decided, to simply find out for sure. If she was very quiet and very careful, she was confident she could put her mind at ease without waking the brute and having to deal with him.

Gently she set down her purse and slipped out of her flats. And then, on tiptoe, she crept up the stairs.

At the top, she paused and peered through the shadows at the bed, which was up in the corner, on a diagonal from where she stood.

He was there, all right. There was no missing him. The moon was shining in the window nearby, bathing him in its silvery glow.

Eden didn't know she did it, but she sighed. When she should have turned around and crept back the way she'd come, she only stared, transfixed.

He was sprawled faceup, one muscled arm thrown across his face. His body was covered with his sleeping bag to the waist. His bare, powerful torso gleamed alabaster in the pale light from outside. Her gaze took in everything, from the ridged hardness of his belly, to the whorling trail of hair down his solar plexus to the soft shadow of the tuft beneath his arm.

Something . . . strange was taking form down inside her, a little bud of need, hot and tender.

Slowly, only half-aware that she was doing it, she approached him.

Far off, way back in her mind where reason was sequestered, there was a voice calling to her, *ordering* her to turn around and descend the stairs and go immediately to her room. But the voice was very far away. It added up to nothing when compared with the sweet siren's call of her own blood.

Before she knew how it had happened, she was standing right beside the bed, looking down at him.

He lay there so still and splendid. Yes, splendid was the word for him, lying there in a spill of moonbeams, looking like a statue of masculine perfection come to life and then fallen asleep on her spare bed.

His hard chest rose and fell evenly. Beneath the arm he'd thrown over his eyes, the grim line of his lips was softened now with sleep. Hardly daring to breathe, knowing she shouldn't, yet unable to stop herself, Eden bent nearer to those tenderly parted lips.

And that was when he reached out with the arm not thrown across his eyes and grabbed her wrist.

Eden shrieked and jumped back. But she didn't get far, because he didn't let go.

Jared dropped the arm that shielded his face. His eyes were open. "Something I can do for you?"

"Let go of me!"

He instantly released her wrist and then actually made a placating gesture. "Look. Settle down. It was only a joke."

"Your sense of humor eludes me. You *scared* me. You're *always* scaring me."

"Sorry. Okay? Finesse is not my strong suit. But I don't want to fight with you. I swear it."

She backed toward the stairs, bewildered by how decently he was acting about this. Not to mention chagrined at her own behavior. After all, he never would have had the chance to grab her and scare her again if she hadn't been sneaking around trying to get a closer look at him while he was supposedly sound asleep.

She clutched desperately for the original issue. And miraculously remembered it. "I told you to leave. You have no right to be here."

"Will you just settle down? Just . . . take it easy, okay?" He sat up. She tried not to look as the sleeping bag fell away a little. "Busy night at The Hole in the Wall?"

"Yes. Very busy." She hitched in a tight breath and forced herself to speak evenly. "And you really must leave tomorrow."

He surprised her by allowing in a perfectly reasonable tone, "I know."

"Y-you do?"

"Yeah. I spoke with my old man. Everything's worked out."

"What do you mean?"

"You're his partner. That's how he wants it. That's good enough for me."

"Oh. I see. Well, good then."

"And you can forget moving out. I've had a little time to think this afternoon and I decided that Heather and Jason Lee can use the money every month for their house payment. From now on, you just make out the rent checks to Heather, all right?"

"To Heather? Well, I—"

He let out a disgusted grunt. "Oh. Right. I forgot. You gotta have a legal document before you'll agree on the time of day."

"That's not it. I—"

"Well, don't worry. We'll write something up tomorrow, before I leave. Fair enough?"

"Sure. Fine. But—"

"But what?"

"Well, I mean, what about you? Where will you live?"

His sculpted, moonlit shoulders lifted in a shrug. "It's not a problem. I won't be staying in town after all."

Eden absorbed this information with a truly ridiculous mingling of guilt and sadness. She had his house and half his inheritance. And now he'd have to go elsewhere to find a place for himself. Good Lord. She almost felt like crying.

"Where will you go?"

He shrugged again. "I don't know yet. Maybe down in the valley. Sacramento, Stockton. I'll work it out."

"You don't have any plan?"

He actually smiled. It was the first time she'd ever seen him do that. The little bud of tender need inside her began to bloom. "Don't worry about me, Miss Parker. I'm a tough customer. I'll get by. And you're right. I shouldn't be here. I came back here after a nice dinner with my daughter and her husband, and I really was planning to take my things and go. But then I couldn't resist getting one more rise out of you before I pulled up stakes. I can stay with my father until I'm ready to leave town. I'll be out of here tomorrow morning."

"Oh." She felt terrible, all achy and crestfallen. What in heaven's name was the matter with her? She heard her own voice weakly proposing, "I'll make you breakfast. Before you go."

"You're on."

"O-okay, then. Good night..."

"Good night, Miss Parker."

She backed halfway down the stairs before she turned and fled to her own room, not even pausing to pick up her purse and her shoes. Then she undressed in a daze and lay down on her bed and tried not to think how much she was going to miss a man she hardly even knew.

"Have you seen baby Bathsheba yet?" Eden asked as she watched Jared pour half a bottle of syrup on his second helping of pancakes. Baby Bathsheba was the two-month-old daughter of Brendan, Jared's brother.

"Yeah." Jared set the syrup down and sipped from his coffee. This morning, she hadn't had to remind him of his manners. He was eating enough for a small army, but he was doing it slowly and with great care.

He was also back to being his old taciturn self. Unlike those few moments in the moonlight last night, he was revealing nothing that she didn't pry out of him first.

Eden, on the other hand, was feeling nervous. Edgy. So naturally, she wanted to talk.

And she did.

"When did you see her?"

"Who?"

"Baby Bathsheba."

"Last night."

"Isn't she beautiful? Did Amy bring her over to Heather's, then?" Amy was Brendan's wife.

"Yes."

"I think Amy looks terrific, don't you? I mean, it's only two months since the baby came and you can hardly tell she was ever pregnant. Brendan is so proud, of both his beautiful daughter and his gorgeous wife. Well, we all know how Brendan is about Amy anyway. But it seems like he's just more in love with her every day. Honestly, it's just incredible to see." Eden pushed back her chair and went to the coffeepot to refill her cup. Still standing at the counter, she held the pot out to Jared. "More?"

"Sure."

She cheerfully trotted over and poured him a cup. "There."

He looked up at her. "Thanks."

"You're welcome." Standing right above him like this, she could smell the shaving cream he must have used when he shaved. She liked it. And his hair, which she hadn't really paid a huge amount of attention to before, was very silky-looking, a rich brown color, threaded very lightly with silver. Also, she could really look at the eye she'd clobbered. It seemed a little better this morning. The swelling seemed to have receded a tiny bit, though it was still a lurid purple.

He was still looking at her, so she ventured, "Jared?"

"Yeah?"

"I'm really sorry. About your eye."

He shrugged. "I'll live."

She realized she'd been standing there, gaping down at him for an inordinate amount of time. So she shook herself and took the coffeepot back to the warming plate. Then she returned to her chair.

For a while, since he volunteered nothing, she managed to sip her coffee and finish her breakfast and be quiet. But soon enough, the silence was too much for her.

"Did Oggie tell you about my plans for the restaurant?"

Jared was just mopping up the last of his pancakes. He looked up. "No."

"Well, it's pretty exciting, actually. Next spring, we're opening a restaurant next door to the tavern. In The Mercantile building? It'll be called The Mercantile Grill, and we'll knock out the walls between the tavern and the restaurant, make them a joint venture, if you know what I mean. Oh, and you don't have to worry about Patrick being cheated out of *his* inheritance, because he's going in with Oggie and me on this particular project."

Jared actually said something of his own accord then. "Patrick, opening a *restaurant?*"

Eden understood his disbelief. Patrick, Oggie's second son, had worked on the county roads, done a stint in construction and was an excellent mechanic. Though he could tend bar when forced to, he was not the kind of man one pictured as a restaurateur. Still, Eden was sure it would work out, because she intended to see that it did.

"I know, it sounds incredible. But don't worry. Patrick won't be doing it alone. In fact, I'm the one who'll really be running things."

"I'll bet."

"Do I detect a note of sarcasm there?"

Jared rolled his eyes a little, but said nothing more.

Eden babbled on. "Well, Mr. Jones. You just wait and see. You come for dinner on the house at The Mercantile Grill. Say, the Fourth of July next year."

Jared stood up. "Fair enough, Miss Parker." He picked up his plate and flatware and carried it to the counter by the sink. Then he stuck in the drain stopper and filled up the sink, adding dishwashing liquid as the water ran.

Eden watched him for a moment before she realized that he intended to do the dishes. She almost told him not to bother, she'd take care of them. But then she decided that his cleaning up after she cooked was a nice gesture. No reason for her to spoil it.

So instead of objecting, she helped him a little, carrying her own dishes over, clearing the table and wiping down the counters. She kept up a pretty steady stream of chatter as the work was done. He said little, only replying when she asked him something directly.

Eden knew she should probably just be quiet. But as the minutes ticked by and the time for him to leave loomed ever closer, she found she felt sadder and sadder. Talking helped her deny the sadness somewhat.

After the dishes were put away, he insisted she write up a short addendum to the rental agreement. It said she was to make out the rent checks to Heather from now on. They both signed it.

Then Jared went upstairs to collect his things. He was back in nothing flat, his sleeping bag slung over his shoulder and his pack in his fist.

Eden was waiting for him at the foot of the stairs. "Have you got everything?"

"Yeah." His voice was gruff. "This is it."

She stood back. He walked past her, into the kitchen and over to the kitchen door. She trailed after him, feeling absurdly bereft.

And then, before she knew it, they were standing at the door facing each other. It was time to say goodbye.

Eden swallowed and started talking. "Well, then. I...suppose I'll see you again, before you leave. I mean, it's a small town. And I'm sure you'll be back, now and then, since your family's here and all...." He was standing very close. She was smelling him again—soap and shaving cream and man. She kept talking. "You'll want to visit Oggie. And Heather and Jason Lee, not to mention all of—"

"Miss Parker—"

"—your friends. You know, I heard you and Delilah's husband, Sam, used to be real drinking buddies. But, of course, as we discussed yesterday, you don't drink anymore, though. I heard you gave it up after, well, after your first divorce, because you loved your wife, Sally, and you wanted to get back with her. And then, you two did work things out, and you got married for the second time, to each other and everything was fine. But then poor Sally got squashed flat by that runaway logging truck and—"

"Miss Parker?"

"Um. Yes?"

"Do you ever shut up?"

"Well, I—"

"I can think of much better uses for that mouth of yours than talking."

Eden blinked at him and the mouth he was referring to dropped open. "Ex-excuse me?"

"I said, there are other things to do with your mouth than talking."

"Oh. I see." She was staring at *his* mouth, which, strangely, seemed to be almost as soft and tempting as it had been last night, during those forbidden moments when she'd spied on him in the moonlight.

"Other things," she echoed idiotically.

"You want me to show you?"

Did she nod? She wasn't sure. If she did, she shouldn't have. Yet if she didn't, she wanted to.

But whether she nodded or not, it happened anyway.

His mouth descended and closed over hers.

Eden gasped. And then softly sighed. She heard a pair of thuds, dimly, in the distance, as his pack and sleeping bag hit the floor. She expected him to reach out, then, and haul her hard and close against him.

But he didn't. He just went on kissing her, his body straining toward her, and his mouth ... oh, sweet heaven, his mouth ...

His mouth tasted her, and stroked her and worked gently, nudging, coaxing, until her own lips were parting, and his tongue was teasing, playing, mating with hers.

Eden groaned. And then she was the one reaching out, twining her arms around his neck and pressing herself hungrily, shamelessly into his heat and hardness. Her breasts flattened against his chest and the cradle of her hips rubbed against his. She could feel how much he wanted her, then, and she groaned again.

That did it. He groaned back. His arms went around her.

Eden sighed her appreciation at being held by him, so tight and close. It was wonderful. It was heaven. It was the kind of thing that only happened in sexy novels and it was happening to her. She wanted it never to end.

But of course, it did.

Jared ended it. He did it very tenderly, sliding his hands to her shoulders, gripping them gently and then slowly, reluctantly, lifting his head.

Her eyes fluttered open and she looked first at his mouth. It was swollen a little, from the kiss. Hesitantly she raised her glance. She saw that his injured lid was opened now to a slit. He watched her through that slit and she felt that his gaze set off sparks where it touched her.

Eden lifted a hand and laid the pads of two fingers on her own lips. Were they swollen like his? They'd have to be, wouldn't they? After what they'd just been through.

Still dazed, she watched as he bent and retrieved his gear. When their eyes met again, she could read nothing in his. The fire had been banked. She looked into cold steel.

"That was a damn fool thing for me to do," he said. "But I've always been a damn fool. Goodbye, Miss Parker."

"Bye..." she said in a croak.

He pulled back the door and went out.

Eden stood in the doorway and watched him drive off.

She was still standing there several minutes after his pickup had disappeared from sight.

She was trying, befuddled as her poor mind was right then, to comprehend the enormity of what had just transpired between herself and her surly landlord. She was trying to fathom the unfathomable: the meaning of a kiss.

She was unsuccessful in her efforts.

All she knew was that the foundations of her reality had suddenly shifted, leaving her perched on an emotional precipice and foolishly longing to fling herself into the chasm below. She yearned with all her heart to chase after his pickup and beg him to come back. At the same time she knew such an action would be totally foolish.

The man was forty years old—she'd learned that last night by asking Oggie a few subtle questions. Jared had always had trouble getting along with people. He'd been married three times—though, to be fair, two of those times were to the same person—and he thought nothing of sneaking into a woman's room in the middle of the night and scaring her to death. Eden could never get anything meaningful going with a man like that. She just *couldn't*. No way...

And, in the end, it didn't matter if she could *or* if she couldn't. Because Jared Jones wasn't going to be around for long. Within a day or two, he'd be heading out of town.

Sighing, Eden went back inside and finished getting ready for work. When her hair was pinned up and her makeup applied, she got into her car and drove into town and parked behind The Hole in the Wall.

Eden went inside and tackled her morning duties. For some reason, though, the mundane satisfaction she usually attained from the simple series of chores was missing today.

She had the chairs on the floor and was proceeding to get the popcorn popping and the cocktail mix set out when Rocky Collins pressed his hangdog face against one of the front windows, in the split between the red café curtains.

Eden glanced up at the big clock over the hall to the back door: 10:48. She really shouldn't let him in, though she knew that Oggie always used to, back when he ran the place himself.

Right from the first, she'd made the rule that the front double doors were unlocked at eleven sharp six days a week, never earlier and never later. Eden believed that starting things off punctually every day gave people an impression that here was a place they could count on. Besides, Eden didn't like to encourage poor Rocky, who spent way too much time here as it was.

But she *was* feeling just a little bit low today. And seeing Rocky looking lower than she felt, Eden's sympathies were roused.

Against her own better judgment, she went and let him in.

"Gee darn, Eden. Thanks a million."

"Have a seat." She gestured at his favorite stool. "But I'm not serving until eleven sharp."

"Hey. I hear you. No problem, I swear." Rocky sat down and gave a luxurious sigh. He was a man who never felt quite at home if he wasn't leaning against a bar. "Hey, Eden?"

Eden measured the oil into the popper. "What is it, Rocky?"

"You got any aspirins?"

"Coming right up." She poured in the correct amount of popcorn kernels, flipped the metal lid closed and then pulled her hand out of the glass enclosure. She closed the glass doors and then she found Rocky his aspirin.

"Hey, thanks. You're okay," Rocky said.

"You're welcome." Eden started scooping cocktail mix into wooden bowls.

Right then, the phone beneath the bar rang.

"I'll get it," Rocky announced.

Before Eden could tell him she preferred to do it herself, he was standing on the rungs of his stool and hoisting the phone up onto the bar. He picked up the receiver.

"Yeah, hullo?" he grumbled into the mouthpiece, causing Eden to cringe. Proper telephone etiquette was another thing she insisted on at the new, improved Hole in the Wall. "Hey, howzitgoin', Jared, my man?"

Eden's heart suddenly rose and stuck somewhere near her throat. And while it was stuck there, it beat out his name.

Jared, Jared, Jared, Jared...

Settle down, she told her heart silently. *Settle down. He's probably just looking for Oggie....*

Rocky held out the handset. "'S for you, Eden."

Eden swallowed, to get her heart back where it belonged, and set down the bowl she was just about to fill. Then she took the phone from Rocky.

"Yes?"

His wonderful, low, sibilant voice hissed in her ear. "Bad news."

"What?"

"The old man."

"Oggie?"

"Yeah. He was cleaning his hunting rifle and—"

Eden felt numb, suddenly. There was a stool right beside her. She sank onto it. "Yes? Tell me."

"He shot himself in the foot."

Relief, as cool and soothing as clear water, coursed through her. She had thought for a moment that Jared would say the dear old coot was dead. "Is he all right?"

"As all right as he can be with a big hole in his foot. I'm at the hospital in Grass Valley now. They're patching him up."

"But is he—"

"Relax. He's going to be fine. Eventually."

"Oh, thank God."

"But he won't be standing up for a while."

"Well, of course."

"And he sure as hell won't be tending bar. In fact, he won't even be leaving the hospital for a day or two. Because of his age, they want to monitor him for a while."

"I understand. And tell him not to worry about The Hole in the Wall. I'll manage things here."

"Well, that's the other thing I called to tell you."

"What?"

"See, the gun went off just as I pulled up in front of his house."

"Yes. And?"

"And I ran in there, and it was—hell, it was a damn messy sight."

"So?"

"So I tried to pick him up, to carry him to my truck and get him here to the hospital."

"Yes?"

"But he wouldn't go."

"He wouldn't?"

"No. Not until I promised him that I'd take over for him at The Hole in the Wall until he was on his feet again."

Eden was silent, a rare thing.

Jared said, "So, I'm just calling to tell you. I'll be in at seven, same time as the old man always is."

"I—"

"We're just going to have to make the best of this, Eden."

Eden. He'd called her Eden. She was positive that was the first time she'd heard her given name on his lips. "Yes, I—"

"And after we shut down tonight, we'll talk. If that's convenient for you."

"Talk?"

"We'll come to an understanding. About how it's going to be."

"Oh."

"What does that mean, 'Oh'?"

"Nothing. Oh. That's all. Just oh."

"You understand, then?"

"About what?"

"About us coming to an understanding."

"Oh. Yes. I do. I understand. About an understanding."

"Tonight, then? After we close."

"Yes. All right."

And then she heard the click at the other end of the line. He had hung up. She took the receiver away from her ear and looked at it.

"Eden? You okay?"

"Why yes, Rocky. I'm just fine." She handed him the receiver. "Here. Hang this up for me, will you?"

"Be my pleasure. But, er, you'll have to give me the phone first."

Eden realized she was clutching the thing against her chest. She coughed. "Certainly," she said, and shoved it at him. He took it, grinning.

Eden turned quickly. With great purpose and dignity, she returned to the other end of the bar where she recommenced filling little wooden bowls with pretzels and nuts and small toasted squares of salty cereal.

Chapter Seven

J ared arrived promptly at seven. He wore a new-looking
pair of jeans, a tooled leather belt, a black vest and a black
long-sleeved shirt. The shirt was open at the neck, the
sleeves rolled neatly to below the elbows. His boots were
dress boots. Eden's silly heart tried to jump out of her
mouth at the sight of him.

And even beyond her personal response to him, Eden
was thoroughly impressed. From a purely business stand-
point, except for his black eye, he looked just great. Casual but professional, wearing a Western costume that was
almost, but not quite, a uniform. It was exactly the image
she was trying to cultivate at The Hole in the Wall. An image that Oggie, in his wrinkled shirts and grimy suspend-
ers, had never managed to achieve.

Which was okay, she quickly told herself, feeling a little
guilty for being critical of her partner, especially now, when
the poor old dear was flat on his back with a hole in his
foot. Oggie, after all, was Oggie. He brought a certain color

and spontaneity to the tavern that would be sorely missed in his absence.

Everyone at the bar seemed happy to see Jared.

"Jared. Hey, heard you were in town."

"Goldurned, where'd you get that shiner, m'man?"

"Hey, Jared. What's the word?"

Jared greeted them all with a wave, as he flipped the hinged counter up and went through, joining Eden on the business side of the bar.

"You look great," Eden told him, meaning it.

The corners of his grim mouth twitched. She knew he was pleased. "Since you seem to be upgrading the image around here, I went through some of the stuff my father's storing at his place and came up with this." He gestured at his outfit.

"That was—" she sought the right word "—thoughtful."

"Yeah. I'm one damn thoughtful guy."

They just stared at each other. Eden knew she was grinning like a borderline idiot, but somehow she couldn't seem to stop herself. Here they were, forced by her partner's injury to work together very closely for the next several weeks.

It was probably going to be sheer hell.

So why was she so glad to see him? And why couldn't she stop smiling?

Down the bar, one of the regulars by the name of Tim Brown groused, "Who do you have to shoot to get a drink around here?"

Someone else piped up, "Anyone but Oggie. He's already down."

A ripple of laughter flowed over the room. By now, of course, everyone knew about what had happened to Oggie.

Tyler Conley, a cousin of Heather's husband, chimed in with, "Yeah, Jared. Tell us. How's Oggie doing?"

Jared went to the wells and poured a whiskey and soda. "Oggie's in Prospector's Hospital for a day or two more. And he is hurting," Jared said, neatly setting the drink on a coaster in front of Tim Brown. "But he'll get over it. He's a Jones, after all." He told Tim the price of the drink.

Eden watched him, amazed. He mixed a drink like a true pro. Quickly and effortlessly, with only the slightest bit of flash and dazzle when it came to squirting in the soda. Also, he'd known Tim's drink without having to ask what it was. That was pretty good, considering Jared hadn't even been in town since early May.

Jared turned then and saw her watching him. "You don't have to look so stunned, Miss Parker. I've been helping out at this bar for longer than I care to remember."

"Well, of course. I can see that now. I just didn't realize, I mean, I thought—" She was babbling.

He knew it, so he saved her by interrupting. "So do I pass muster as your substitute bartender?"

She nodded. "I think you'll work out fine."

"Good. Then how about if you play cocktail waitress, and I'll handle the bar?"

Eden had no argument with his plan. It was the way she and Oggie always did it, unless things piled up, in which case Eden helped with the fancier drinks. "Fair enough."

The night was a busy one and it seemed to fly by. Jared wasn't like Oggie, who kept everybody laughing and who would sometimes talk more than the most loquacious of his customers. Jared was cool and businesslike and never missed an order. Working with him, Eden found that she herself became more outgoing.

With Oggie, Eden was the one who kept things running smoothly, while the old man supplied the personality. But with Jared, if there was going to be any personality supplied, Eden had to deliver it. Jared worked, and he worked hard, but he was simply not the kind of man who kept people in stitches with the latest traveling salesman joke.

So Eden spent more time with the customers. And, all in all, it worked out just fine.

She also stayed right through until closing time, partly because it was Saturday night and so busy. And also because of the *understanding* Jared had said they must reach together once they'd closed the doors.

At two-fifteen, Eden escorted the last customer, Rocky Collins, to the door. There, Eden stood for a moment and watched as Rocky tottered down the street. She was relieved when he made it safely to the North Magdalene Grocery Store, above which he rented a small apartment. He grasped the railing to the stairs that ran up the side of the building and pulled himself toward the floor above. When he reached the top, he swayed in front of his own door for a few moments. At last, he succeeded in getting out his key and fitting it into the lock. He disappeared through the door.

"Kind of sad, isn't it?" the low voice said from behind her.

Eden didn't turn to look at him. She was afraid that if she did, he would walk away. She asked, carefully offhand, "Sad? Rocky, you mean?"

"Yeah. He wasn't always like that."

Eden looked up at the tall pine trees on the surrounding hills. It was cooling off now. She breathed deeply of the fresh air, which still seemed warm, and sweet too, after the air-conditioned smokiness in the bar. "What made him change?"

"Hell. What makes anybody change? Life. One too many busted dreams."

Eden folded her arms over her breasts and leaned against the shingled outside wall. She wanted to ask, Were *you* ever different, Jared? And if so, what made *you* change? But she didn't. She had heard from everyone in Jared's family that he had always been a hot-tempered, unapproachable kind of guy. And more than that, such a personal question would probably put a quick end to this lovely moment of peace and near-companionship they seemed to be sharing.

He said, "You're very quiet, Miss Parker."

"Enjoy it while it lasts."

He chuckled then, a kind of rusty-sounding chuckle. She thought that chuckling was something he probably didn't do often. And then he leaned against the building, too, and looked up at the shadowed trees. They were quiet together. Eden thought it was a friendly silence and didn't mind it at all.

Eventually he spoke. "Sometimes, when the people around here are driving me up the wall, I forget what a nice little town this is."

She closed her eyes for a moment. "North Magdalene's much more than nice. It's the home I've always dreamed of."

"It is, huh?"

"Oh, yes. I knew it the first day Laurie brought me here." Eden smiled to herself, remembering. "It was late spring and everything was still green. There were poppies along the road and the locust trees were in bloom. And people were friendly. It was like I was never a stranger."

Jared made a low noise in his throat. "There's a flip side to how friendly folks are, you know. They can also be nosy and interfering as hell. That's why I like this town best in the middle of the night, when the streets are empty and there's not a soul in sight."

"Oh, come on, Jared."

"Oh, come on, what?"

"Well, I mean. Saying you like this town best in the middle of the night is like when a mother says she likes her kids best when they're asleep. Everyone knows mothers are only joking when they say things like that."

"Wrong. Everyone wants to *believe* a mother is only joking when she says things like that."

"You are such a cynic. And besides, loving North Magdalene in the middle of the night is so *limiting.* There are only four streetlights, so you can hardly even *see* it in the middle of the night."

"I don't need to see it. I've got it memorized."

"Is that why you don't miss it when you're gone, because you've got it memorized?"

"Who says I don't miss it?" There was an edge to his voice. Then he said, "Come on. We're wasting time. Let's get things cleaned up. Then we can talk."

Eden sighed. She would have remarked, "I thought we *were* talking," but he didn't give her the chance. He had already ducked back in through the double doors.

Jared cleaned up as efficiently as he tended bar. They were ready to head out the back door in twenty minutes flat.

Then he asked, "You want a drink or something?"

She found she dreaded what was coming, so she tried to keep things light. "Will I need one?"

But that one rusty chuckle he'd given her earlier had apparently been about all the humor he could deal with in one night. He answered without even a trace of a smile, "That's up to you."

"Well, no then. I'll . . . take it straight."

"Suit yourself."

He took down two of the chairs they'd already put up and sat backward in one. She took the other, though she didn't really feel like sitting. He looked at her for a moment.

Then he began, "Er, Miss Parker . . ."

It was too much. She felt edgy and awful again, like she had last night—or was it night before last, by now?—when she'd realized he was actually leaving town.

She snapped, "Look. Could you just call me Eden? Please?" She couldn't sit still for another second, so she stood up and looked down at him. "I mean it's too strange, your calling me Miss Parker. Face it. We're going to be tending this bar together for the next several weeks." She threw out both her arms. "You can at least call me by my given name." She realized how widely she had gestured and dropped her arms. Then, feeling totally foolish, she sat back down again. "Okay?" she asked meekly.

"Fine," he said, his good eye looking wary. "Eden."

"Thanks a lot."

"You're welcome. Where was I?"

"Not very far," she said tartly. "I think you got to 'Er, Miss Parker' and that was about it."

"Hell." He raked through his hair with his fingers and then rubbed the back of his neck.

Eden decided that waiting around for him to figure out what to say was worse than having him actually say it. "Oh, for heaven's sake. I can't stand this. Let's just...get it over with."

"I'm trying." He really did look miserable. He was gazing off toward the pool table.

"Oh, why is this happening to me?" Eden muttered. "Shall I help you? Is that what you want?"

Now he actually turned those bullet gray eyes on her. His expression was nervous, but hopeful. "Well, I—"

Eden wished she hadn't volunteered. But it was too late now. "It *is* what you want, right?"

"Hell."

"All right. Fine." She stood up again. This was not a task she wanted to tackle sitting down.

She began, "Let's see. *You* want *me* to be aware that you are not in the market for any kind of relationship with a woman. You are through with women, forever. And, even though you kissed me recently and both of us liked it *a lot*, we have to learn to put that behind us and just be...what?

Friendly colleagues? Is that right? I mean, to work together and be nice to each other but only in a very professional way?"

Slowly he nodded.

"Okay. So we're going to be buddies on the job and nothing else, until Oggie gets over shooting himself in the foot and you can do what you really want to do and leave town again." She took a breath. "Is that it?"

He looked up at her from his chair. "Right on the money, Miss —er, Eden."

"Okay." For some completely incomprehensible reason, she wanted to cry. But she was not going to cry. "Fine with me," she said brightly. "I mean, it's pretty obvious you and I are hardly a match made in heaven, right?"

"Exactly."

"Shake on it?" Eden stuck out her hand. He stared at it for a moment, then his own engulfed it. She resolutely ignored the heat that shot up her arm. After a couple of teeth-rattling pumps, he let go.

"See you tomorrow night, then. Seven sharp," she said.

"You bet."

Eden turned and got out of there.

At home, she went right to bed. Her dreams were sad dreams, in which she wandered, feeling lost and alone.

She woke at seven when her alarm went off and wished she could simply throw the darn thing across the room and go back to sleep. But she wanted to see Oggie before she went to the tavern, to make sure he was okay and find out if there was anything she could do for him.

So she dragged herself from her bed and stood for several minutes under the cold spray of the shower. After a good breakfast and some heavy-duty primping to disguise the circles under her eyes, she began to feel as if she just might make it through the day and night to come after all.

At a little before nine, Eden pulled into a parking space in the Prospector's Hospital lot. Inside, the front desk clerk gave her directions to Oggie's room.

When she peeked around the door at the old darling, he was sitting up in the adjustable bed. His right foot was propped in front of him, wrapped in what looked like a small mountain of gauze bandaging. His seamed face lit up at the sight of her.

"Well, what's that there? A ray of sunshine on a damn gloomy day! Get on in her', gal." He waved her into the room.

Eden smiled widely and scooted around the doorframe. She held up the flower arrangement she'd brought with her.

"Not bad," he said. "'Course, I woulda preferred a case of whiskey."

"I'll bet. Where should I put it?"

"Aw, hell. How 'bout over there?"

Eden set the flowers on the windowsill and then took the chair by his bed. She looked at him for a moment before she said anything. Then she squeezed his bony shoulder. "Oh, Oggie. Are you all right?"

He snorted. "Hell, no. I'm wounded for life. And in the worst possible place, too—my pride."

"Jared said you were cleaning your hunting rifle and—"

"Yep. It went off. *Blam.* Right through the foot."

Eden thought about this as he described it and something odd occurred to her. "But, Oggie, I thought people cleaned guns with the barrel up. I mean, when you hear about gun-cleaning accidents, you always hear about injuries to the upper part of the body."

Oggie looked chagrined. "Well, see, like I've explained to Sheriff Pangborn and just about every other damn person who's come in this room, I thought I'd taken out all the shells. I had the rifle pointed down at the floor and I was... Aw, hell. It don't matter how I explain, I still come out a damn fool. At least if I *had* shot myself in the head, I might not have to live through the razzing I'm gonna take when I get back on my feet.''

"No one's going to razz you, Oggie." She patted his hand. "I won't let them."

Oggie chortled. "I feel better already, knowin' you'll stand up for me—since I myself ain't gonna be standin' up at all for quite a while."

"How long will it be until you're really over this?"

"Too long, like I said. The doctor says I'm lucky the bullet only snapped one little bone and went on through, but still it's gonna take weeks and weeks to heal."

Eden thought of that, of weeks and weeks of laboring side by side with Jared. Some foolish part of her was disgustingly gleeful at the prospect, while her wiser self knew the best she was going to get out of this deal would be a tension-filled work environment.

"Eden? Something on your mind, gal?"

"No, no. I was just wishing you were over this, that's all."

Oggie's grizzled brows drew together. "Did my boy, Jared, leave you alone to handle things all on your own last night? Is that it? If he did, I'll—"

"No, no, Oggie. He showed up right on time and he...he was great. You know, actually, he's an excellent bartender."

"Damn straights. Who d'ya think taught him everything he knows?"

Eden smiled and nodded. She was thinking that she'd like to ask her partner a few questions about the way he'd misled her when it came to his oldest son—in saying that Jared wanted nothing to do with the bar, and swearing that Jared wouldn't be the least upset to hear his father had taken on a partner.

But right now, she was looking at an old man with a painful injury. And somehow, now didn't seem the time to take him to task. She'd have it out with him later, when his wrinkled face didn't look quite so gray with pain and tiredness.

"I can't stay long, you know," she told him.

"Lucky you," he muttered dryly. "This place is a prison, don't let anyone tell you different. One more day, maybe two, and I'm outta here. 'Course, then I gotta go stay with Delilah for a while. That'll be a trial. But it can't be helped. Since school's out now, she's got time to take care of me." Oggie's only daughter was a teacher. "On second thought, maybe I'll just stay here in prison for a while."

"Oh, come on, Oggie. Delilah will take wonderful care of you."

Oggie looked at her from under his brows. "You ain't known Delilah for too long, Eden. And besides, since she married Sam, she comes across a lot different than she used to. Fulfillment will do that to even the most hard-hearted of women. But there was a time, and it wasn't too long ago, when I'd a shot myself in more than the foot before I'd ever let myself be put helpless into Delilah's hands."

"Oh, Oggie. You're exaggerating."

"You go ahead and believe that, Eden. You're a sweet, bighearted gal. A gentle woman like you don't even want to consider the bloodthirsty inclinations of her less civilized sisters."

Eden couldn't help laughing. "Whatever you say, Oggie."

"This ain't no laughing matter, Eden."

"All right, all right."

"Damn. What I wouldn't give for a smoke."

"Oggie, listen. What I really came for is to see if there's anything I can do for you. You know, anything I can bring you, or any errands I can run?"

"Yeah, hustle over to my house and bring me that box of cigars I left on the coffee table in the living room."

"Now, now, Mr. Jones." A nurse bustled into the room just as Oggie finished talking. "We already told you there is no smoking in the hospital. And besides, you're old enough to know what smoking does to you."

"Yeah, if I'd a known I was gonna live this long, I mighta taken better care of myself."

The nurse winked at Eden. "Isn't he a card?"

Eden nodded. "Yep."

"Now, Mr. Jones. The doctor will be coming by shortly and I think we should remove the dressing on that foot, so he can have a look at it."

"How 'bout you just remove it by yourself?" Oggie asked.

The nurse looked puzzled. "Yes. That's what I said."

Oggie cackled, pleased with himself to be one step ahead of his nurse. "What'd I tell you, Eden? It's hell here."

"I can see they're really making you suffer." Eden stood up. "I'll leave you two alone. But before I go, Oggie, I want you to tell me seriously. What can I do to help out?"

"Aw, hell. I told you what I want. A good cigar. And a six-pack would be nice. And maybe a couple of blondes to help me drink the beer." He looked hopefully at the nurse. She only shook her head. "See? What I want, they won't let me have. So just don't be a stranger while I'm down and out and I'll be happy."

"You're sure?"

"Yep. And take care of business."

"You know I always do."

He spoke to the nurse. "And she ain't foolin' neither. It was my lucky day, when Miss Eden Parker came to town."

The nurse nodded and smiled.

Though she should have known better, Eden still found her heart melting a little at the old flatterer's words. "Thanks, Oggie." She bent over and placed a kiss on his grizzled cheek. "You take care, now."

Oggie made a face at the nurse. "See? With a business partner like this, what the hell do I need with a couple of blondes, anyway?" Oggie grabbed Eden's hand and gave it a squeeze. "Work hard. Make us lots of money."

"I will. I promise."

"And be patient with poor Jared. He ain't had an easy life, you know."

Eden forced a cheerful smile, thinking that only Oggie could get away with bemoaning the troubled life Jared had led, when the old man himself was at least partly to blame for Jared's current problems. She promised, "I'll do my best."

Oggie cackled. "That's just what I'm depending on." As he spoke, Eden thought she detected a crafty glint in her partner's eyes. But if she did, it disappeared as fast as it had come. She hesitated, thinking maybe she should ask him exactly what was going through that scheming mind of his.

But then the nurse coughed and Eden realized that Oggie probably preferred privacy for the unbandaging of his mangled foot.

Eden moved toward the door. "Okay, then. You call me if you need me. Otherwise, I'll drop in tomorrow, and stay a little longer." Tomorrow was Monday, and The Hole in the Wall would be closed, leaving Eden more time for visiting.

Oggie placed a hand over his heart. "I'll be countin' the hours." Then he spoke to the nurse. "Okay, gorgeous, I'm all yours."

To Eden's surprise, things went pretty well at The Hole in the Wall that night. Jared arrived, looking sharp, promptly at seven. At first, when he moved behind the bar and their eyes met, Eden had an awful, sinking feeling in her stomach.

Why *him?* she thought desperately. Out of all the nice, openhearted guys there are in the big, wide world, why did it have to be *him?* I can't do this, I simply cannot do this.

But, somehow, she *did* do it. She waited on the customers and bantered with the regulars while Jared mixed the drinks and kept the bar looking shipshape. And within an hour or so, she found she was *almost* able to forget what he'd looked like, magnificent in the moonlight, as he feigned sleep in her spare bed just two nights ago. Not to mention the shameless way she'd responded the next morning when he kissed her at the kitchen door.

And since it was Sunday and a little slower than the night before, Eden was able to turn the place over to Jared at eleven and go home. That spared them those moments alone together that couldn't be avoided when she stayed to the very end.

The next day was Monday and she didn't have to work. Eden puttered around the cabin in the morning and then drove to Grass Valley to make the bank deposit. Since Oggie had been released from the hospital, she stopped by Delilah's house to see him in the afternoon. The old dear was as sweet and amusing as ever.

But she was nervous through the whole visit, fearing that Jared might drop in. She would have felt so awkward, having to sit and make conversation with Oggie, while Jared stood there and glowered, or acted impatient for her to be gone, or worst of all, behaved as if he couldn't care less whether she was there or not.

When Amy appeared with baby Bathsheba to say hi to Grandpa Oggie, Eden took her chance to make a quick getaway. She went home, where she did her laundry and cleaned up the cabin.

Laurie, who was working full-time for the summer at the restaurant where she and Eden had met, called from Sacramento in the evening.

"Hey, pal. I just talked to Heather. She says Great-uncle Oggie shot himself in the foot."

Eden, who'd been feeling a little down, perked up at the sound of her friend's voice. "Yes. It's true. The poor old dear."

"Have you seen him yet?"

"Oggie? Um-hmm. Yesterday and today. He's doing fine. Driving everyone nuts, of course. But that's to be expected."

"Yeah. I'll bet. I've got a day off Wednesday, so I figure I'll drive up and drop in on him."

"He'll love that."

"Heather also said her dad wasn't too thrilled to hear his cabin was rented."

"You could say that."

"So. What do you think of him?"

"Who?"

"C'mon, Eden. Heather's wild-man father. I know you're stuck working with him until Oggie's better. Heather told me that, too."

Eden felt her spirits sinking again. There was just no escaping Jared Jones. Either she was working with him, dreaming about him, or discussing him with one of his relatives. In fact, now that she thought about it, she realized what a bind she was in. The friends she'd made over the past several months were wonderful. But unfortunately, they all seemed to be related to the man she was trying not to think about.

"Eden?"

"What?"

"I asked what you think of Cousin Jared."

"Of Jared?"

"Are you feeling all right?"

"Fine. I'm just fine. And I think your cousin takes some getting used to."

"Oh, Eden. You really are a sweetheart. He's driving you up the wall, right? But you're determined to make the best of the situation, for Oggie's sake."

"Well..."

"Hey. Say no more. I know cousin Jared. He's just one of those guys who was born about a century too late. He should be out fighting mountain lions with his bare hands, building log cabins with only an ax, settling the west. You know, stuff like that."

"Right. It's so limiting for him, to have to act like a reasonable human being."

"Oh, wow. You *are* having a rough time with him."

Eden sighed. "Oh, I'll get through it. One way or another."

"Eden?"

"What?"

"Is there something... going on here?"

Eden could have kicked herself. Laurie wasn't her best friend for nothing. Laurie *sensed* things. Eden should have been more circumspect. Venting her frustrations about Jared had been foolish.

"Eden?"

"Hmm?"

"Did you hear my question?"

"Yes. I heard you." Eden swallowed. "And what do you mean, going on?"

"Honestly." Laurie sounded mildly annoyed. "I mean, is there something romantic going on between you and Jared?"

"Who said that?"

"Nobody. You just seem ..."

"What? I seem what?"

"A little defensive about him."

"Defensive? I am not defensive. I'm really not. Not at all."

"Okay, okay."

Eden knew she should change the subject right there, but she wanted to make certain Laurie got her point loud and clear. "How could there be anything going on between your cousin and me?"

"Well, I was only—"

"He's old enough to be my father."

"Well, not quite. I mean, you're twenty-six and he's forty. That's fourteen years. I suppose technically, a guy can be a father at fourteen, but that would have meant he'd have been about thirteen when he—"

"Why are we talking about this?"

"Well, Eden. You said—"

"I said there's nothing whatsoever going on between your cousin and me. He's too old for me and he has a terminal bad attitude."

"He *is* kind of surly." Laurie was trying to be fair.

"And he's been divorced twice."

"Oh, come on," Laurie said. Eden could tell by her friend's tone that she shouldn't have brought up both divorces. "That's not fair. His first divorce doesn't count and you know it. He and Sally remarried and things were going just fine between them when—"

"Laurie. Why are we talking about this? I don't want to talk about this."

"Eden, I—"

"I mean it. I really don't."

"Sheesh. I've never heard you like this. You've never been one to let a man bother you. I mean, let's be frank here. You hardly even *date*."

"I'm a businesswoman," Eden said, as if that explained everything. "I've been busy all my life, making a place for myself. I don't have time for *casual* relationships with men. I've told you that."

"Okay, fine. All I'm saying is, this is *me*. Your best friend. If I'm nosing around where I shouldn't be, I'm sorry. But please remember I'm here, if you need me. And

I really *can* keep my mouth shut in terms of the family, if that's what's worrying you."

Eden felt contrite. Laurie was right. If Eden couldn't trust her own best friend, where did that leave her? "Thanks, pal," she said. "I'll remember that."

"Good."

"And, the truth is..."

"Yeah?"

"The *sad* truth is, there's nothing to tell."

"What's *nothing*, exactly?"

"Zero. Zip. Jared and I have an *understanding*."

"Yuk. Sounds grim."

"We work together a few hours a night. And that's all."

"But *you* want more?"

"Oh, Laurie."

"I'm listening."

"I'm attracted to him...."

"But?"

"But he's not the kind of man I pictured myself falling for. I always thought I'd find someone friendly and easygoing. A nice, good-natured, hardworking guy."

"Well, you're okay on the hardworking part. Cousin Jared's always been a hardworking man."

"Great. But what about friendly, easygoing, nice and good-natured?"

"No comment."

"My point precisely."

"So what will you *do*?"

"Grin and bear it."

"What fun."

"What else can I do?"

For a moment there was silence on the line. Then Laurie asked, "Do you really want to know?"

Eden shrugged. "Sure. Hit me with it."

"Well, it seems to me you've got a golden opportunity here."

"Oh, a golden opportunity. Right."

"Do you want to hear what I have to say? Or would you prefer to just go on being sarcastic?"

"Sorry. I want to hear, I really do."

"Then let me finish, please."

"All right."

"Okay. You've got a golden opportunity. You're working with the guy every day but Monday for the next several weeks. And then, unless something happens to make him change his mind, he's outta here. Right?"

"So?"

"So it's perfect. If things don't work out, he's going to be gone anyway."

"Well, they *haven't* worked out, that's what I'm telling you. And he *isn't* gone. Not for weeks yet. And I've got to see him every night until then."

"Okay, so don't waste the time you have left."

"What do you mean, waste? What is there to waste? It's over before it even started."

"I mean, why don't you take advantage of the situation? Since you're thrown together every night, make it your business to get to know the man better. Just in case he *is* the one you've been waiting for."

"Get to *know* him. Please. He's *your* cousin. How can you say that? You know how he is. The master of the one-syllable response."

"Was I finished? I didn't think I was finished."

"Sorry. All right. Go on."

"Fine. So I'm not sure *how* you do it, but you do it. Become *friends* with him. Don't push, just be receptive, any time he's willing to open up a little. Slowly you'll get to know more about what makes him tick."

"Yeah?"

"And then..."

"Yeah?"

Laurie sighed. "Oh, never mind."

"What do you mean, never mind?"

"Oh, well."

"Oh, well *what?*"

"It would never work."

"What are you saying?"

"That you're right."

Eden gave a little groan. "About what?"

"About my cousin Jared. I mean, no matter how positive I try to be about this, I can't help remembering who we're talking about here. And cousin Jared never opened up to anybody in his life. You really want the advice of a friend?"

Eden didn't, not really. But it was too late to say so now. She bleakly conceded, "I said I did, didn't I?"

"Okay, then here it is. Forget him. Keep it strictly business for the next few weeks. And be waiting at the door to help him into his coat when he heads out of town."

Eden felt like a pricked balloon. But she knew her friend was right. "Yeah." The word was glumness personified. "You said it. And I know it."

"So do it."

"I will."

And Eden fully intended to. At least consciously, anyway.

But deep in her secret heart, she still nourished a futile longing for the man she knew she ought to forget. Thus, it was Laurie's original advice that stuck with her.

Later, as she lay in bed, she couldn't help wondering just how a person would go about getting someone like Jared Jones to open up a little....

Chapter Eight

Jared didn't know how the hell it happened, but after he and Eden had been working together for a while, he began telling her things. About himself. About his life. About his *feelings,* for godsakes.

It started out as a sort of joking remark she made, during a lull on that first Tuesday night after Oggie's injury. That night had been pretty quiet to begin with. And at about nine the place emptied out, except for a few real diehards at the card table in back.

Eden went out to the tables and began gathering the empties on a tray. Then she trotted over to the bar and set the tray down.

"Okay, Jared," she said out of nowhere, as soon as the glasses and empty beer bottles stopped clinking together. "We've got a spare five minutes here. Why don't you tell me your life story?"

He gave her a look, a look he'd practiced a lot in his life. The look said, *"Back off."*

Eden shrugged and came around to join him behind the bar. Then she began washing the glasses. He assumed he'd shut her up.

He assumed wrong.

She said, very offhandedly, "Okay, forget your life story. After all, if this keeps up, I'll head on home. So you'd better save your life story for some night when I'm trapped here."

He'd grunted then. Though he was really watching it with her, keeping strictly to the terms of their understanding not to get involved, it was hard not to respond to her.

She was so tall and sparkly and full of the oddest, gawky grace. A damn gorgeous flamingo of a woman, with those neverending legs and that flame-gold hair and that mouth that could smile like no mouth he'd ever seen before.

Then she asked, "But how about . . . the happiest day of your life? So far."

And he said, "The day Heather was born," before he even realized that he'd opened his mouth to speak.

She swooped the pair of rocks glasses she was washing through the rinse water and turned to give him a quick, melting look from those Kahlúa-colored eyes of hers. "I can understand that."

And that was all. She didn't make too much of it. She didn't say, like a lot of women would, *So tell me all about it, every itsy-bitsy detail of how you felt and what you felt and why you felt it.* Just that soft look and *I can understand that* and that was all.

It surprised the hell out of him, to tell the truth. He'd never thought that she could back off like that, that she could hear what he'd said and let it be, because most of the time Eden Parker was such a damn motor-mouth. And also because he'd assumed she was just like any other woman, that she'd fall all over herself at the slightest opportunity to get him to "communicate."

In Jared's experience, most women said they adored a man who was strong and silent and self-contained. And then they were somehow always after him, nagging him, because he wouldn't "open up" with them.

But Eden Parker never urged him to "open up," and she never nagged because he didn't. She just... invited him to. And damned if he didn't find himself accepting her invitations, as often as not.

"I've got a moment here, Jared," she'd announce. "Name your favorite song of all time."

And he'd be answering some idiotic thing, like "Blue Velvet," before he even realized that he *had* a favorite song.

She'd say, "Well, that's not bad. Not bad at all." And he'd want to ask her, *"Not bad compared to what?"* But by then he would have remembered that he was supposed to be keeping things distant and professional when it came to her. So he'd say nothing. Until later, when she'd pop out another harmless question and he'd answer it before even stopping to think.

"What's your favorite color?"

"Something that doesn't show the dirt."

She'd chuckled when he said that.

Then, later, she demanded, "Favorite kind of movie?"

And he hadn't missed a beat. "One with lots of action and not too much talk."

She asked, "Favorite card game?"

He answered, "Seven card draw."

"Favorite food?"

He grunted at that. "Whatever's in front of me."

She laughed. And then she wondered, "If you could take back one thing you said or did during your life so far, what would it be?"

He told the truth. "Hell. There's no way I can pick just one."

She moved on. "Name an exotic place you'd like to visit."

"How 'bout Tahiti?"

"Fine with me. Name something in this world that you love, not including people."

He thought about that one and then told her, "Peace and quiet. A hawk soaring. The way the wind makes ripples on a mountain pond."

"Hmm," she said after that and walked away with that soft smile on her face.

Later she asked, "What do you hate, Jared? I mean *really* hate?"

"The national debt. A broken promise."

"Got any enemies?"

"Sure. But my enemies don't worry me."

"Why not?"

"A man knows where he stands with his enemies and his friends. It's everyone else you have to watch out for."

When did the questions become less than harmless?

Be damned if he knew.

Maybe it was that night she knocked a glass off one of the tables and he went out with the broom to sweep up the pieces for her.

She was kneeling, her bright head bent, carefully picking up the larger shards. She looked up at him, her wide mouth as soft as a flower in full bloom, her brown eyes like velvet. "Were you scared as well as happy the day Heather was born?"

He stared down at her and hardly realized he was answering until he'd already said, "You bet. Scared as they come."

"Yes. I believe that."

He found he wanted to elaborate. So he did.

"Sally had a hard time of it—with the birth, I mean." His voice sounded gruff, unpracticed. But still he wanted to say more. He continued, "And I was a drinking man in those days. Nineteen years old and a stone alcoholic. Sally and me were having our problems because of that. But not that day."

"You were sober that day?"

"Yeah. I don't remember now how I managed that. Maybe that was during one of those times when I promised Sally I'd quit. Who the hell knows? What matters is, I was sober and they let me be there, at the end, to see my daughter born."

Jared leaned on the broom and shook his head. "Damn, she was ugly. It's hard to believe sometimes, when I look at her now, but Heather Jane was about the ugliest baby I ever saw in my life. I remember I mentioned how plug-ugly she was. And Sally said, 'You wouldn't look that great, either, if you'd just been through what *she's* been through.' And we laughed together. Then I said to Sally, 'I'm real proud.' And she kinda whispered back, 'Me too.' "

Jared flexed his fingers around the broom handle, wondering where the hell all those words had just come from. "It was a good day," he finished. And since he didn't know what else to do, he held out the dustpan.

Eden Parker didn't say anything. She only smiled and took what he offered her.

He told her about Belle and the boys a few nights later, when they were a week and a half or so into their temporary partnership.

She asked what was the *worst* day of his life.

And he said, "There have been many."

"Worst of the worst?"

He answered, "I suppose there were two of those."

"And they were?"

"The day Sally died. And the day I came home from work to find an empty house and a note from Belle saying she was taking the two boys and going back to the man she loved—that was her first husband, Dale."

"Taking the two boys," Eden repeated his words in a quiet voice. "Your stepsons, right?"

"My stepsons, T.J. and Lucas. Right."

Right then, a man and a woman, strangers in town, came in separately. They took places at either end of the bar. They each ordered a rum and cola. And then the man looked at the woman and she looked back.

The woman smiled.

The man said, "Put the lady's drink on my tab." And he moved to her end of the bar.

Jared and Eden settled in at the other end. Jared was drying glasses. Eden was tidying up, consolidating bowls of cocktail mix, wiping down the bar, things like that.

Jared didn't know what made him say it. But it was inside him, just itching to get out.

He told her, in a voice low enough that the other couple couldn't hear, "The truth is, stepfathers have got no damn rights at all."

"They don't?"

"No, they don't."

"Why not?"

"If the kids aren't yours by birth and you didn't manage to adopt them, then it doesn't matter what you've done for them." Jared turned and started putting the glasses away on a shelf, one at a time. As he set each glass down, he heard his own voice listing the little things, the everyday things, that make a man a father.

"So what if you walked the floor the nights they were sick? Or drove them to the dentist every time they had to go? Or made sure they got to their T-ball practice on time twice a week? Or fed them, or paid for the clothes on their backs?" He set the final glass on the shelf and then turned to pull the plug so the dirty water in the sink would drain.

He watched the murky water disappear and went on with his list, with all the little things that, in the end, had counted for nothing at all. "And who cares if you were the one to teach them how to tie their shoes? So what if you were tough when you had to be and said 'no' sometimes, because you knew it was the best thing for them, even though it damn sure didn't get you any points with them."

Jared rinsed the last of the dirty soapsuds down the drain. "You could have loved them with everything that's in you. And it doesn't mean squat, it doesn't mean a thing. If their mother wants to take them back to be with their *real* father, well, she can just go ahead. No court in this land will allow you a claim on them. They're nothing of yours. Just stepkids. That's all." Jared dragged in a deep breath and flipped on the faucet to refill the sink.

The room seemed very quiet then. The other couple wasn't talking, they were just staring into each other's eyes. And even the guys in the back room seemed to be keeping it down.

In that silence, Jared knew himself to be a fool. The worst kind of fool, one who talks too damn much. He started to turn away.

But then Eden asked, keeping her voice low, "Do you know where they are now?"

He felt the strangest thing. A kind of sweet relief. She wasn't going to say how sorry she was for him. She had only listened to him, accepted both his self-indulgence and his pain and then moved on from there.

He answered her. "Yeah. I know where they are."

"Did you ever try to see them?"

"Yeah. It was a mistake."

"Why?"

"Because Belle didn't want me around. And Dale didn't, either. And it confused the kids. It only caused problems. From what I understand, they're working things out as a family. And I...I wish them well." Miraculously, as he said the words, Jared realized they were true. The crippling bitterness he'd known for too long really was fading. He volunteered, "They teach about letting go, you know. In Alcoholics Anonymous?"

"Yes."

"So I'm learning. To let go. In this case, I think it's the best thing. Hell. Maybe it's the only thing I *can* do. Because like I said, I've got no damn rights with those kids anyway." He thought about Heather then, about how she was all grown up now and had her own life.

His expression must have told Eden something, because she asked, "What?"

"Just thinking. About raising kids."

"What about it?"

"If there's anyplace you have to let go, it's when you're raising kids. Maybe I just had to let go of Lucas and T.J. a little sooner than usual, that's all."

"Maybe," she said. She looked thoughtful. Then she asked, "So you married Belle because you liked her children?"

Jared actually laughed then. He had a lousy laugh and he knew it. He hadn't had a lot of practice at laughing during his life. "No, liking the boys came later."

Down the bar, the man and woman stopped staring at each other and glanced their way.

"'Nother round," the man said.

"Coming right up."

Jared went and mixed their drinks while Eden wiped down the tables and re-racked the pool cues. Then she went into the back room to check on the poker players there. She returned with four orders, including the usual tequila shooter for Rocky Collins and a whiskey and soda for Tim Brown. She set them up and Jared poured out.

Eden was leaning on the bar, waiting for him to finish, her chin in her hand. "Then why did you marry Belle, if not because of the kids?"

He didn't even hesitate. He said, careful only to keep his voice down so no one else would hear, "Because I wanted to have sex with her." He set the drinks on the tray.

Eden said, softly, "Hmm," and nodded, the way she did sometimes when he told her things, as if she were just storing them away, but making no judgments at this time. He watched her long, slender fingers with their pink-tipped nails as she moved the drinks around so the tray would balance. Then she slid the tray onto her left hand.

He heard himself adding before she could leave him, "I don't believe in sex outside of marriage. I've never had sex with a woman I wasn't married to first."

He expected her to laugh. Hell, he *wanted* her to laugh, to think he was joking, which he was not. If she had only laughed, it would have put some much-needed distance between them. It would have been a proof of a sort that she was not as sensitive nor as keen as he was beginning to believe.

But she didn't laugh. She only nodded again. "I see," she said and smiled the sweetest, most understanding smile. And then she turned to give the guys in the back room the drinks they had asked for.

And when she came back, she asked if he would mind if she called it a night. It was after ten and things were quiet. "Of course," she added, "I'll stay if you want me to."

And he realized he wanted more than anything right then to tell her to stay. But he remembered their understanding—the understanding that, as the nights went by, was getting harder and harder to keep in mind.

"Sure. Go on home," he said.

And she did.

It was after that night that the tension began to build between them again.

Jared tried to figure out exactly how it all came about, but he couldn't get it straight in his mind. He just knew that they'd come to an understanding, and there had been a time when they'd been careful of each other, distant with each other.

And then there had been a week or so when some connection beyond the way she turned him on had been forged.

That connection happened when she got him talking. God knows, he still had no idea how she did that. Even his sweet Sally had never been able to get him to talk. But Eden did it. And once she got him talking, she just listened, or said only what needed to be said to *keep* him talking.

But whatever the hell she had done, whatever had happened between them as he talked and she listened, it somehow made the denial of his desire for her all the harder to bear. Because he started to see her as an equal, as a contemporary. It got harder and harder to remember that she was closer to his daughter's age than his own, that he didn't have a damn thing to offer her, that he never intended to marry again anyway. And that he still held to his belief that it was wrong to have sex with a woman who wasn't his wife.

Not only did he want her more, on more levels than before, he also began to feel more protective of her. Objectively he knew this new protectiveness was uncalled-for. She didn't need or want his protection. She could handle herself.

But wanting her so damn much and knowing he was not going to have her was putting more and more pressure on him as each night crawled by. And it just didn't help his attitude at all when other men would look her over.

He found himself realizing that it was very damn possible that some night a man could come strolling into The Hole in the Wall and walk out with Eden on his arm. Hell, it might be a perfectly suitable man. A decent, unattached man with a good job and a shining future. A real winner of a guy. And if this prize of a fellow liked Eden, and she liked him back, then there would be nothing to stand in the way of the two of them getting together. And that would be good; it would be for the best.

Eden was just what his father had said: a great gal. A hardworking woman with a good attitude and a terrific head for business. She deserved to hook up with a winner.

Jared just prayed to holy heaven that Mr. Terrific didn't dare show his face in North Magdalene until after Oggie was back on his feet and he was long gone. Jared wanted the best for Eden. And the best would be someone else, he understood that. He just didn't want to have to watch it happening.

In truth, he feared that if he *were* forced to watch it happening, he wouldn't be watching for long. He'd be leaping over the bar and beating the daylights out of some poor fool whose only fault was that he was just the kind of sharp, successful guy that Eden Parker deserved to fall in love with.

And then, on top of everything else, there was Oggie, driving Jared right up the wall with his never-ending questions and his sly remarks.

"How's Eden?" Oggie would ask the minute Jared arrived at Delilah's to visit him. "You treatin' her right? You ain't lettin' her work too hard, are you? That gal is a workin' fool, you know. It wouldn't do for you to take advantage of that."

"I won't take advantage of her, Dad."

Then came that damn cackling laugh. "Hell, son. I didn't say don't take advantage of her personally, just don't let her work too hard. If you want to take advantage of *her*, well, you are two adults and there's nothing that I can do to—"

"Drop it, Dad."

"I got a right to have my say."

"Sure you do. And I got a right to turn around and walk right out of here."

"You don't like Eden?"

"I like Eden just fine."

"Then what's the big deal if I ask you how she's doing?"

"No big deal, Dad."

"Good, then." And there'd be more of the same.

Somehow, Jared never seemed to be able to pay his father a visit that the old fool didn't ask him how Eden was doing, or how Eden was feeling, or how he and Eden were managing together. As if Oggie didn't know exactly how Eden was, since she went to visit him nearly every day.

Yeah, Oggie was driving Jared crazy, all right. It was beginning to seem like a toss-up to Jared as to where he'd be more likely to lose his temper first: while watching some punk put the make on Eden, or while listening to his father go on about how damn wonderful she was.

Jared knew he was getting close to the brink. And he did not want to go over. One of the things he'd told himself when he came in from the woods this time was that he was not going to get in any fights. His goal was to make peace with the world, not beat the holy hell out of it. Too bad that when he set that goal he hadn't known about Eden Parker. If he'd known about her and her long legs and wide mouth and those big brown eyes that lately seemed to be looking at him even in his dreams, he might have just stayed in the woods.

But it was too late now. He was here. And he was stuck here until his old man could walk again. And, by God, he was going to keep himself under iron control, if it killed him to do it.

But by Saturday night, two weeks after Oggie shot himself in the foot, Jared was ready to snap.

There was a hotheaded street fighter down inside Oggie Jones's oldest son. Jared had battled that troublemaker all of his life. And now, because of Eden, the battle with his own violent self was worse than it had ever been. He was determined to win out over it.

But he was losing.

The sad truth was that it wouldn't take much, now, for the street fighter to rule the day once more. He was only

waiting. Waiting for the right excuse to take on any idio
who made the crucial error of looking at Jared—or Ede
Parker—cross-eyed.

Chapter Nine

The final Saturday night in August started out the same as the two previous ones. The place was humming when Jared came in at seven.

He went right to work mixing drinks so Eden could concentrate on playing waitress. They worked smoothly and swiftly for an hour or so, which was just fine with Jared.

Jared liked it when business was brisk. Not only did they bring in more money, but time went by faster. Even better, when things were hopping, Jared found that it was *almost* possible not to think for a while about how much he wanted Eden.

And tonight, all the trade they were getting really was a lifesaver. Because tonight it was even harder than usual not to think about Eden. She'd worn something different, a sort of Annie Oakley outfit, a Western shirt and fringed skirt and vest, along with a pair of white cowboy boots. The skirt wasn't that short. It ended just above her knees. But on Eden, a skirt didn't have to be short. Her legs were so damn gorgeous a man found himself staring at them even when all he could see was the little stretch of calf between her boot tops and her kneecaps.

Jared reminded himself to talk to her later. He'd tell her to stick with the black slacks and white shirt from now on— or else. And then he silently admitted that he'd do no such thing, because there was nothing wrong with the cowgirl outfit except that she looked great in it. He couldn't fault her for looking great, unless he was prepared to admit exactly why it bothered him. And no way was he going to do that.

So he worked fast and hard and told himself to be grateful it was a busy night.

At around eight, Rocky Collins, who was sitting on his favorite stool right by the little rubber mat where Jared poured the drinks, suddenly announced, "Well, lookit who's coming. Ain't that a sight?"

Jared glanced toward the window in time to see his sister Delilah and her husband, Sam, approaching the double doors to the bar. Sam was pushing Oggie in a wheelchair.

"Oggie!" Eden cried out. "Jared, look. It's Oggie."

Jared grunted. What a thrill, he thought.

He couldn't see what she was getting so excited about. After all, it wasn't as if they never saw the old geezer. Jared had visited his father at Sam and Delilah's house that very day and got a slew of unwanted questions and advice for his trouble. The questions, as usual, had been all about Eden. And the advice had been disgustingly personal.

"A man like you really needs a woman, son," Oggie had suggested. "'Cause sexual frustration can be a hell of a problem for a man in his prime. Matter of fact, sexual frustration can make a man a real trial to everyone who cares about him."

"Who the hell gave you the right to lecture me about my sex life, Dad?"

"*Your* sex life? Who said I was talkin' about *your* sex life. I said a man *like* you."

"Right."

"And as for the rest of it, well, that was scientific fact and that is all. When a man goes too long without sex, a pressure begins to build up, a pressure that has been proven by science to have to be let loose somewhere, and—"

"I never hit a man in a wheelchair, Dad. But there's a first time for everything."

Oggie cackled gleefully then. "See what I mean? Something's got to give, son, or before you know it, *ka-blam!* You're just gonna explode."

Jared had left soon after that. He figured he'd seen about enough of his old man for one day.

And Eden saw plenty of Oggie also. She visited him at Delilah's whenever she got the chance—or so Oggie and his sister were always telling him. Jared himself had never run into her there. And he knew why. She was being careful to go at times when she thought she wouldn't meet up with him.

North Magdalene was a dinky little town. However, since he and Eden had reached their *understanding,* Jared hadn't run into her even once outside of the hours they were forced to work together.

At first, he'd been grateful that she gave him a wide berth whenever possible. But recently, as she'd drawn him out and got him talking during business hours, the way she avoided him the rest of the time had begun to irritate him. He knew his irritation was unreasonable. It was his own fault that she was staying out of his way. He had no right at all to be bugged about it.

But he was. He was damned annoyed.

Right that minute, she further annoyed him by clapping her serving tray on the end of the bar and rushing to prop open the double doors as if royalty had come to call. Oggie, with his bad foot leading the way, was then wheeled in with a lot of clucking and fluttering from Eden and Delilah, and with Sam doing most of the work of getting the old man's chair over the doorjamb.

"Hey, Jared." Sam saluted him. "How goes it, buddy?"

"It's been worse," Jared answered. He even attempted a smile for Sam's sake, in spite of his dark mood.

Jared and Sam went back a long ways. And beyond that, Jared couldn't help feeling respect for the man who had married his sister. Jared knew Delilah, after all. And he had a pretty good idea what kind of a man it would take to sleep with Delilah at night and still walk around smiling in the daytime the way Sam did. So Sam got a real greeting from Jared.

On the other hand, when Oggie called out, "Good to see you workin' so hard, son," Jared felt hard put to spare him a wave.

Once he was inside, Oggie was set up at the best table in the house. He ordered a whiskey on the rocks. Sam wanted a beer and Delilah asked for a vodka tonic. Then every damn customer in the place had to have a fresh drink so they could all propose toasts to Oggie's recovery and make bad jokes about people who shoot themselves in the foot.

Personally Jared thought the whole routine was a pain in the butt. But he gutted it out anyway, even raising his cola can once or twice at the toasts.

And then, just when things started to settle down a little, in came Brendan and Amy. They explained that they'd left the baby with Amy's teenage sister for the evening, so the grown-ups could have a little fun.

More chairs were pulled up at Oggie's table. Amy wanted a cherry cola and Brendan asked for his usual whiskey straight up.

When Eden came over to the bar to get the drinks for them, her eyes were shining so bright she looked like a kid on Christmas Eve. Eden was just nuts about the family and

Jared hadn't the faintest idea why. If you asked him, he thought they were all more trouble than they were worth.

But then, no one was asking him.

As soon as Amy and Brendan were settled in with their drinks in front of them, some damn fool dropped a quarter in the jukebox and there was Patsy Cline singing "Crazy." And then what? Brendan pulled Amy to her feet. Sam grabbed Delilah. The two couples went swaying out onto the little square of floor by the curtain to the card room.

Jared was careful not to look at them. It was enough to make a man sick. No four people had a right to look that happy in a screwed-up world like this one.

A few minutes later, Jared's middle brother, Patrick, came in. Thankfully, as far as Jared was concerned, Patrick was alone. Jared didn't think he could stand looking at another happy couple right then. Patrick joined the family table and ordered a drink to be sociable, but Jared thought he looked a little down.

Which made sense. Patrick's ex-wife had recently taken their two daughters and moved out of state. Also, Chloe Swan, who'd been in love with Patrick for years, had run off a couple of months ago with a stranger. Since their messy breakup a decade ago, Patrick had kept Chloe at a distance, insisting she and he were no more than friends. But ever since she'd gone, everyone said Patrick had been mooning around like a motherless calf.

For a few minutes after the glum Patrick's arrival, Jared felt a little better about things. It was a welcome relief to see another man without an ear-to-ear grin on his face.

But then Oggie and Eden got to talking about the restaurant they were going to open next door come spring, and Patrick perked up. Apparently, as Eden had mentioned a couple of weeks ago, Patrick was in on the restaurant deal and enthusiastic about it as well.

Jared's spirits grew darker.

More customers came in. It was turning into one of the busiest nights Jared could remember. And there were almost as many women in the place as there were men. The Hole in the Wall was now the kind of bar where a man could bring his lady and not worry if he'd end up having to protect her honor from some yahoo who'd had one drink too many. That was due to Eden's influence, of course.

Yeah, Eden was a damn wonder, all right. Jared scowled and mixed more drinks.

Around ten, when the atmosphere was more like that of a large, successful party than a busy night at a bar, three single men came in together. They were all big and young—college buddies out in the sticks on a camping trip from the look of them. Jared knew their type on sight. Their bulging muscles and good-natured arrogance gave them away. Jocks. Probably football players from the size of them.

Over near the curtain to the back room, three single women were sitting together, sharing a girls' night out and seeming to be having a pretty good time. The three jocks homed in on the women and had them surrounded in seconds flat.

The ladies put up not even token resistance. They smiled and flirted and helped the jocks find three spare chairs—precious commodities in the filled-to-capacity bar.

Eden slipped through the crowd to take orders from the newcomers. Jared, who was mixing more drinks right then, watched her out of the corner of his eye. He knew how careful she was about getting ID from anyone who looked to be under thirty, and he was a little uneasy about how she was going to handle these guys. You just never knew about jocks, especially when they'd just found themselves some women to impress. They might get hostile about having to show they were old enough to drink.

But Eden proved equal to her task. From that distance, Jared couldn't hear what was said. But he saw that she smiled and made some kind of joke, because both the jocks and the women laughed. Then the three men were whipping out their wallets and handing her their ID's. She gave each one of the ID's a good look before she handed them back in the order she'd collected them.

As Eden returned the final ID, its owner grabbed her hand, turned it over and planted a kiss in the heart of her palm. He looked up at her and said something. Eden's slim back stiffened.

Jared set down the shaker of margaritas he was mixing. His gut was clenching, his whole body gathering . . .

And then Eden pulled her hand away and made some light remark that sent another wave of laughter over the group at the table. The big jock who'd kissed Eden's hand laughed the loudest. The woman sitting next to him, the most attractive of the women, didn't laugh at all.

Eden turned and left the table. The big jock watched her go. Jared knew just what that college boy was looking at. For the last two weeks, he himself had looked at exactly the same thing whenever he forgot to stop himself.

Jared remembered his job. He picked up the shaker of margaritas and poured them out swiftly into salt-rimmed glasses. "Hey Jared, what about *my* drink?" Rocky complained.

Jared poured out a straight shot of tequila, grabbed the salt and a wedge of lime and put it all down in front of Rocky. "There you go, Rock," he said in a voice so patient and low that poor Rocky, cringing back, almost fell off his favorite stool. "Will that take care of it?"

"Er, uh, yeah. That's it. You bet. Thanks a bunch. That's great—"

Jared turned away before Rocky could finish groveling. He set the margaritas before the customers who'd ordered them and watched as Eden approached him.

She smiled. "A pitcher of the dark stuff for the all-Americans back there. And another round for the ladies. Plus two tall ones for the guys at the pool table." She was already setting up the glassware for him to use. The woman was so damned efficient it set his teeth on edge sometimes.

He poured the drinks. He told himself he was not going to ask, "What'd he say to you?" But somehow, he did.

"What did *who* say?" She was busily arranging the drinks on the tray, looking extremely unconcerned. But she gave herself away when her hand hit one of the drinks and it nearly spilled.

Jared steadied the drink and captured Eden's evasive gaze. "Don't play dumb. Just tell me what he said."

She looked at him for a moment. Then she gave up her pretense that she didn't know who he was talking about. Her wide mouth pursed. She spoke very quietly. "Stop it. I handled it."

His voice was equally soft. "What did he say?"

"Let it go."

"Tell me. Now."

Eden said nothing.

Over at the family's table, Oggie was in the middle of a long, involved joke about a salesman and a pair of silk stockings. Down the bar, someone called for a refill. Behind the curtain to the back room, a winner at the poker table crowed in triumph. The jukebox droned on, a sad song about a desperado who would not surrender to love.

Neither Jared nor Eden noticed any of this. The boisterous crowd all around them had spun away. There was only the two of them, will to will.

They had an *understanding*. They were temporary business partners and no more. Yet he wanted to know what the other man had said to her. And she would not tell him, for fear of a fight.

Then Eden said in a low, even whisper, "Please, Jared. It honestly was not that bad. And it's over. It's done. Don't make trouble. Please."

Jared's fist, clenched on the bar, slowly and reluctantly relaxed.

Damn her, he thought. She *would* have to go and ask him so nicely. What the devil could a man do when a woman said please, except give her what she wanted?

And hell, in spite of how tight he was wound up, he really didn't want to spoil things for her. He knew she was as proud as a peacock over the way the place was cooking tonight. And she had a right to be proud. It was her triumph, her proof that she'd done real wonders with his father's dingy saloon. A fight would spoil everything, and he knew it damn well.

"All right," he said.

"Thank you." Her smile was tremulous, brimming with silent gratitude. Jared drank in her shining eyes, her petal-soft mouth and sweetly flushed cheeks—and that heated, hungry longing down inside him almost took control.

The urge was on him to reach across the bar that separated them and wrap his hand around her soft nape. To pull her toward him, just enough that he could put his lips against hers.

One quick, hard kiss. That was all it would take. And every man in the place would know who she belonged to. And anyone else who messed with her would do it at his own risk.

"Jared?" Her smile had changed. Her sweet mouth was slightly parted.

Damn her. She *knew*.

And she *wanted* him to do it, to stake his claim on her.

He thought of Sally, who had died and left him. And of Belle, who'd betrayed him and then taken the two boys he loved from him without a single backward glance.

He reminded himself, as damn near impossible as that was to do while he was looking at Eden, that he was never going to put his heart and soul in a woman's frail hands again. And besides, he had to remember that he had nothing left to offer a woman anyway. His heart was a dried-up husk, and he was an unemployed lumberjack, his prospects dim at best.

"Serve the drinks," he told her. Then he turned to take an order from a man who'd just slid onto the only vacant stool down at the far end of the bar.

He knew she stared after him, for the briefest of moments. But Eden Parker was a pro. Before he could mutter "What'll it be?" to the man at the end of the bar, she had hoisted her tray of drinks up high and was off to weave her way between the full tables.

Jared kept an eye out as she served the six at the back table. He didn't miss the speculative sideways looks that the biggest of the three men kept giving her. But the college boy said nothing this time, and Eden was careful never to look at him. And then the woman beside him, not pleased at all with the interest he was showing in their waitress, tugged on his arm. The big jock turned to the woman with a slow, sexy grin, and Eden slipped away.

Oggie caught her as she passed the table where he still held forth, keeping everyone in stitches. "Give us all another drink, gal. And make it snappy."

Eden laughed, a bright, sparkly sound that seemed to prod at Jared's empty shell of a heart. "Watch it, partner. You are in no position to get pushy."

Sam advised, "She's right, Oggie. You get pushy, and I'll be pushing you . . . right out the door."

"All right, all right. Jeez. What's the damn world coming to? A man can't even be an s.o.b. in his own damn bar." He pretended to look sorry. "Could we all have another drink. Please?"

Eden agreed that they could.

Midnight approached and went on by. Everyone was having a hell of a time. Brendan and Sam pushed the tables back a little more from the small section of cleared floor, and more couples ventured out to dance to the jukebox. Eden moved, swift and sure, between the tables, stopping to take an order, or to laugh at a joke. And Jared waited on the people at the bar and mixed the drinks and made sure there was plenty of cocktail mix and fresh popcorn.

At the back table, three romances appeared to be in bloom. The all-Americans and their new girlfriends danced and laughed and drank a bit more than was good for them. Jared almost quit keeping tabs on them. The one who'd tried to make a move on Eden was plenty busy as the night went by. He seemed thoroughly absorbed in the woman who had pulled him down next to her when he and his buddies first entered the bar.

She was a pistol, that woman. Small and slim, with a pretty, catlike face and short brown hair. She'd set her sights on the big blond college boy and she wasn't letting him slip through her paws. She pulled him onto the little section of dance floor and she plastered her trim little body up against him. As the jukebox played on, she clung to him like a new coat of paint.

Jared actually had to suppress a grin when he watched that little pussycat of a woman stalk her all-American prey. His opinion, the more he watched the two of them, was that the college boy didn't stand a chance.

In fact, seeing that the catwoman was going to keep the college boy from getting anywhere near Eden, Jared felt his mood improve marginally. He began to believe that he might make it through this night without busting anybody's teeth after all.

But then Eden dropped off her tray, grabbed her purse from behind the bar and made the high sign that told him she was taking a bathroom break. She disappeared down the back hall to the ladies' room, which was all the way out back, through an outside door off the parking lot.

Not five minutes later, he noticed that the catwoman was sitting at her table all alone.

* * *

Eden was too flushed with the success of the evening to pay any attention to who might be watching when she went outside. And she was also in a hurry. She was the only waitress on a very busy floor. She wanted to relieve her bladder and run a quick comb through her hair and get back to work.

She gave a little grateful sigh when she got out to the parking lot and saw that there wasn't a line. Even better, the door to the ladies' room opened right then. Angie Leslie, a beautiful brunette who lived across the street from Sam and Delilah, stepped out.

Angie smiled. "Be my guest." She held the door.

"Thanks." Eden smiled back.

Then she slid around Angie into the ladies' room and latched the door behind her. Quickly she relieved herself, washed her hands and straightened her hair. She glanced at her watch. Only four minutes since she'd left Jared alone in there.

Thinking of Jared, she couldn't help smiling. Her face in the mirror blushed as pink as a strawberry daiquiri. He'd wanted to beat some sense into that smug jerk at the back table, for her sake. And he hadn't done it, also for her sake.

Even better, she had seen the look in his eyes after he'd agreed to leave well enough alone. He'd come *that* close to grabbing her and kissing her. She knew it.

Soon enough, he *would* kiss her. She knew that as well.

And, oh, how she was longing for it to be sooner rather than later.

The fact was that over the past two weeks, Eden Parker had come a long way in admitting to herself what she wanted.

"Okay, okay," she said to her own reflection in the mirror. "Settle down there, girl. So you're in love. With an absolutely impossible man. Love finds a way. Give it time. Let it happen."

She glanced at her watch again and realized she'd wasted two minutes grinning like a lovestruck fool and talking to herself in the mirror. She fumbled in her purse until she found her lipstick. After freshening her lips, she hooked her bag over her shoulder and pulled open the door.

There was another woman waiting her turn outside. Eden exchanged a quick smile with her and the woman disappeared inside, latching the door behind her as Eden had done.

And then Eden turned for the back door to the bar, only to be brought up short when she collided with a man coming out.

"Hey, baby. Been looking for you. Where're you going in such a big hurry?"

It was the big all-American jerk. The floodlight over the door to the bar clearly illuminated his chiseled features.

Eden didn't bother to suppress her groan of annoyance. "It's none of your business where I'm going."

She slid to the side to go around him. He moved to block her path. "My name is Lew. What's yours?"

"Get out of my way," she instructed wearily. Eden had spent a lot of years tap-dancing away from overly amorous creeps. Since she'd come to North Magdalene, it hardly happened anymore. She suspected that was because of her connection with the Jones Gang. Generally, in North Magdalene, it was considered downright foolish to invite the wrath of any one of the Joneses. People just didn't do that.

But Lew hadn't been in town long. He waxed poetic. "God, you are gorgeous. I've got a thing for leggy redheads, you know."

"Look. I'm not interested. Step aside, please."

"Call me Lew. And like I said inside, I'd like to find out if you're a redhead everywhere..." He reached out.

Eden stepped back and avoided his grasp. "I said I'm not interested." She was stalling, thinking she only had to hold him off for a moment or two. Someone was bound to come outside.

And she was right. Eden had barely finished thinking someone would come, when someone did. The back door to the bar swung open on a long squeak.

Eden started to breathe a sigh of relief. But her sigh caught in her throat.

Beyond the threshold stood the one person she didn't want to see right then: Jared. His eyes were as cold as steel, his mouth set and grim.

Suddenly the fight she'd managed to avert earlier seemed distressingly imminent all over again.

Chapter Ten

Eden was sure the big jock would turn to see who was standing in the open door.

But right at that moment, the man was oblivious to all but the object of his desire. "My name's Lew. Say it. And give me a kiss. And then *maybe* I'll let you go."

Had she still been alone with Lew, Eden might have become nervous at that point. But Jared was there. Suddenly dealing with Lew seemed the least of her problems.

Right then, in that unnerving way that Jared sometimes had, he vanished from beyond the door and reappeared directly behind the big man. Jared tapped him on the shoulder.

Lew's amorous expression became one of mild surprise. He turned. "Huh?" He looked Jared up and down. "What's your problem, barkeep? Can't you see the lady and I are having a little talk?"

Jared spoke to Eden. "You have anything more you want to say to Lew, here?"

The relief Eden felt was lovely. Jared was being reasonable after all. "No," she said quietly. "I've got nothing more to say to him."

Lew's square jaw clenched. "So what? I've got plenty to say to you."

Jared cut in. "You're not getting the message, Lew. What *you've* got to say doesn't matter, if the lady's not interested."

Lew's face grew flushed. "She's interested. She's just not admitting it yet. And besides, it's no business of yours. You stay out of this, barkeep, or I'll..." Lew left his threat unfinished, as if to emphasize the gravity of it.

Eden suggested, "Look, fellas, if we could just—"

Jared waved a hand at her for silence. "You'll what, Lew?"

Lew threw back his big shoulders and stuck out his already imposing chest. "I'll be forced to adjust your attitude for you."

"Jared, let it go, I—"

Jared didn't even acknowledge that Eden had spoken. He asked Lew, "Oh? And how will you do that, exactly?"

"You want me to show you?"

"Showing's better than telling any day of the week."

Lew grinned, displaying an alarming expanse of big white teeth. "All right, barkeep. You asked for it."

"No. Stop this, I mean it..." Eden insisted.

Neither of the men listened. Lew drew back his huge fist and sent it rocketing toward Jared's jaw.

Unfortunately for Lew, Jared didn't wait around for the blow to connect. Instead, moving so fast that what he actually did seemed invisible, he managed simultaneously to block the punch *and* kick Lew's legs out from under him.

Eden heard her own voice demanding once more, "No, Jared, don't!" as the big man went down.

Jared gave her his frozen gunmetal glare. "Go inside," he instructed in that hissing whisper of his. "Now."

"No, I will not. I want this to stop, and I—"

"Damn it, Eden..."

Jared's curse trailed off as he glanced down at his opponent. Lew had pulled himself to his knees. He was rubbing his scraped hands together and shaking his head.

"Go, Eden. I mean it," Jared said.

But Eden remained firm. "Forget it. I'm not moving."

"What the hell?" Lew seemed unable to fathom how he'd ended up on the ground. He looked up at Jared and asked, "What are you, crazy?"

Jared said, "Around here we don't like it when a man forces himself on a woman."

"You *kicked* me," Lew complained.

"Jared—" Eden began, but got no farther.

"Damn straight I kicked you," Jared said to Lew. "Your manners suck." He shot Eden a grim look. "And since the lady won't go inside like I told her to, I want you to apologize to her. Now."

"Huh?"

"I said, say you're sorry. Now."

Lew looked from Eden to Jared and back again. He let out a kind of low, bellowing noise. It seemed he had decided that he was the one who had been wronged. Then he snarled at Jared, "Why you..." and he sprang upward, straight for Jared, aiming his head at Jared's midsection.

Jared feinted back and kicked sideways, nicking the side of Lew's head with his boot. Lew grunted, but didn't go down this time. He reassessed his target and charged at Jared like a bull at a red cape. Jared moved aside.

Lew didn't notice that his target had shifted. He ended up ramming his head into the front grill of Owen Beardsly's Ford Explorer.

That stopped him for a moment.

But only for a moment. He shook his head to clear it, turned and charged again, snorting like the bull he resembled.

Eden watched, hopping from one foot to the other, trying to decide which one of them she should grab to stop this insanity.

Just then, the woman inside the rest room pushed the door open. She took one look at Jared, crouched and waiting, and Lew barreling toward him headfirst, and let out a piercing scream, pulling the door closed on herself again.

Eden tried once more to inject a plea for reason. "Jared! Stop it. I mean it, stop this right now!"

The only answer Eden got was a sickening thud and an agonized "Oof!" as Jared jumped back and kicked Lew a good one right in the breadbasket. Lew crumpled, holding his stomach. Jared stepped in, hit him on top of the head and then kicked him in the chin with a knee.

The woman hiding in the ladies' room peeked out and screamed again as Lew fell over backward and Jared jumped on top of him. There was a tangle of legs and arms and fists and a lot of awful grunting and groaning.

And then, somehow, Brendan and Patrick and Sam were there, pulling Jared off the other man. And then Lew's friends were there, too, hauling Lew to his feet. A small group of spectators had appeared out of nowhere as well.

Jared cursed his brothers and demanded they let him go. But the Jones boys held on.

Then Sam said to the strangers, "Get him out. And don't let him come back. Understand?"

The other two were not nearly as aggressive as their friend. They nodded and dragged Lew away.

Lew struggled and protested, but Eden thought it was more for pride's sake than anything else. He was staggering, his nose was bleeding and his lip was cut, whereas the worst thing about Jared's face was the scowl on it—and the last fading remnant of the black eye Eden had inflicted on him over two weeks before.

After Lew and his buddies had disappeared around the side of the building, the woman in the bathroom slid out and made a quick getaway of her own.

Then Sam asked, "Is it going to be safe to let go of you now, Jared?"

Jared made a low, growling sound.

Patrick and Brendan and Sam exchanged looks. Brendan suggested, "You just tell us when."

For a few moments they all stood there, Eden glaring at Jared, while Brendan, Sam and Patrick held him still. The small crowd that had gathered muttered quietly to each other. And then Jared grunted.

"All right. Let me go."

Slowly, warily, the other three released him. They stood back from him.

"Go on inside, folks," Sam said to the spectators. "The show's over."

The onlookers began filing back into the bar.

Meanwhile, Jared brushed the dust from his sleeves, tucked in his shirt and rubbed his chin, which, Eden saw now, had been cut. It was bleeding. She took a handkerchief from her purse and stepped up to him.

He gave her his narrow-eyed scowl.

"Oh, for heaven's sake. Take this and wipe it up," she said. She was thoroughly disgusted with him—and very glad that he hadn't been badly hurt.

He took the handkerchief from her hand and blotted his chin with it, while she glared at him and he glowered back.

"What the hell's going on out there?" Oggie called from inside.

"We'd better go on in," Sam said, "Or he'll be wheeling himself out here, even if he has to batter down the walls in the hallway to do it."

Brendan and Patrick made sounds of agreement. Jared and Eden, each glaring at the other, paid no mind to Sam's advice. "Don't be long," Sam warned, as he led the othe men back in. "You've still got a full house in there."

"We'll be right in," Eden promised, though she kept he eyes locked with Jared's.

When the door had closed behind the brothers, Ede opened her mouth to tell Jared Jones exactly what sh thought of his behavior. But then she realized that if sh once started telling him off, she might never be able to stop

She glanced at her watch: a few minutes shy of one. Jus a little over an hour to go and they could close the doors o the most successful night they'd seen since Eden becam half owner of The Hole in the Wall.

Okay, so she hadn't managed to prevent a fight. But i could have been worse. Much worse. If they went right in side now and picked up where they'd left off, everything would work out just fine from a business point of view anyway.

She could give Jared Jones the dressing-down he de served after hours.

Jared, who was watching her expression, chose that mo ment to let out a rare chuckle. "Are those dollar signs I se shining in your eyes?"

She stuck out her chin at him. "Don't push me, Jared You're just lucky I'm a businesswoman first."

He was smiling. She didn't like it. He *never* smiled. He held out her handkerchief, which was now stained a vivi crimson in more than one spot. "I think I ruined it."

She didn't care about that. She took the cloth from hin without looking at it. "You could have been hurt."

"I'll be hurting all right. Tomorrow. I'm too old to be getting in fights."

She wanted to demand, *Then why did you?* But she held her tongue. She'd demand a lot of things. Later.

She went and pulled back the door. "We've got work to do."

Docile as a lamb, he preceded her inside.

PLAY

BIG BUCKS

ONE MILLION • ONE MILLION

AND YOU COULD WIN THE

$1,000,000.00

PLUS JACKPOT!

SILHOUETTE

YOUR *PERSONAL* GAME CARD INSIDE....

EXCLUSIVE PRIZE # 4L 964923

BIG BUCKS

$

TWO WAYS TO WIN BIG BUCKS!

1. Uncover 5 $ signs in a row. . . . BINGO! You're eligible to win the $1,000,000.00 SWEEPSTAKES!

2. Uncover 5 $ signs in a row AND uncover $ signs in all 4 corners . . . BINGO! You're also eligible for the $50,000.00 EXTRA BONUS PRIZE!

HURRY!
This Jackpot must be claimed!

Scratch Here →

LUCKY CHARM GAME!

Claim 4 FREE books AND a FREE Mystery Gift!

YES! I have played my BIG BUCKS game card as instructed. Enter my Big Bucks Prize number in the MILLION DOLLAR Sweepstakes III and also enter me for the Extra Bonus Prize. When winners are selected, tell me if I've won. If the Lucky Charm is scratched off, I will also receive everything revealed, as explained on the back of this page.

235 CIS ANTM
(U-SIL-SE-05/94)

NAME _____

ADDRESS _____ APT. _____

CITY _____ STATE _____ ZIP _____

NO PURCHASE OR OBLIGATION NECESSARY TO ENTER SWEEPSTAKES.

Million Dollar Sweepstakes III, 3010 Walden Ave., P.O. Box 1867, Buffalo, NY 14269-1867. Limit: One entry per envelope.

BUSINESS REPLY MAIL
FIRST CLASS MAIL   PERMIT NO. 717   BUFFALO, NY

POSTAGE WILL BE PAID BY ADDRESSEE

"BIG BUCKS"
MILLION DOLLAR SWEEPSTAKES III
3010 WALDEN AVE.
P.O. BOX 1867
BUFFALO, NY 14240-9952

NO POSTAGE
NECESSARY
IF MAILED
IN THE
UNITED STATES

* * *

He didn't stay docile for long. Within a half an hour, he was scowling again and glaring at anybody who got too pushy about wanting a drink.

Part of his ill humor was probably caused by the unpleasant incident that occurred shortly after he and Eden went back inside.

They'd gone straight to work, filling drink orders and trying to get back on top of things. In her rush, Eden still managed to spare a glance for the back table. The three women who'd been sitting with Lew and his friends were gone.

Eden had barely had time to notice their absence, when one of them, the petite brunette who'd been after Lew all night, was back.

She came storming through the front door like a mini-hurricane, stomped right up to the bar and pointed a red-nailed finger at Jared.

"You." She poked the finger at the bar. "Right here. Now."

Hesitantly Jared approached.

The little brunette jabbed the bar once more.

Jared moved into place.

The brunette stuck her pert nose right into his scowling face. "You are an animal," she told him. "And you leave Lew alone from now on, or you will answer to me. Understood?"

Jared went on scowling.

"Understood?"

Grimly he nodded.

"Good," the brunette announced. And then she whirled on her pointy-toed high heels and got out of there.

Over at his table, Oggie let out a loud guffaw. "And they try to tell us that *men* run the world!" Then he added, "A round on the house!"

After that, Jared's mood grew progressively darker. To Eden, it seemed as if there had been pressure building in him all night. The fight with Lew had worked like a safety valve, releasing enough steam that Jared had actually relaxed for a minute or two out there in the parking lot, when he'd teased her about the dollar signs in her eyes. But the reprieve had been short. The brunette came in and gave him a hard time and the pressure started building all over again.

By the time Sam finally wheeled Oggie out the door and everyone else went home, Jared was spoiling for a fight all over again.

By then, the only one left to fight with was Eden. And that was just fine with her. She was fed up with him anyway. And now that the big night was over, she had every intention of telling him so.

At first, in the silence after everyone was gone, they ignored each other. Eden cleared all the tables and wiped them down, while Jared cleaned the bar and washed the glassware. Then Eden took the register drawer into the card room and counted what they'd earned that night. It was a stunning amount. She should have been thrilled.

But she was so preoccupied with what she was going to say to Jared that she couldn't even appreciate what a triumph the night had been. She blamed Jared for that, too, for stealing her pleasure in their success.

She set up the drawer for the next day and went back to the main room to return the drawer to the register where it belonged. Jared, she noticed, was already mopping up by then. She pointedly didn't speak to him, but instead took the rest of the money next door to the deserted Mercantile building, where she locked it in the safe that was hidden behind a false cabinet there.

She came back to find him sitting at the counter with a drink in front of him.

He must have taken note of the way her eyes widened when she saw the tall glass, and realized she was thinking that the night had driven him to drink. He toasted her with the sweating glass and then took a long swallow.

After that, he admitted, "Relax, it's only tonic water," before polishing off the rest. Then he stood up. "About time to call it a night, wouldn't you say?"

To Eden, his words amounted to an outright taunt. "No," she said, pushing the single syllable out through her clenched teeth. "I wouldn't say that at all."

The flap was up at the end of the bar. He went through there and tossed his ice cubes into the steel sink. They clattered loudly. "Well, then. What *would* you say?" He set the glass in the sink to be washed tomorrow.

She hardly knew where to begin. But she managed. "You were way out of line, out there in the parking lot tonight."

Idly, as if he were wandering aimlessly rather than moving with absolute purpose, he came back around to her side of the bar. "Oh, was I?"

"Yes. You were."

He flipped over the stool he'd been sitting on and placed it on the bar with the rest of the stools. "That's not how I saw it."

Eden reminded herself to stay calm. She wanted to explain to him very reasonably just what an overbearing oaf he'd been. She took in a long breath. "I have worked very hard, Jared, to make this bar the kind of place where everyone can come and have a good time without worrying that they'll get their heads bashed in. *Anyone* who starts a fight here is sabotaging all the progress that's been made. I believe that you understand that."

He looked away, then looked back at her. Then he said, very patiently, "I didn't start that fight. And you know it."

"Right. Because *he* threw the first punch, *you're* not to blame."

"That's about the size of it. And anyway, nothing happened in your precious bar. We took it outside, so it didn't hurt your business one damn bit."

"It was totally unnecessary."

"Wrong."

She gaped at him. "What do you mean, wrong?"

"I mean it *was* necessary. Both you and I bent over backward giving that bastard a chance to get lost. But he wouldn't take a hint. He needed a lesson in how to behave."

Eden couldn't believe what she was hearing. "You have all the reasoning abilities of a Neanderthal, Jared Jones."

"Call me names if you want. But that's one fool who won't be bothering you again."

"You aren't listening. I said it was completely uncalled-for. Picking a fight with that guy was like ... putting out a trash fire with a nuclear warhead."

He folded his arms over his chest. "It was necessary."

"It *was not.* I did not need your help. I had everything under control. All it required was for me to stall him until someone came out."

"Someone did come out. Me."

This was not going as Eden had planned at all. The man actually *refused* to admit that he was the one in the wrong. She put her hands on her hips and moved closer to him. "I was doing fine handling that guy, admit it."

He just looked at her, his eyes like flint, his thin lip slightly curled.

She took another step, until she stood nose to nose with him. "It's my job to deal with people. I've been doing it since I was sixteen years old. And I've been handling creeps in bars since I was old enough to serve alcoholic beverages. I was in no danger from that jerk, and you know it. You're just *jealous,* that's all...."

The minute she said the word, *jealous,* Eden wished she could bite her tongue. It was a taunt, pure and simple. And taunting was beneath her, since she considered herself to be the righteous one here.

But what was done could not be undone. Jared dropped his crossed arms to his sides.

Eden backed up a step. "Um, Jared, I—"

Now he was the one moving in. He closed the distance she'd created. His eyes had changed, gone from flint to curling smoke. "Jealous, am I?"

"Never mind. Really. I shouldn't have said that." She backed up again and started to turn away.

But something had happened to Jared. Something had finally snapped.

"But you did say it." He reached out and wrapped his hand around the back of her neck. Her skin tingled. His touch was electric.

"I—"

"And why the hell shouldn't you say it? It's only the damn truth."

She licked her lips. It was so hard to think, when his hand was there, warm and rough, cupping the back of her neck. "Jared, I . . ."

He pulled her toward him, so there was no more than a hairbreadth between their bodies. Then he lowered his mouth until it almost touched hers.

"You can bet those sweet, long legs of yours that I'm jealous." His rough whisper slid along her nerves like a physical caress. "As jealous as they come. And that's why it was necessary, what I did to that fool. Because I don't want *anyone* to touch you. Not anyone but *me.*"

Eden gave a small, sharp gasp. Though what she'd just heard was only what she'd been waiting, *longing* to hear, it still stunned her to have him actually say the words at last.

She stared into his eyes like a woman mesmerized. How long had she waited for him to admit that he wanted her? It seemed like forever.

At last, the waiting was over. He had confessed his desire.

And in the space of an instant, the whole world had changed. The fight with Lew, the threat to her business, none of that mattered.

What mattered—*all* that mattered—was that, at last, he was going to kiss her again. She knew it with every fiber of her being. He'd confessed his desire. And the kiss would come next.

She longed for that kiss.

And yet she feared it, too. Now that it was really here, the exact moment when . . .

With a low groan, Jared put his mouth on hers.

Eden stood stock-still at the shock. And the wonder. And then she sighed.

He pulled her toward him, into his hard, muscled length.

He murmured something against her lips, some sort of denial, a low, harsh, "This is wrong. . . ."

"Don't stop," she begged, and wrapped her arms around his neck.

He groaned again, a hushed, hungry sort of sound. His tongue traced her lips.

She opened, sighing once more. And then his tongue was inside her mouth, roving, until it found hers and twined with it, in a secret, sparring dance as old as time. Eden gloried in it. This kiss was something she'd waited for her whole life.

His hands moved down her back, stroking, learning every curve as his mouth kissed her with a hunger and a need that stole her breath and left her gasping, overwhelmed, wanting more.

Before, on that aeons-ago morning, when he kissed her at the door of the cabin, he had been careful with her. His hands had been mannerly.

But his hands were not mannerly now.

I want more. More. Her blood seemed to beat the word through her veins. She groaned, as he cupped her buttocks and pulled her up even tighter against him, so she felt him, and knew exactly what he wanted of her. He muttered her name, chanting it, into her mouth, as he went on kissing her and pressing her against him.

And then he was turning her, as he shoved the upturned stools on the bar out of his way. He lifted her, a fleet, seamless movement, so she sat on the bar. Her skirt billowed out around her. He moved, swiftly, before she could grow shy and close her legs against him, and he stood between her knees.

And then he cupped her face in his big, rough hands and kissed her so sweet and long that she feared she would die with the pure, carnal beauty of it.

And then, miracle of miracles, his hands were sliding downward, over her neck, which she arched for him. His lips followed his hands lower... lower. She braced her own hands on the bar, and leaned back on them.

"Eden." He kissed her name into the soft hollow at the base of her throat, at the place where her collar gaped open. He nibbled at her skin there, causing her to release a long, shuddering sigh.

"Jared. Yes..." Was that husky, hungry murmur her own?

His hands slid lower then, nudging aside the little fringed vest she wore, until they found the shape of her breasts. He cupped them gently. Her nipples, through the layers of her shirt and bra, hardened for him. She knew that he must be able to feel them, firm with yearning, wanting more.

He put his head there, between her breasts, and nuzzled her. She brought one hand forward and held his head, pulling him against her, cooing "Yes..." as she stroked his silky brown hair.

And then he kissed her, through her shirt and her bra, a moist, suckling kiss. His mouth sought and found her nipple, closing on it through her clothing, taunting it, arousing it, until it ached and yearned for even more.

His hands strayed down, stroking, seeking, first gliding over her skirt, then caressing her bare knees. And then—she gasped and moaned—sliding up, to the hem of her panties, tracing the elastic there....

And then he froze.

"Jared?" She forced her heavy eyelids to flutter open.

He was watching her, desire still there in his eyes, making them look slightly glazed.

"This is wrong." He was pulling back, smoothing down her skirt over her knees. "I don't believe in—"

She threw her arms around his neck, brought her face right up to his and made no effort to hide the desperation she was feeling. "Take me home, Jared. Take me to the cabin. And make love to me. Please."

He put his hands on her waist in a distancing gesture. "Damn it, Eden, you don't know what—"

"I know exactly what. I want you. You want me. And we...like each other, don't we?"

"Damn it, Eden."

"Don't we? Don't you...like me, Jared?"

He let out a shuddering breath. "Yes."

She hurried on. "I knew it. And I...feel for you. So let's give it a chance. That's all people get in this world, Jared. A chance."

"There's no point. And it's wrong."

She took his face between her hands. "No, it is not wrong. It is *not*. It's never wrong, when there's love."

He blinked. "Love? What the hell are you saying, Eden?"

Eden looked into his eyes. This was it. The moment when she could play safe and lie, or tell the truth and put her poor heart at his feet.

She chose truth. She lifted her chin. "I'm saying that I love you, Jared."

He swore low and feelingly and pulled loose of her gentle grasp. He turned away.

"Oh, Jared, please. Look at me."

He faced her again, but what he said was not encouraging. "You're crazy. You know about me. I'm not the kind of guy a woman like you should waste her love on."

Eden refused to waver. She kept her chin high. "That's my decision."

"I'm through with love, Eden."

That hurt. That really hurt. But still, she did not let her shoulders slump. "I'm not asking for your love. Did I ask for your love?"

His gray gaze was wary. "No."

"Okay, then. I'm just telling you how it is for me. You don't have to do a thing about it, Jared. That's okay. But you do admit you like me. And want me. Right?"

"Right." The word was a low growl.

"And this really isn't working out—our *understanding,* I mean. Is it?"

"Hell. All right. No, it's not."

"So maybe we'd be better off to go about this a different way."

"What way?"

Eden opened her mouth to tell him.

But a flood of agonized embarrassment overcame her. No. She couldn't. Wouldn't. It was bad enough that she'd revealed her love to him, only to be told it would never be returned. But to baldly suggest that they become lovers until he left town again...

It was too much. That far she would not go.

Looking away from him, she jumped down from the bar and smoothed her skirt. Then she turned to straighten the stools that he'd pushed every which way in those few glorious moments of passion they had shared.

From behind her, he demanded again, "I asked you, what way?"

She went on fixing the stools. "Never mind. Let it go. We'll sleep on it tonight, and—"

He touched her shoulder. "No."

She froze. "Excuse me?"

"I said no." He turned her to face him, wrapping his hands around her upper arms. He looked hard into her eyes. "All my damn life I've tried to do the right thing. Do you understand?"

His grip was so warm and strong. Ah, how she longed to...

"Eden. Do you understand?"

She nodded.

"And somehow," he continued, "the right thing just about always went wrong."

She nodded again.

"In A.A., they have a saying. *One day at a time.* Have you heard that?"

"Yes."

"So maybe that's how you and I should take it. One day at a time. Starting with tonight."

"What are you telling me, Jared?"

The flinty eyes were turning once more to smoke. "I'm not telling. I'm asking."

"Asking what?"

"Asking if we could go back to a few minutes ago, to what you asked me a few minutes ago."

"What I asked you—?"

"To take you home to the cabin and—"

Eden felt hope glowing warm in her heart. It was a start. A rocky one maybe, but a start nonetheless.

She said, "Take me home to the cabin, Jared. And make love to me. Please."

His warm hands slid up over her shoulders. He cupped her face. "Damn. What's a man to do when a woman says *please?*"

Chapter Eleven

They drove the short distance together, in Jared's pickup.
Eden sat close to him, her head on his shoulder, her hand
resting on his hard thigh.

At the cabin, he parked where he'd parked before, beneath the fir tree by the front deck. After he stopped the
truck, he sat for a moment, looking at her through the
gloom of the cab.

"Do you want to back out?"

She couldn't see his eyes in the darkness, but she could
feel his gaze nonetheless. "No. Why? Do you?"

"Hell, no." He chuckled. Eden relished the sound. His
chuckles were so rare. "I never wanted to go through with
anything as much as I want to go through with this. You're
sure you don't plan to get smart and call this off?"

She leaned toward him and breathed in the manly scent
of him. "No way." She kissed him, on the side of his chin,
near the place where he'd been cut in the fight with Lew.

He made a little growling noise, and his arms went around her. His mouth sought hers.

Outside, a slight wind came up, causing a low, sweet sighing in the trees. But the sound was not nearly as sweet as the sighing that went on in the cab of Jared's pickup right then.

Reluctantly he pulled away. "Let's go in."

"Okay."

They walked up the stone steps to the kitchen door with their arms around each other.

Eden flipped on the overhead light once they were inside, regretting the action the moment it was accomplished. After the soft darkness, she had to squint just to get her bearings in the sudden, harsh brightness. She almost flicked the light off again, but then restrained herself. She should probably offer him some refreshment—didn't a woman always offer a man a drink first?—and she'd look pretty silly stumbling around in the dark trying to get him a cola.

She turned to Jared and pasted on a smile. "I'm not, um, really experienced with this." It was the understatement of the year, but he would find that out soon enough.

He took the words at face value. "That makes two of us."

She realized exactly what he meant. Jared Jones had only made love with two women, both of them his wives. He was strict with himself, in terms of his beliefs. Eden liked that. She didn't want a man who held lovemaking cheap.

She felt her stiff smile relax a little. She even dared to brush at a lock of his hair that had fallen over his forehead. "Should I offer you a soda or something?"

He smiled back. His smile was a wonder to her, unpracticed and so very real. "If you offered, should I take it?"

She looked down. "Never mind. Let's skip the soda."

"Good idea." He flipped off the harsh light, casting the room once more into night shadow.

They stood facing each other. And then he asked through the darkness, "Where the hell were we?"

"Excuse me?" She had no idea what he meant.

And then she felt his finger, very lightly, hooking under her purse strap and sliding it off her arm. He whisked it away and set it on the floor somewhere nearby. She didn't notice where. And she didn't much care, either.

She felt his touch again, on her shoulder, right where the purse had hung. The touch trailed down. He took one small piece of her vest's fringe between his fingers and he gave a tug. She swayed against him, sighing.

"I said, where were we?" He guided the vest off her shoulders and set it aside. She heard it land on a chair by the table not two feet away.

She swallowed, thinking, *Here I am in the dark with this man I've grown to love, this man I want so much—and yet fear a little, too....*

Her body felt strangely languorous. And weightless as well. As if she were floating upright in some deep, warm pool.

His strong hands were at her waist. He waltzed her backward, quickly, effortlessly. Until she came up short against the kitchen counter.

"I think we were right about—" he lifted her "—here."

She found herself sitting on the counter, just as she'd been on the bar earlier. Her skirt billowed out again. Jared moved swiftly into the same place he'd been before, close up against her, between her parted knees.

He captured her mouth then.

"Oh, yes," she heard herself sigh against his parted lips. "Right about...here."

His lips played on hers in a long, lovely kiss, while she stroked his hard shoulders and kissed him joyfully in return. He pulled her even closer, so that she could feel his heart beating, strong and swift, against her own.

Then down below, his hands closed on her thighs beneath her skirt. His touch was warm, both a promise and a demand. Eden drew in a long, shaky breath as he guided her legs, gently, inexorably, wider. And then his palms slid around to cup her buttocks and pull her even tighter against him, so that her womanhood was pressed to his hardness.

Her senses heated even more than before. Her whole body knew only one yearning, to be closer to him, to be one with him. Not even realizing she did it, she wrapped her legs around his hips, hooking her boots together.

His hands slid under her thighs.

She moaned as he lifted her. She held on for dear life, still lost in his kiss, as he reeled backward from the counter. She could feel him fully, as she settled onto him, once the counter no longer supported her. He was so hard, pressed against her at her most secret place. His hands cupped her thighs, and his mouth demanded everything from hers.

He carried her like that, kissing her, holding her tight and high against him. Out of the kitchen, through the main room and into her own bedroom they went. And then he turned. She felt her back come in contact with something solid. Her heavy eyelids opened a little. He held her pressed against the wall, in the small space between one of the two windows and her vanity table.

Slowly he let her legs down, until she was standing again. Then he put his hands on the wall to either side of her head and he kissed her some more, his whole body caressing her, just as she pressed and rubbed against him.

Eden was in ecstasy. And when he reached up and cupped her chin and then tenderly stroked her cheek, she took his hand and guided it down, until it was between her breasts.

She forced herself to look at him. The soft glow of starlight from the window showed his eyes to her. His eyes were pure smoke right then. A woman could lose herself forever in eyes like those.

At her breasts, she felt his hand moving, doing as she'd prayed he might, slipping the buttons of her shirt from their holes. He smoothed the shirt open, sweetly, gently, and guided it off her shoulders and away.

Then he stood back a little and he took off his own shirt and vest, tossing them aside as soon as he was out of them. She saw the hard, sculptured planes of his upper body, the little trail of hair that ran down his belly into his jeans. She remembered the night she'd watched him sleep. That night, she had almost let herself imagine doing just what they were doing now....

He bent, never letting go of her gaze, and he pulled off his boots and socks. Then he stood. From his back pocket, he took three condoms. He turned, walked to the bed and set them on the little table there.

Eden watched him, unmoving. She'd known about the condoms, of course. Before they left the tavern, he'd acquired them from the machine in the men's room. That machine was another of Eden's improvements. She'd seen enough in her life to have come to believe in safe sex.

Jared returned to her. Looking in her eyes once more, he unbuttoned his jeans and slipped out of both them and his briefs at the same time.

Then he straightened and stood naked before her. Eden thought he was beautiful, as a man can be beautiful, lean-muscled, sculptured, poised for displays of power and grace. His manhood stood out rigidly, proof of his desire.

Eden knew a slight apprehension when she saw that most private part of him. She thought of what would happen, very soon. But she believed in her love, and she believed this night would be magic for her. She drew in a deep breath and pushed her anxiety aside.

She reached behind her to unclasp her bra. It came undone easily, the cups falling loose from her breasts. But somehow, just to toss the thing away seemed more than she could manage. In a last gesture of shy modesty, she held the scrap of lacy fabric close to her chest.

A knowing, tender smile played on Jared's lips. He lifted a hand. Then, his eyes still locked with hers, he slid the straps, one at a time, from her shoulders. He gave a tug.

She released the bra. It fell away. And she was naked before him from the waist up.

With the same hand, he caressed the side of her face, just a whisper of a touch. And then his fingers strayed behind her head. He pulled out the comb that held her chin-length hair up in the back. The soft, short curls fell around her cheeks.

He put both hands on her shoulders and slowly brought them down, over the swells of her breasts. He cupped her breasts, one in each hand. With a low moan, he lowered his head. He licked a nipple, then blew on it.

Eden sighed and squirmed in delight. He took the nipple fully into his mouth. She groaned. And then he lavished the same attention on the other waiting breast.

His hands, meanwhile, drifted down, over her waist and then around to the little hook and the zipper at the back of her skirt. The hook came open, the zipper parted. The skirt slid to the floor. Her half-slip quickly followed it.

Eden felt the night air on her skin and knew she was standing, naked but for her panties and cowboy boots, in front of Jared Jones. His roving hand dipped into the waistband of her panties. She gasped. He eased the panties off and helped her to stand while he got them over her boots. After that, he knelt to remove her boots and socks, too.

And then he was pressing himself against her again. His hand returned to the vulnerable center of her, dipping in, feeling her readiness and making her more ready still.

Eden, lost in wonder, rolled her head back and forth against the wall and let the sensations his touch aroused have their way with her. He said something low and unintelligible.

She said, "Yes," in return. It didn't matter to Eden what he said. Her answer would always be, forever, "Yes . . ."

She felt him then, kissing his way down her stomach. She stiffened.

He pleaded, "Eden, don't hold back. Let me . . ."

And she let him. How could she not let him? She *wanted* to let him, though the kiss he gave her then was a kiss she'd never known before.

It was the most intimate of kisses. She gloried in it. She opened for him and pushed herself against him as he knelt before her, put his mouth on her and drove her higher and higher, to the top of some magical, mythical cliff.

She hovered there, moaning. And then she fell, a falling that was also a soaring, out and over, higher and higher, into an explosion of heat and light. She cried out once, a long, keening sound.

And then she slowly relaxed, feeling that the whole, beautiful world lay beneath her, ready to fold her against its heart as she drifted slowly, sweetly down.

Jared stood, kissing his way back up her body, as she returned to the real world. He pressed himself against her. She felt the wiry roughness of his chest hairs, the heat of his skin, the hardness pushing at the juncture of her thighs. He smelled of that soap of his that she liked and of the smoke from the bar, and of himself, a man-scent, slightly musky with desire.

His mouth covered hers. She tasted herself. She was boneless and liquid, hardly knowing how she remained upright, except that his hard body held her there against the wall.

He said against her lips, "I want you now. You're ready for me now. Open and soft. Now, Eden. Now..."

She said the only word she knew right then. "Yes."

He cupped her bottom and brought her up against him again. She wrapped her legs around his hips and she felt him, against her entrance, straining at her with his own readiness. He carried her that way, over to the bed.

He laid her down, then came down quickly with her. Then he fumbled for a moment with a condom. When that was done, he poised himself above her.

Eden lay beneath him, grateful for the sweet lassitude that had stolen over her limbs after the fulfillment he had just given her. She looked up into his face. This was what she'd wanted, what she'd waited for. She was doing the right thing, she was sure of it.

She could see the glaze of hunger and desire in his eyes. He was far gone in it. And she was glad. Because she wanted him to claim her. And if he knew her secret too soon, she feared he'd call a halt.

He said her name, braced above her on his extended arms.

She gave him her answer, her only answer, "Yes..." Then she brazenly wrapped her legs around him and pulled him down to her.

She felt him, there, at the entrance to her womanhood. He moved, finding the right angle.

And then he thrust into her.

Crying out at the sharp, burning pain, Eden drove upward to meet him, gripping his hard buttocks, taking him fully inside, though her eyes teared and her untried body protested such a sharp invasion.

Jared froze. And then he bucked up onto his arms once more. His lips drew away from his teeth. He glared down at her.

"What the...?"

Eden whimpered a little—both at the way it burned down there, where he felt so very large, buried in the tender heart of her—and in response to the look in Jared's eyes.

"You're a *virgin*..." It was an accusation.

She bit her lip and forced herself to answer. "Not... anymore."

Chapter Twelve

Jared threw back his head and groaned at the ceiling.

He poised himself to withdraw.

And then Eden moved, a slow, sweet rolling motion, beneath him.

He groaned again, before he could stifle the sound. He tossed his head and gritted his teeth. He knew he must break this off now. He jerked back.

She held on and pressed herself closer against him.

"No, Eden..."

"Yes, Jared..."

"I should..."

"...never stop..."

He swore then, a poignant oath.

"Please never stop..."

He glared down at her.

"Please..."

He felt himself weakening. "Eden..."

"Yes. Please..."

He hovered there, as if on a precipice, clinging in fading hope to what he knew he should do, while bewitching desire lured him down.

Her soft, final "Please..." finished him off. Jared, enveloped by her, sheathed in her, admitted that the moment for withdrawal had slipped away.

He let go of what he *should* have done. Desire took him down.

She moved again. He moaned in response.

She whispered, "Yes," once more. He drank the word from her sweet, wide mouth.

He didn't deserve her, not even for the limited alliance they'd agreed upon. He shouldn't have taken her. But he couldn't, in the end, refuse the heat and wonder she offered him so freely, with no holding back.

In all his life, bound by duty, lured by violence, he had never known such a woman as this. Who talked too much and listened too well, and whose smile pierced him in a place he hadn't really known he possessed.

He surrendered.

With a low, hoarse cry, he submitted to his own feral nature. He plunged into her hard and fast, pushing himself ever deeper, into the center of her sweetness, calling out her name.

She held him to her, opened herself wider, letting him claim all of her, though he knew it must hurt her, virgin that she was.

But Jared couldn't control himself by then. He was lost. Gone. Finished. He bucked up, and then surged into her, deeper than all the thrusts that went before. He felt his seed spilling, pumping out of him in that culminating ecstasy that turned a man inside-out.

And then, with a long, shuddering sigh, he sank upon her. Relaxing along the smooth, satiny length of her, he tangled his fingers in the bright spill of her hair.

It seemed to him that a sweet eternity passed as he lay there, listening to her breathing and his own, feeling the wonderful softness of her, idly stroking her hair. The skin of his hand felt rough against the short, silky strands. He wrapped a lock around his index finger.

And then he allowed his touch to roam the little distance to her neck. He caressed the soft flesh there and put his thumb, possessively, on the deep pulse of her throat.

She was lying very still. He sensed an apprehension in her. A slight tension.

Well, she *should* be tense. She had lied to him. If not with words, then with what she'd *failed* to say.

She was what? Twenty-six, he thought she'd said once. In this day and age, there weren't a lot of twenty-six-year-old virgins around. She must have known he would assume she'd been with a man before.

And she'd probably also known that there was no way he would have taken her if she'd told him the truth. To bed an *innocent,* let alone a woman who was not his wife, was the kind of thing only a womanizer would do. And Jared Jones was no womanizer. A troublemaking unemployed over-the-hill alcoholic, maybe. But a seducer of innocent women?

Never. No way.

Which was why she *hadn't* told him.

So if she was worried he might be mad, well, she *ought* to be worried.

But *was* he mad?

He nuzzled her neck, ran a hand down the slim curve of her ribs to her waist.

How the hell could he be mad? She'd just given him all he'd ever known of heaven. A man couldn't be mad at a woman for that.

"Jared?" Her voice sounded hesitant, a little scared.

"Yeah?"

"Are you . . . angry at me?"

He smiled to himself and rolled slightly to the side. As he did that, he slipped out of her. He felt the wetness along his thigh and looked down.

The starry light from the window above the bed shone down on her bare thighs. There was a dark trail across them: blood.

"Oh," she said softly, looking at the blood, too.

"I'll be back." He rose from the bed.

He went to the bathroom, got rid of the condom and moistened a towel with warm water. Then he returned.

She'd slipped beneath the sheet while he was gone. Modestly covered, she was peering at him, her brown eyes wary. He thought she looked more like a virgin, right now when she was no longer one, than she ever had waltzing around The Hole in the Wall acting as if she knew everything there was to know about men and their ways.

He approached her, carrying the towel. Her eyes widened. He smiled, reassuringly he hoped, though he'd never been very good at smiling.

He carefully kept eye contact with her as he took the hem of the sheet and pulled it back, revealing her slender, pink body. She allowed him to uncover her, biting her lip the whole time.

He knew exactly why she was keeping that poor lip caught between her teeth. To keep from babbling. She was nervous as hell now. And when Eden was nervous, her jaws started flapping like crazy, as a rule.

And, oh, she was beautiful. As long and slim as a willow wand. With high, firm breasts and a waist made for a man's hands. The curls on her mound were darker than those on her head. He couldn't see in the dim room if they were auburn or light brown, but he knew how silky they were. He'd felt that for himself. His gaze drifted lower, to her legs. They were a damn poem, those legs of Eden's. He was getting hard again, even at his age, just looking at them.

Carefully he put one knee on the bed and half knelt there beside her. Then he gently began to use the moistened towel, to wipe the traces of blood from her thighs.

He concentrated on what he was doing and didn't glance at her face, both because he enjoyed it and because he wanted to give her a moment of privacy, a moment when he wasn't looking in her eyes. He felt her body relaxing as she realized that he only meant to tend to her comfort. Her legs parted slightly. He tenderly stroked the blood away there, too.

And while he stroked the signs of her lost innocence away, he tried his damnedest not to think that no other man would have that of her. That in this at least, he would always be the only one. He had no right to think that, because his whole intention, as they both knew, was to get out of her life as soon as his father was back on his feet.

When he was done, he took the towel back to the bathroom. And then he returned to her and slid under the sheet that she'd once again pulled up.

"Jared?" she asked, once he was settled in, with his arm beneath her head and one hand cupping her breast.

"Um?"

"You didn't answer me. *Are* you angry?"

"No. I'm not angry." He toyed with her breast a little, felt the nipple grow in quick response. He liked that, the way she responded to him. Her breathing had changed a little. It was quicker, shallower.

He thought of taking her again, but then realized how sore she probably was. He could wait. They had time.

Yeah, but not forever...

He blocked out the taunting voice. This was just for now. One day at a time. As they'd agreed.

"I thought you wouldn't...make love to me, if you knew." She arched a little toward his teasing hand.

"You were right, I wouldn't have." He shifted, pulling his arm from beneath her head and canting up on an el-

ow. He stroked her hair again. "And hell. I guess I'm glad
ou tricked me."

She smiled then, a burst of sunlight in the moon-dark
oom. "Oh, Jared. I'm so *glad* you're glad."

He smiled back, the third or fourth time tonight. Damn.
He was turning into a grinning fool. He'd never smiled as
much in a year as he had in the last two weeks, since this
all, enchanting creature had taken over his house and half
of his inheritance.

He looked at the clock on the bed stand, the clock she'd
clobbered him with that first night. It was late. Very late.

She read his mind. "Um. Snuggle down." She fitted
herself against him as if she's been sleeping with him for
years.

He closed his eyes and thought of how he really did want
to ask her about how she could look the way she looked,
handle herself as she did, and yet still have been a virgin a
few hours ago.

He wrapped an arm and a leg around her. She snuggled
even closer.

It was late, he decided. He could ask those questions
later. They had time.

But not forever, the taunting voice in his head whispered.

Jared pretended not to hear the voice. He was wrapped
up in his woman's arms and halfway off to sleep.

Morning came too soon.

Eden hadn't remembered to set the alarm, but she'd left
all the curtains and windows open. The gradual lightening
of the room did the trick. That and the incessant squawk-
ing of a group of mouthy blue jays outside the window.

Jared awoke looking at the clock. It was eight-fifteen.
Groaning, he brought up an arm and covered his eyes. And
then, as the events of last night stole into his mind, he

smiled. He turned his head toward Eden's side of the bed and raised his arm enough to look at her.

She wasn't there.

He realized then that there was water running in the bathroom. She must be having her shower.

He dropped his arm and sat up.

And every muscle in his body shouted at him never to move again.

"Ugh," Jared grunted, rubbing the small of his back and shaking his head.

He thought of the fight with Lew and felt some regret. He was still young enough to come up with the moves when he had to. Unfortunately he was also old enough now to have to pay the price later on.

Carefully he eased his legs over the side of the bed and put his feet on the little woven rug there. He rubbed his jaw, feeling the tender place where Lew had clipped him a good one. Then, cautiously, he stood up.

He felt as stiff as an untanned hide. Slowly he stretched, forcing his muscles to stir and respond, though they seemed to be screaming at him to get back into bed and not move for a week. He knew he'd done more damage to Lew than Lew had done to him, but he couldn't console himself with thoughts of how Lew must be feeling right now.

Lew, the lucky stiff, was twenty-five at most. At that age, Jared could have taken on ten idiots, slept the night in a ditch and still arisen in the morning ready to fight again.

Jared forced himself to bend at the waist. It was pure agony. He cursed Lew and his youthful resilience, as he felt each of his vertebrae crack in agonizing turn.

This getting old, Jared decided, was *not* the most fun he'd ever had. On a morning like this, he could *almost* feel sympathy for his father, who was constantly complaining that his aging bones didn't work the way they used to.

Jared was so concerned with getting his body loosened up a little, that he hardly noticed when the shower stopped.

running. Had he noticed, he would have slipped into his jeans before Eden could emerge from her shower and see him in the altogether by the bright light of day. Jared was a modest man by nature. Besides that, last night had been Eden's first experience with to-the-limit lovemaking. He would have put on some clothes in consideration for her tender sensibilities.

But he didn't notice. And so when Eden opened the bathroom door she found herself staring at a naked man doing push-ups on her bedroom floor.

Her first reaction was more of appreciation than embarrassment. Jared was a marvelously put-together specimen of a man. There really wasn't an ounce of fat on him. Eden watched the muscles of his arms and back flex and release as he raised and lowered his entire body. She thought that it was really a delightful plus that she'd ended up loving a man who was so very nice to look at. She blushed a little, as her roving gaze traveled lower and she was looking at the rocklike hardness of his buttocks and his strong, hair-dusted thighs. Also, she could see his manhood. It looked much different than it had the night before when he'd been making love to her.

Right then, he caught sight of her, out of the corner of his eye. He fairly leapt to his feet.

"Good God, woman!" He flew to the little chair, where he'd tossed his jeans last night. He shook out the jeans and shoved his legs into them, buttoning them up as if his life depended on it. Once he was covered, he barked out gruffly, "You surprised the hell out of me."

Eden felt her slight blush turn to crimson. She gathered her robe closer around her. "Oh. I'm sorry. I . . ." She gestured, rather ineffectually. And then she started babbling. "I went ahead and took my shower first. But I was careful not to use all the hot water. There's plenty left. So you can go ahead, if you want. And take yours. And I'll go get breakfast started. I thought maybe French toast. Do you like French toast? Because if you don't, I can just make eggs and bacon, or whatever you—"

"Eden."

She hitched in a breath. "Huh?"

A slow smile was curling his mouth. Oh, she really did like it when he smiled. And then he was coming toward her, soundlessly on his bare feet. She looked at his chest, at the beautiful, sculptured hardness of it, at that little tempting trail of hair that went down toward his jeans.

He tipped her chin up with a finger. She saw that there was a bruise on his jaw, beneath the place where Lew had broken the skin.

"French toast is great. Whatever you make is great." His eyes looked into hers, seeing everything, *knowing* everything.

She looked at his mouth. For a man who'd only made love with two women before her, he really knew how to kiss. But then, he could have done a lot of kissing, couldn't he? He could have been a kissing fool, kissed every woman he met, and not have made love all the way with them. Just because you kissed someone didn't mean you had to sleep with them, after all.

"What are you thinking?" he asked softly.

"You have a bad bruise on your chin."

Well, it was the truth. She *had* been thinking that. Before the other about how many women he might have kissed.

"That bruise is the least of my problems. You should feel the rest of me."

I have. You felt wonderful, she thought but didn't say. "Serves you right. For fighting. Nothing ever gets solved by fighting." She tried to sound reproving.

"I know."

"You do?"

"You bet. I *oughtta* know, if anybody does. I've been in enough fights."

"So why did you get in a fight last night?"

"Haven't we covered this ground already?"

"Yes," she agreed. "I guess so."

"Then can we leave it behind?"

"Yes. All right. That's fine."

"Good." He gave her one of those smiles that she enjoyed more each time he bestowed one on her. "But I will say this much."

"Yes?"

"I'm really working on it—staying out of fights, I mean."

"I'm glad."

His mouth covered hers then, his hands slipping down to wrap around the collar of her robe and pull her closer. Eden let out a long sigh as his tongue slipped beyond her lips.

She let her neck relax. His hand left her collar to cradle her head, holding her still for more of his arousing, blood-heating kisses.

Then, just when she was thinking how close the bed was, he drew slightly away. "If I don't take that shower now, I'll probably never take it."

She smiled up at him. She knew her eyes were shining and that he'd felt her arousal in the way she'd melted like butter in the sun when his lips touched hers. She didn't mind that he knew what she felt for him. It was obvious that he wanted her, too. And beyond that, she was giving all of herself to him, unashamed, in the brave hope that her love and her passion would be enough to make him surrender his wounded, hardened heart.

She kissed him once more, a swift, sweet peck on the lips. "Well, go on, then. I'll make breakfast." She turned him around and pointed him toward the bathroom door. Then she hurried to get dressed.

He joined her in the kitchen twenty minutes later and helped her put the finishing touches on their breakfast.

They sat down and ate. Then together they cleaned up after the meal.

Eden felt that there was a certain tension in the air through all of this. Jared was quiet, though whenever she looked up, she found him watching her. And she was constantly on guard against talking too much, so it was a silent breakfast, for the most part.

By the time they got to washing up, Eden had begun to wonder if something was wrong.

She was putting the final dish away as Jared finished rinsing out the sink. She turned to find him drying his hands, looking at her.

"What time do you have to be at work?"

"Ten-thirty."

He shot a glance over his shoulder, at the clock on the wall behind him. "Not for over an hour, then?" He was looking at her again.

Suddenly she knew what was making him so quiet.

She felt a kind of warming, a lovely weakening down in her lower belly. He wanted to . . . make love again, that was it. Before she left.

He hung the towel up and then he took the few steps to where she stood. Slowly he ran the back of a finger down the side of her cheek.

"Are you sore?" He asked the question gently. "From last night?"

She swallowed and nodded.

"How sore?"

"A little. Not too much."

His hand was sliding back, clasping her nape, creating those lovely, tingling sensations. He bent close, yet he kept his body slightly away from hers.

"I should leave you alone now." His lips brushed hers, insistent, yet restrained.

"Jared . . ." She dared to touch him, to put her hands on his shoulders and massage the hard muscles there.

He went on kissing her, a tormenting, teasing, promising kiss. And he spoke against her lips as he kissed them. "I want you. And it'll be a long day without touching you. Say no now, or..."

"Jared..."

"That's not no."

"Jared..."

"Say it, damn it. Say it now."

"But Jared. I...I want you, too."

He let out a low, eager sound. And he took the comb from her hair as he had last night. She heard the clatter it made as he tossed it on the counter. Her hair curled around her face. He smoothed it with his hands. And then he slid one arm behind her knees, wrapped the other around her shoulders and swung her high against his chest.

He carried her to the bedroom and laid her down on the bed.

She stared up at him, dazed, as he stripped off his clothes with such swiftness that it seemed one minute he was fully dressed—and the next he was wearing nothing at all. Then he came down beside her and began helping her out of her own clothes.

They were naked in no time. And he was guiding her down and kissing her until she felt her whole body was on fire, a flame of pure longing. For him.

The slight burning from the loss of her virginity faded to no more than a memory as he touched her and kissed her, making her ready for loving once more. His fingers did things, wonderful things. And then he kissed her there, at her feminine center as he had last night, so that she was open and receptive, longing to have him fill her.

Then, pausing only to slide on protection, he rose above her. She took him inside her easily this time, in one smooth, slow stroke.

And when he was in, he lay there for a while above her, joined with her but absolutely still. His breathing was careful as he let her feel him and know him and get used to having him there.

She stroked his back and cooed wordless things in his ear. And he kissed her, his lips so warm and good against her mouth, whispering how much he wanted her, how much he wanted *this.* . . .

And then he began to move.

She knew what heaven felt like, when he began to move.

Eden moved with him, at first slowly, then faster, then slowly once more.

"Oh!" Eden cried out. Her eyes flew open in surprise. This was different than last night. Last night she had not felt her body rising toward completion while he was inside her.

Jared was watching her, knowing what was happening to her. He lifted his hips and brought them to meet hers once more.

"Oh, yes . . ." Her eyes drifted closed.

Their bodies rose and fell as one. Soon, Eden felt herself spinning out and away, shattering into a thousand tiny stars of delight. She tossed her head back on the pillows and felt her body closing around him, milking him, as fulfillment shimmered through her.

He found his own satisfaction just as hers began to fade to afterglow. He drove into her, insistent, lost to all thought.

"Eden . . ."

"Yes . . ."

She opened herself utterly to him, meeting his every hungry, wild thrust. He drove deep. He groaned.

And then, with a long sigh, his muscular body relaxed on top of hers.

She held him gently, stroking his back as his breathing found its regular rhythm. As he'd done last night, he combed her hair with his hands.

Eden, who'd been seeking a true home all her life, found herself thinking that she'd found her home at last. Her home was right here, in this man's arms.

And then the phone rang.

Jared muttered a low curse against her ear. "Don't answer it."

She pushed at his shoulders a little, so she could meet his gaze. "Why not?"

"It'll only be my father. Or some busybody or other. I'm not up to dealing with any of them now."

"But Jared—"

"Fine." He slid to the side and landed on his feet by the bed. Eden looked at him, stunned as usual at the lithe splendor of his body and also bewildered by his abruptness. The mood had been so lazy and lovely until just a few seconds ago.

"Jared, wait...."

The phone went on ringing.

"If you're going to answer it, then do it," Jared said over his shoulder. He was already halfway through the bathroom door, his jeans in one hand.

The phone rang again and Jared closed the door.

Eden stared at the door he'd shut on her, wondering how a moment so beautiful could have vanished so quickly. Then she picked up the phone.

"Ha. I caught you. I know you're probably just heading out the door, but—"

"Laurie." Eden pulled the sheet over herself and combed her tangled hair with her free hand. "Hi. Look, it's okay. I'm ... running a little behind today."

"Well, I won't keep you. But it turns out I've got a day off tomorrow. I thought I'd come up, see my folks and Great-uncle Oggie. The usual, you know." Sacramento, where Laurie lived, was an hour and a half away. She went on. "And I was thinking, since tomorrow's Monday, that you'd be off, too. We could go to dinner in Nevada City or something. What do you say?"

Eden's mind balked. Since last night, her whole life had changed. Now Jared seemed to fill every corner of it. And yet they had agreed to take things one day at a time. And they hadn't discussed what they'd tell everybody, about the two of them.

"Eden? You still with me?"

"Yes, I'm here. Just thinking. Listen, why don't you come here to the cabin for dinner? I'll fire up the barbecue and toss us a salad and we'll split a bottle of wine."

Eden could hear Laurie's smile. "How you do read my mind. I'll bring the wine."

"Done."

"About six?"

"Perfect."

"Bye, then."

"See ya."

Eden hung up the phone.

"Who was it?" Jared stood in the doorway to the bathroom, wearing his jeans and a scowl.

"Laurie."

"Did you tell her about us?"

"No, I—"

"What did she want?"

"She's coming to town tomorrow. I invited her for dinner here." Eden gave him her warmest, most open smile. "I hope you'll join us, of course."

He didn't smile back. "I didn't think about this, last night. About everyone knowing."

She spoke gently. "I know. Neither did I, really. But it's okay."

"What do you mean, okay? The whole damn town will be buzzing."

"Oh, Jared. Come on. It can't be that big a deal."

"Oh, can't it?"

"No."

He sauntered into the room and dropped into the little chair by her vanity table. He stared off toward the wall, rubbing the bruise on his chin.

"I've gotta think," he said.

"About what?"

"This is no good. I should have considered this. There'll be nothing but talk, if I start staying here with you."

Eden blinked. "Is that what you were thinking of— staying here?"

He stopped staring at the wall and looked at her. "You don't like the idea?"

She looked down at the sheet she was clutching to her breasts and then back up at him. "No—I mean, yes. I do like it. I just, well, you hadn't said anything, before now."

He looked at the wall again. "I know. It was a bad idea."

Eden felt crestfallen. Now she'd had a moment to consider it, she liked the thought of him staying with her. She liked it a lot. Yet he was already saying he wouldn't. "But why?"

He cast her a patronizing look. "I just told you. Because people will talk. It's not so bad for me. I'm used to it. But it won't be good for you. Your reputation will be ruined."

Eden rolled her eyes. "Oh, Jared, please. This is not 1950, for goodness' sake. A woman's private life is her own business."

"Not in North Magdalene, it's not."

"Jared—"

He stood and began gathering the rest of his strewn clothing. "Look. I should get my truck out of here before someone sees it. And you'd better get moving if you want to be at The Hole in the Wall by ten-thirty. We'll talk about this. Tonight, after closing time. Or tomorrow, when we both have a day off."

"But—"

He was already headed for the door. But before he went through, he turned and pointed a boot at her. "And don't tell anyone about the two of us, until we settle this."

"But Jared, I—"

"Where are your car keys?"

"In my purse, but—"

"Where's your purse?"

"In the kitchen, I think. But I—"

"I'll get your car here in the next half hour. I'll leave the keys in the ignition."

"Jared, why don't you just—"

"Drive you to work? No way. Someone might see."

"Jared—"

"I mean it, keep your mouth shut," he warned again. And then he was gone.

Chapter Thirteen

As Jared had promised, her car was waiting when Eden went outside a half an hour later.

She was ten minutes late for work, but she hurried to get set up and managed to open the doors on time anyway. And then, once she had the place opened, time slowed to a crawl.

It was Sunday, and Sundays were always quiet. However, today seemed even worse than usual.

Eden tried to make the time go faster by cleaning everything in sight. She wiped the dust from the bottles on the highest shelves, bottles containing obscure liqueurs and other spirits with weird names that people rarely ordered. She cleaned the popcorn machine. She even took an old knife to the undersurface of the bar itself, in an effort to scrape free the numberless wads of chewing gum that thoughtless customers were always sticking there.

Owen Beardsly, whose wife taught school with Delilah, was sitting at the far end of the bar when Eden started in on the chewing gum. "Aw, come on, Eden," Owen complained. "Everyone in town admires you for what you've done with this place. But there's such a thing as a step too far. Scraping the gum from under the lip of the bar falls in that category."

Eden looked up. "I want to keep busy." Each time she stopped working, she thought of Jared and the way he'd left her this morning. Everything was so up in the air. She wouldn't see him again until seven tonight. She missed him already.

"So do something that matters and give me another shot," Rocky suggested from his usual spot on his favorite stool.

"Yeah," Owen chimed in. "I'm ready for another drink, too. And I mean it. Put that knife away. Please? Watching you do that is making my ulcer act up."

Eden wanted to tell Owen that he shouldn't be drinking anyway, if he had an ulcer. Also, it was Sunday morning and why wasn't he in church? His wife, Linda Lou, was probably fit to be tied that he was hanging around the bar at this time of day.

But Eden kept her mouth shut. She knew she was just feeling edgy about Jared. It would be bad business to take her personal frustrations out on her customers.

She put the knife away, washed her hands and served Rocky and Owen their drinks.

Somehow, she got through the day.

But, as Jared had warned her, people certainly did talk. The fight in the parking lot the night before seemed to be common knowledge today. Everyone had a remark or a question about it.

"Hey, Eden. Heard about the fight last night. What exactly was that all about?"

Eden knew how to handle such talk. She turned it right back on the questioner. "Oh, you heard that, did you? From who?"

"It's all over town, I'm telling you. The word is that Jared Jones and some big blond kid beat the hell out of each other."

"Oh, really?"

"Yeah, really. And you still didn't tell me. What was it about?"

"Well, I wasn't in the fight. You ought to ask Jared. Or that big blond kid."

"But I heard you were there. I heard they were fighting over you."

"You heard that, did you?"

"Yeah. Is it true?"

"No. It was about common courtesy. That big blond kid had no manners."

"Aw, come on, Eden. Tell the truth. It was over you."

"Is that what you think?"

"Yeah. That's what I think."

"Well, what goes on in your head is up to you. Here, have some cocktail mix. And take this half-dollar and play something good on the jukebox. It's too quiet in here."

All the prying questions and knowing grins did get a little old after a while. But Eden was handling it fine, all in all. Maybe it would be harder to take if they knew that Jared had gone home with her last night. But she doubted it. A love affair between her and Jared Jones would be more likely to be discussed in whispers, behind her back.

And Eden couldn't have cared less what people said behind her back. She was perfectly capable of just ignoring such stuff. But she feared Jared wasn't.

And she feared right.

When he came in at seven, he was scowling. Eden felt a quick thrill all through her body at the sight of him. She couldn't help remembering what had passed between them in the dark last night *and* today in the bright morning light.

But the grim set to his jaw and the flinty look in his eyes was distinctly unloverlike. She greeted him. He grunted in return. They switched places. He came behind the bar, she moved out on the floor.

They had enough business the first hour that it was bearable, but more than one man asked Jared about the fight with Lew. Jared answered in terse syllables.

"He needed a lesson. That's all I want to say." Or, "Drop it. You want a refill?"

By eight-thirty, his scowl seemed worse than when he'd come in. Eden bore such surly behavior for as long as she could take it.

Then, when there was a lull, she went around behind the bar and whispered to him, "Please meet me in the back room. Now."

She trotted through the door behind the bar itself, to the little hall that led to the storeroom. She half expected him to ignore her demand, to leave her waiting back there with the cases of whiskey and gin until she gave up and returned to the main room. She sat down to wait on the little stool that they used to reach the supplies on the top shelves.

A moment later, she looked up and he was there, standing in the doorway to the hall.

"What is it?" His voice was low and gruff. "We've got people out there, you know."

She stood up and immediately wished she hadn't. Her knees actually felt weak at the sight of him.

He seemed to be keeping a careful distance from her, staying there in the doorway, where he could turn and bolt at a whim. "Well?"

"I . . . just wanted to talk to you for a moment. Because you've seemed so angry, ever since you came in tonight. What's wrong?"

He looked at her—a piercing look. She thought he was going to be frank with her, but then he seemed to change his mind.

"We can talk about this later." He started to turn away.

She reached out and grabbed his arm. "Wait."

He froze. He looked down at the hand that was clutching his arm and then back into her eyes. Eden felt his look, burning all through her body. She realized then that, whatever was bothering him, he still wanted her. She suspected that he was exerting iron control over himself to keep from grabbing her.

"What?" His eyes were molten.

"Tell me." She licked her lips because they suddenly felt so dry. "What's making you angry?"

He looked down at her hand on his arm again, a pointed look, one that clearly said, *"Let go."*

Her hand fell away. He started to leave again.

She insisted, "Please, Jared. What is it?"

He stopped and turned to pin her with another look.

She met his gaze, unwavering.

At last he gave out grudgingly, "It's just what I knew was going to happen. The damn story of the fight last night is all anybody's talking about."

"So?"

"And I made the mistake of visiting my father today. He said he called his house this morning early, the house where *I'm* supposed to be staying, and I wasn't there."

"Oh, Jared. You're making a big deal out of nothing."

"The old geezer did a lot of chortling and leering about where in the world I could have been at seven this morning. It was disgusting. He's on to us. I'm sure of it."

"So what?"

"It's not right. Not good for you. You're...a pure woman. And I've ruined you."

"Jared. You really have some seriously outdated ideas here. You have to get over this. Get past it. It's—"

She didn't get a chance to finish. In one of those lightning-swift moves of his, he reached out and grabbed her. She suddenly found herself pressed against his chest. She gasped, then blinked and stared up at him.

"Jared? What *is* it?"

"I should marry you," he said into her upturned face.

"You . . . you should?" Eden's mind, dulled by the pull his body exerted on her senses, struggled to comprehend his words. They were words she'd been secretly longing to hear for a while now. "Do you mean that?"

Staring at her lips as if he yearned to devour them, and seeming not to have heard either of the questions she'd asked, he continued, "But that would be a rotten thing to do to you. You could have any man. And soon enough you'll realize that. And then you'll hate me, for taking advantage of you in your moment of weakness."

Please, take advantage of me, her heart cried. But she tried to make what she actually said more rational. "I'm a grown woman, Jared. I'm old enough to know who I love and to make my own decision about who I want to marry."

"You say that now."

"Because it's the truth!"

"You don't know what the truth is now. You're confused by this *thing* between us."

"No, Jared. *I'm* not the one who's confused. I know exactly what I want and I'm—"

"Yoo-hoo! Anybody back there?" The voice came from down the hall. Someone was shouting from out in the bar.

"We're getting thirsty out here!" a different voice called in a syrupy singsong.

Jared let go of her. "We have to go. Now." He turned.

"But, Jared—"

"We are parched out here!" It was a chorus of voices now.

"Can it! I'm coming!" Jared shouted back.

"Oh, Jared—"

But as usual, she was speaking to thin air.

Things stayed reasonably busy until eleven, and then the place pretty much cleared out. Jared, by that time, was so withdrawn and uncommunicative that Eden felt a bottomless weariness every time she glanced his way. He seemed farther away from her now than he had two weeks ago, when they'd made that futile agreement to steer clear of each other.

She had no idea what to do to get through to him.

And, for tonight anyway, she decided she was just plain tired of trying. A good night's sleep would probably be the best thing for her right now. And they didn't have to work tomorrow. There would be time to hash out this whole mess then.

Since Rocky and a few other diehards were still hanging around, she spoke in an offhand way, "Jared, if you don't need me, I think I'll go on home."

He turned and looked at her, searing her, as he always did, with his gaze. But his answer was as casual as her request. "Sure. Go ahead. I can handle this."

She wiped the tables and washed up the dirty glasses and took one more round of orders from the boys in the back room. By eleven-thirty she was waving goodbye.

Ten minute later, she pulled into the little garage by the cabin. She left the car, trudged up the stone steps and went straight to the bedroom, shedding her clothes as she went.

She took a long, relaxing bath. And then she put on her sleep shirt and crawled into the bed she hadn't even had time to make that morning.

It was a warm night, though not as warm as that first night, when Jared had sneaked into her room and frightened her so badly. She pulled up the sheet and a light blanket to cover her.

The sheet smelled of their lovemaking. And her pillow smelled of Jared.

Eden snuggled down and put her arms around the pillow. She was fast asleep in minutes.

When Jared left The Hole in the Wall at 2:23 a.m., he knew very well what he *should* do. He should drive straight

to his father's house and go right to bed in the spare bedroom. That was where he belonged while he was staying in
North Magdalene.

But Jared wasn't doing much of what he *should* do lately.

And tonight—hell, this *morning* by now—was no ex-
ception. He found that his damn pickup suddenly had some
kind of a magnet attached to it. The magnet pulled him,
relentlessly, to the cabin by the river.

He stopped underneath the fir tree, which seemed to have
become his parking space now, since her car was in the garage. He shut off the engine and lights and just sat there in
the dark for a while, staring at the shadow of the cabin beneath the star-dusted sky.

This was bad. This was hell. He wanted to throw back his
head and howl his longing at the moon.

But there was no moon. It had gone down hours ago.
And he'd been through enough in his life that he should
have known better than to let this happen to him.

But some men, evidently, were fools their whole lives
long. They never learned their lesson. And Jared was becoming more and more certain that he was one of the fools.

He had loved his first wife. Sally had been his high school
sweetheart. He'd married her right after they graduated.
Loving Sally had been like breathing, the kind of love he
never even questioned. With Sally, he was doing what a
man did: find his woman and marry her and provide for the
children he got from her. Both his mother, bless her soul,
and his rogue of a father had taught him that.

If he'd had resentments at the way duty ruled his life, he
had conquered them, when he conquered drinking with the
help of A.A. and regained his wife and child. Things had
been fine.

Then he'd lost Sally to cold death.

He'd gone on. And he'd met Belle.

He'd wanted Belle. And he'd married her to have her,
because that was what a man did. Marry. And provide.

He'd lost Belle—and the boys—to another man.

And he'd sworn he was done with women and the traps they laid.

But now there was Eden.

And he was captured, thoroughly ensnared. And he knew, in spite of his own prejudices, that she was a good woman, a woman who would stand by him, as Sally couldn't and Belle wouldn't.

Eden Parker was a woman who would keep any promise she made. Even after the magic of desire melted away and she found she was married to a man who was too old for her, a man with nothing to offer her but a pair of hard-working hands, she would keep any vow she had made to him.

And that was the problem. He'd managed somehow to survive losing Sally and Belle. But to have Eden look at him one day as nothing more than a promise she must keep would be the end of him. His dry husk of a heart would shrivel up and blow away.

Jared straightened in the seat and put his hand on the ignition key. He had to get out of there. He started the truck and flicked on the lights and drove as if demons pursued him back to his father's deserted house.

But he'd no sooner stepped down and slammed the door than he realized that the magnet he'd thought was attached to his truck, was in reality inside himself. And it was pulling him....

He didn't even bother to get back in the truck. He didn't want to park it at her place anyway, where someone might see it, and know what was going on between them. In this, at least, he could protect her, though he'd taken her innocence when he'd had no right at all to do such a thing.

Jared ran into the dark trees, not even bothering to stick to the roads. This was the country of his childhood, after all. He knew every hillock, every rise and gully. He covered the distance between Sweet Spring Way and Bullfinch

Lane without breaking a sweat, burst out of the bushes near Sam and Delilah's place, and then crossed the road and plunged into the shadowed trees once more.

He followed the meandering curve of the river until he reached the end of Middle Fork Lane. Breathing hard, he emerged at last from the trees into the cleared space around the cabin.

He let himself into the dark kitchen, stopping to find a glass and take a long drink before moving soundlessly through the main room to the door of her bedroom. He paused there, in the doorway, looking toward the bed.

She lay beneath the covers, her cheek resting on an arm. Her strawberry-blond hair seemed silvery in the starlight. Her skin shone like the inside of one the fancy china cups his Grandma Riley used to display in a glass cabinet in her dining room. Dire consequences had always been threatened if any unruly boy dared to get too near those precious cups.

Jared thought of the first night he'd seen Eden, when he'd come into his cabin and found her asleep in the same place she lay now. She'd been sleeping without a cover. Jared had stood and stared at her, at her long, incredible legs and the china-cup beauty of her skin. He shouldn't have done that, stared at a woman he didn't even know while she was helpless, fast asleep, unaware of him. But he'd somehow been unable to stop himself.

He'd approached the bed hardly knowing that he moved. And he'd stood there for a long while, endless minutes, just watching her sleep.

The strangest thing had come into his mind, standing there, staring in forbidden longing at a woman he didn't even know. He'd heard his own voice, inside his head, clear as if he'd spoken aloud.

The voice said, *Too late. You've found her too late....*

And for the first time since Sally died, Jared Jones had felt the thick heat of tears in the back of his throat. In the middle of the night in his own bedroom, while he watched a strange woman sleeping, he'd nearly broken down and cried.

And then she'd awakened and thrown a clock at him.

He'd managed, for a couple of weeks to push those moments when he watched her from his mind. But now, they were back with him, as he watched her once more.

Too late. You've found her too late....

On the bed, Eden stirred.

"Jared?" She sighed and turned over and then she sat up. "Jared, is that you?" She pushed her hair back from her forehead by combing her fingers through it. And then she focused on him, in the doorway. "Jared. Come to bed." Though the light from the window was behind her, he knew she was smiling.

"I shouldn't—"

She cut him off. "Jared, just for now, could you please stop talking about what you *shouldn't* do?" She yawned and stretched, as contented as a well-rested cat.

"Hell."

She reached out a willowy arm and beckoned him. "Come here. Come on."

He felt like a boy, suddenly. His mother used to do that—reach out to him when something was bothering him. And he'd go and she'd pull him against the side of her tall, slim body and kiss the top of his head. She'd tell him that she loved him, not to take life so seriously, that everything would be all right. Bathsheba Riley Jones had been a steadying influence on the whole crazy Jones gang. It was too bad for all of them that she'd died so young.

"Jared." Eden's voice was infinitely patient. She didn't drop her arm.

He left the doorway and went to her. She slid over a little, making room for him. He dropped to the side of the bed. Suddenly nervous, she plucked at the sheet a little, her eyes focused on his face.

"I tried not to come here," he said.

She said nothing, something of a rarity for her.

He hitched a leg up on the bed, so he could face her more fully. "I couldn't stay away."

"Good." She nodded, a satisfied little nod. "I'm glad you couldn't."

"It's just going to get worse, the more we go on with this."

Eden sighed. "But we *will* go on with this. Won't we?"

He looked at her for a moment, then said, "Yeah. Until one of us has the sense to break it off."

She sat up straighter, as if she'd come to some sort of decision within herself. "Okay, then. Can we make a deal, for as long as we're together?"

"What deal?" He peered at her sideways. He was a man who expected to pay full price for things. He was wary of *deals*.

"Can we please *enjoy* it while it lasts? Can you quit walking around with a frown on your face, mumbling about my reputation and acting as if someone is going to carve a scarlet letter on my forehead if they ever find out about us?"

He considered her request. "All right," he said after giving the matter the serious thought it deserved. Then he added a condition of his own. "But we're going to keep it low-key."

"What does that mean?"

"It means we won't tell anyone. About us."

Eden shook her head. "No. I won't do that. I won't pretend I don't...care for you." He didn't miss the way she hesitated over the word *care*. He knew the word she'd wanted to use, but hadn't. And he despised himself a little for yearning, once more, to hear that word from her lips.

"Oh, Jared." She put her hand on the side of his face in a tender caress. "Don't ask me to lie about how I feel.

Please. Don't expect me to work side by side with you every night and act as if you're nothing at all to me. I couldn't bear that."

He caught her hand. "Damn it, Eden."

"Please. Can't we compromise on this?"

"What kind of compromise?" He wasn't sure he liked the sound of this.

"Well. Could we let people know we're together, but just not let on *how* together?"

He frowned. He was beginning to get the picture.

She hastened to clarify what he already suspected. "I mean, let them think we're dating, but keep it to ourselves that we're...lovers."

He thought about that. It just might work. The cabin was off to itself, at least a quarter of a mile from the nearest house. As long as his truck wasn't parked there all night, who would guess what went on inside?

"Personally," Eden added in a tart tone, "I think you're making a big thing out of nothing."

"You didn't grow up here."

"No, I didn't. And I respect your feelings. I do. If it's so important to you to keep our private lives private—"

"It is." When he left, he wanted her to be totally free of him, which she'd never be in North Magdalene once everyone knew he'd slept with her.

"Then, okay," she said. "I'd be willing not to tell anyone exactly how *together* we are, as long as you don't treat me like a stranger when you come to work at night. Agreed?" She stuck out her hand, to shake on it, as she had that night they'd agreed to stay away from each other.

He looked at her hand, his thoughts bleak. What made her think that this agreement would fare any better than the last one they'd made?

"Jared, please..."

Her voice was so soft, so full of hope and tender concern. How could he ever refuse her, even for her own good?

"Jared . . ."

"All right, Eden. Agreed." He took the hand she offered him.

Chapter Fourteen

"Whoa. Can this really be happening? It's time for one serious reality check here." Laurie, who was stretched out on a lounge chair on Eden's deck, took a fortifying sip from her glass of wine and looked probingly at Eden through the gathering darkness. Dinner had been cleared off a half an hour before. Jared had just left them, saying he wanted to go over to Delilah's and check on his father.

Laurie went on. "Now tell it to me slowly. You and my cousin Jared—"

"Are dating. That's all." Eden gave her best imitation of an unconcerned shrug.

"That's *all?*" Laurie wasn't buying. "I gotta tell you, pal. The air sizzles when you two look at each other."

"We're dating," Eden said again, and knew there was a slight edge to her voice. "Period."

Laurie put up a hand in a pacifying gesture. "Okay, okay. Whatever you say."

Eden looked away.

There was a silence, one that flooded quickly with the sounds of twilight in the mountains: the chirruping of crickets, the croaking of frogs, the warning whine of biting insects. A wind set the trees to whispering.

As the silence drew out, Laurie got up from her lounge chair and went to the patio table in the corner, where she poured herself another glass of wine from the bottle she'd brought.

As she poured, Laurie ventured, "I thought you said you two had an agreement...."

Eden tried her best to keep her tone offhand and casual. "We did. And it wasn't working. So we decided to, um, spend a little time together, to let things sort of... evolve...."

Laurie sipped from her glass. "I see."

"What does that does that mean, 'I see ...'?"

"Wow. You *are* defensive about this."

"I'd just like to know what you meant when you said 'I see,' that's all."

"Well, Eden, I meant just what I said, that I understand. But—"

"But what?"

"Well, I guess that letting things *evolve* just doesn't sound like something anyone could do with cousin Jared." Laurie gestured with her glass. "He's sort of an all-or-nothing kind of guy, if you know what I mean."

"No, I don't know what you mean," Eden lied. She was finding she already hated her new agreement with Jared. She wanted so badly to confide all the wonder of what she was feeling to her friend. But that was denied her, because no one was to know the true nature of what she and Jared shared.

"I mean—" Laurie dropped into her chair again "—he's sort of a caveman, cousin Jared is. You know, *Me-Tarzan-you-Jane*. It seems like he'd either be with a woman or not.

Letting things *evolve* would be a little subtle for a man like him."

"Maybe you don't know him that well."

Laurie ran her finger around the rim of her glass. "You're right about that. I mean, I mostly think of him as Heather's wild-man dad. And then, there are all the family stories about him. But he's not the kind of person too many people ever really get to know." Laurie took another sip and then added, "Of course, Heather says he's a big pussycat, that he's really just a good man whose life didn't work out the way it should have."

Hearing what Heather thought of Jared, Eden felt a little better. It was reassuring to think that her opinion of the man she loved was also held by his only child.

Laurie snared Eden's glance. "So I've read things all wrong here, then?"

"What do you mean, all wrong?"

"I mean, it's just a casual thing."

"What do you mean, casual?"

"I mean, no grand passion?"

Eden, who was leaning against the railing, picked up a pine needle that had fallen near her elbow and pulled it in two.

"Oh, wow," Laurie said softly. She sipped again from her glass. "You told him you wouldn't talk about it, right?"

Eden nodded, staring down at the two sections of pine needle as if she didn't know how they'd gotten into her hands.

"You love him?" her friend asked. It wasn't really a question.

Eden nodded again.

"Does he love you back?"

"I believe he does. He's just . . . fighting it."

Laurie said quietly, "If he hurts you, I'll murder him. The rest of the family will help me."

That made Eden laugh.

"Believe it," Laurie told her. "It's true. If he breaks your heart, he's done for."

"Heather's right about him, Laurie. He's a good man. He really is."

"Nobody said he wasn't."

"But he's absolutely sure he's through with women and with love."

"So what's he doing with you, then?"

"He's confused. He's attracted to me. But he thinks he'd be bad for me, in the long run."

Laurie set her glass on the small deck table near her chair. "Eden, I have to tell you. When it comes to running a restaurant or a tavern there's no one as savvy as you are. But in romance, we both know you're no expert. And cousin Jared is not The Hole in the Wall. You can't . . . renovate a broken-down heart."

Eden forced a smile and slapped at a mosquito that had landed on her arm. "It'll work out. I'm sure of it." She straightened from the railing and went to pick up the wine bottle. "And let's go inside, okay? Before we get eaten alive out here."

"Wait."

"What?"

"I'll say it again. If you need someone to talk to . . ."

"I know, and thanks. But really. Everything will be fine."

When Laurie left at a little after ten, Jared still had not returned. Eden walked her friend out to the driveway and then stood waving goodbye as Laurie drove away.

When Laurie's taillights had disappeared around the first bend in the road, Eden turned for the cabin. Her breath caught as she saw Jared, standing at the top of the stone steps, silhouetted in the light from the kitchen door.

Her blood quickened in her veins. He must have been waiting, out in the trees, for Laurie to be gone.

Eden hurried to meet him, all her worries and doubts about where this thing between them might be going submerged in her joy that he had come back to her once more.

At the top of the steps, they embraced. When Jared's arms went around her, Eden sighed in pure happiness. He kissed her. She felt, once again, that she'd found her true home at last.

They went in through the door together and paused, just inside, to share another kiss.

And then he was waltzing her backward, through the main room to her bedroom. Eden went joyfully, unhesitating, grateful for every moment they might share.

He undressed her swiftly and brought her down upon the sheets. Eden cried out as he entered her. And then she forgot everything but the feel of him inside her. The world whirled away to nothing. There was bliss, and that was all.

The next several days were happy ones for Eden. It was a golden time. She and Jared were together night and day. She felt that they grew closer as each hour passed.

He never parked his truck under her tree again. Also, he was careful, though he virtually lived at the cabin with her, never to answer the phone or leave signs of his presence where a casual visitor might detect them. But it wasn't as unpleasant as Eden had thought it might be, because the cabin was isolated anyway. They didn't have to be too sneaky to keep what they shared a secret.

As they grew more comfortable with each other, he began to ask her questions about the life she'd known before she'd come to North Magdalene. He asked about her parents.

"They divorced when I was four," she explained. "And both of them remarried, my father once, my mother twice. I have six half sisters and four half brothers, not to mention all the stepbrothers and sisters from my stepmother's and stepfathers' previous marriages. I spent most of my growing up years bouncing between my mother and father. Whichever one of them could handle an extra kid right then, got me.''

"It was tough, huh?" Jared tenderly smoothed her hair with his hand. They were lying in bed early on Friday morning, just a week after they'd become lovers, snuggling and talking softly together as they had yesterday and the day before that. To Eden, sharing these precious moments at the very start of the day seemed like something they'd been doing for years.

She cuddled up closer to him. "Not that tough," she mused. "I mean, they really did do their job of raising me. I was never hungry, and I was never abused. And I knew that they loved me. I just...never felt like I really *belonged*, you know?"

He made a low noise of understanding.

She continued, "And because no one paid much attention to me, I learned the habit of independence early. I realized that if I wanted to get anywhere in this life, I'd have to get there on my own steam. No one was going to do it for me. I think that's an important thing to learn."

He grunted. Her head was on his chest right then, and she heard the sound as a low, agreeable rumble against her ear. Then he asked, "What held you back, from men, until now?"

Eden smiled to herself, touched by how tactfully he was asking her why she'd stayed a virgin until she met him. "Well, it's partly because I've had plenty to do. There's hardly been time for romance. I worked long hours to save my money, so I would be ready to move, or invest, or whatever was required of me when I finally found what I was looking for."

He chuckled then, a warm, rumbling sound. Eden basked in it and told herself he was a much happier, friendlier person now he had found her.

"What you were looking for," he playfully scoffed. "To live in North Magdalene and partner up with my father in his tumbledown saloon?"

She kissed him on the chest, reveling in the way the wiry hairs there tickled her nose. "Exactly. North Magdalene and The Hole in the Wall are just what I'd been looking for. And when I found them, I was ready...."

"...because you hadn't wasted any of your young life on falling in love, right?"

"Right. I'd earned the money I needed. And when your father offered me a partnership, I jumped at the chance." Jared's outside arm rested on her waist. She stroked the hard muscles with an idle hand. "Also, in this day and age, a woman has to be careful. Working in restaurants and bars, I've really seen firsthand what not being responsible about romance can lead to. That's why I put the condom machine in the men's room, even though your father ribbed me about it unmercifully. I like to hope that somebody will be saved from an unwanted pregnancy—or much worse—because that machine is there. You see?"

She felt his nod against the top of her head. "And what else?" he asked. His voice was slightly gruff.

She knew what he meant. *What else had kept her a virgin until the age of twenty-six?*

The answer, of course, was quite simple. He must already know it. Because she'd never found a man she loved before.

But somehow, her heart balked at giving him the words outright. She'd told him of her love that first night they spent together, but had not said the words since.

The truth was, she was keeping them back. Somewhere deep in her heart she was waiting, longing to hear the words from him before she uttered them again herself.

She sighed, thinking that to give all of herself to him in the hope that he could give himself fully to her must include the precious words of love as well. Especially now when he'd as much as asked to hear them.

She began, "Because I never—"

And he cut her off. "Shh." He lifted her chin with a tender hand, and she found herself looking into his steel-and-smoke eyes. "Never mind. I've got no right to ask," he said in a slightly ragged whisper. "Forgive me."

"But—"

She got no further. His mouth covered hers. His hand found her breast. She moaned. The kiss deepened.

She let her body express what she hadn't managed to say in words.

Later, as she was rushing to finish her hair and makeup so she could get to The Hole in the Wall on time, she decided that she wasn't going to let it bother her that he had stopped her just before she could tell him again of her love.

They were making progress. She was sure of it. Everything was going just fine. Soon, he would come to her and tell her they didn't need their silly agreement anymore. He would admit that he was through trying to keep their love a secret. He'd want to shout it from the rooftops, just as she had all along.

Eden realized she was frowning at herself in the mirror. She ordered her face to relax. But inside, she couldn't help feeling anxious.

She had visited Oggie yesterday. The sweet old coot was getting around part of the time on crutches now.

True, it would be weeks yet before her partner could work again. But when that time came, if Jared hadn't decided that what he and Eden shared could last a lifetime, then Jared would leave, as he'd always sworn to do. And his going was something she couldn't bear to consider.

Eden had believed, until Jared came, that she'd found her home in this lovely little town. But now she knew better. Home was where Jared was. And if he left, well, somehow she'd live through it. She was a strong woman, after all. But if he was gone, she'd have to start all over again to find the place she'd sought her whole life: the place where she belonged.

Eden caught her thoughts up short. What was the matter with her this morning? Nothing had changed since yesterday. She and Jared were doing just fine.

But for some reason, she kept remembering the haunted look in his eyes when he'd stopped her from saying she loved him. She kept recalling the ragged harshness of his whisper when he'd said, *"Never mind, I have no right to ask."* And she kept having the strangest feeling that what she and Jared shared would soon be coming to an end.

Which was silly. Everything was going along just fine. She just had to stop letting negative thoughts control her, that was all. She smoothed her hair one more time and quickly applied her lipstick. Then she rushed out through the main room to the kitchen.

Jared was sitting at the table there, drinking his second cup of coffee and reading the *North Magdalene News.*

He glanced up as she flew toward the door. "Hey. Don't I rate a kiss goodbye?"

She went to him and bent to swiftly press her lips to his. As so often happened between them, the brief kiss drew out. Eden sighed and felt his smile against her softly parted lips.

After a moment, she straightened up and gazed fondly down at him. Her lipstick was on his mouth. She wiped it away with a caressing thumb. "If you keep that up, I'll just have to stay home for the day."

"You'd never forgive yourself if you did that," he teased, putting his big hands at her waist and looking up at her, his silver eyes gleaming. "You'd lose a day's income, not to mention give customers the idea that they can't depend on you."

"You're right," she agreed, enjoying the feel of his hands spanning her waist. She idly combed his hair with her fingers. "Consistency is everything."

He chuckled. "So you're always telling me." He turned back to his newspaper, though he kept an arm loosely draped around her waist.

"Which is why I'd better get going." She started to edge out of the circle of his arm.

He pulled her a fraction closer. "Hold on just a second. I want to show you something. Look at this." He pointed at the newspaper, which was spread out on the table in front of them.

"Jared, I really have to—"

"Come on, this won't take a minute. Read."

Eden quelled her impatience to be gone and did as he asked.

He was pointing to an ad in the *News*'s scanty Classified section.

Position Sought

I am dependable, hardworking, 23 years old. Seeking entry-level job in any local company. Fast learner, flexible, will work any hours. Inquire at SANTINO'S BB&V 555-2435. Ask for Nick.

Jared explained, "I know the Santinos. They're all good workers. Sam hired their youngest son, Marty, over at his gold sales store. He says Marty's the best clerk he's ever had. Now, Nick would be the Santinos' middle son. He's been out of town for a few years, as best I can remember. But it looks like he's back now and looking for a job."

"So?"

"So I'll bet he'd make a damn good bartender. And we could really use one more pair of hands around The Hole in the Wall."

Eden backed away from him just enough that he dropped his arm from around her waist. "We're managing."

"Just barely," he reminded her gently. "Come on, Eden. You're overworked. You're at that bar up to eighty hours a week sometimes."

"I like to work, especially when I'm working for myself."

"I know, but—"

"Jared, your father handled the place alone for years."

"Right. And you remember what it was like when you became his partner. Half the time, he was so worn-out, he didn't even bother to go in until late afternoon. He was barely getting by. And look what happened when he shot himself in the foot. If I hadn't been around to cover for him—"

"I would have managed." Eden really didn't want to hear anymore. The truth was, she'd been planning to hire another bartender next spring, when the busy season started again. And she probably would have hired someone when Oggie hurt himself, if Jared hadn't been there to fill the gap so perfectly.

With her shrewd head for business, Eden knew that what Jared was suggesting made complete sense. They were bringing in nearly three times the money that Oggie had made alone. And they were often busy four or five nights of the week now. They did need someone to take up the slack. The way it was now, if either she or Jared—or Oggie, once he was back on his feet—got sick, the business was bound to suffer.

But Eden knew very well what having someone else to help out would mean. That Jared could leave even sooner than she'd thought. And she didn't want him to be free to leave until *after* he'd decided he wasn't going anywhere.

"Eden," Jared said quietly. "Just talk to Nick, okay? I know you won't want to pass up the chance to hire someone like him."

She turned for the door. "I'm late."

"I'm calling him as soon as you leave. And I'll bring him in around noon if he's willing, so you can meet him. The weekend's coming up, and Monday is Labor Day." They'd already decided to stay open on their usual day off this week, to take advantage of the heavy holiday trade on the last big weekend of the summer season.

"Unless we interview him today," Jared went on, "we won't have another chance until Tuesday. And if there's anyone else in town who's looking for good help, he'll be unavailable by then. I think we should move on this now."

"I have to go, Jared."

He grabbed her hand. "Say yes."

No, her heart cried. *Never! Not until you swear you'll love me forever, and never ever go away....*

"I have to go."

"Say yes."

What could she say? He was right. And her heart was breaking in two.

"All right, fine. Call him, and I'll talk to him today."

Chapter Fifteen

Jared brought Nick Santino into The Hole in the Wall at twelve-fifteen that very day. Eden saw immediately that the young man was just what she'd hoped to find when she started interviewing for a helper. He was big and bright and handsome, with a ready smile and a steady hand. And there was a calm levelheadedness about him that Eden found instantly reassuring.

She told him that the pay would be low to start out, but that they were planning on adding a restaurant in The Mercantile building in the spring. Nick could "grow" with them if he found he liked the work. If he learned about both the bar and restaurant ends of the business, there could very well be a manager's job for him eventually.

Eden didn't say so, but she had big plans for farther into the future. Grass Valley and Nevada City were nearby, after all. Eventually she intended to open more restaurants in those larger neighboring towns.

Nick, who'd returned to North Magdalene with the hope of settling down permanently, was eager to start as soon as Eden thought she could use him. They agreed on a salary and that he would begin work right after the holiday. He'd be taught how to open the place first, get his initial training during the day, when things were generally less hectic.

"I'll meet you right outside the back door then, ten-thirty Tuesday morning." Nick stood up from the table where Eden had led him to conduct the interview.

"Sounds good." Eden reached across to take the hand he offered. "See you then."

Nick gave her a nod and turned to go. Eden stared after him until the doors swung shut behind him. She felt strangely at a loss. She knew she'd made a sound business decision.

And yet she wanted to cry.

"Hey."

Eden blinked and smiled at Jared, who had taken over the bar so she could talk to Nick. "Hey, what?"

"Take a break, that's what. Go on over to Lily's, why don't you, and get yourself some lunch? I'll handle things here."

Eden never ate lunch out. She'd either bring it to work with her, or call down to the café and have something delivered. She started to decline Jared's suggestion without even stopping to consider it. But then she decided that getting outside on her own for a little while might be an excellent idea right now.

"Thanks, I think I'll do that." She got up and started to go behind the bar to get her purse.

Jared got it for her. He picked it up and plunked it right down in front of her. "Get lost."

She took the purse and made a mock-sour face at him. "Yes, sir."

Out on the street, she made herself walk slowly. She looked around and reminded herself how much she loved this little town.

Since she was being purposely observant to keep her mind off her vacillating emotions, she found herself noticing the maples that lined Main Street. They looked different than they had just a few days ago. Their leaves weren't quite as green as they had been. They weren't changing yet, so much as fading, like summer, a little at a time.

Thinking back to last night, she recalled how she'd wanted her sweater the minute the shadows came. Strange, in the space of the week that she and Jared had been lovers, summer seemed to have found its apex and to be fading now toward the autumn of the year.

The thought saddened her, brought the tears that she was keeping down a little nearer to the surface.

Oh, what was the matter with her? Somehow, today, everything seemed to speak of changes.

It was ridiculous. Very little had really changed. She'd hired a much-needed employee. So what? It was something that was bound to happen sooner or later. And it didn't mean that Jared would be packing up his gear and heading out of town tomorrow.

And yet Oggie was on crutches now. Autumn was on its way. And Jared had stopped her from declaring her love. He'd said he had *no right* to hear the words from her....

"Allow me, Miss Parker."

Eden shook herself and realized that she'd reached the café and then stood there, absorbed in her thoughts, blocking the door.

She pushed back her self-pitying tears and murmured "Thank you," to Sheriff Pangborn. He pulled back the door.

Eden sat down in the first empty booth she came to. Heather was there before she even had a chance to look at the menu.

"Hi, Eden. What are you doing here this time of day?"

"Your father kicked me out of The Hole in the Wall. He made me take a break."

Heather laughed. "Well, good. Want coffee?"

"How about iced tea?"

"You got it." Heather bounced cheerily over to the beverage station and poured the iced tea, pausing to call out Sheriff Pangborn's order through the cook's window on the way. Heather returned with the tea. "There you go."

"Thanks."

"You want a few minutes?"

"No, I'm ready." Eden ordered a sandwich and cole-slaw.

Heather wrote down the order and then stuck her pencil behind her ear. "Say, Eden . . ." She leaned in closer.

"Hmm?"

"You know, I've been thinking . . ."

Eden smiled at Jared's daughter. "What?"

"Maybe you and Dad could come over for dinner. Maybe this Monday night, on your day off?"

Eden felt the tears come again. She held them back by smiling wider. She was touched. She knew exactly what this invitation meant. It was Heather's way of telling Eden that she approved of the idea of her father and Eden together. It also meant that people in town were starting to see the two of them as a couple. And that was good, as far as Eden was concerned. That was just wonderful.

Eden drew in a breath. "That would be great. As long as Jared says yes, too. But it would have to be the Monday after this one. We're staying open for the holiday."

"Okay, then, Monday after the one coming up. Say, six o'clock?"

"Sound's fine. As long as Jared—"

"Eden. Do me a favor."

"Anything."

"Don't *ask* my dad. *Tell* him. You'll save yourself a lot of grief."

Eden laughed at that. "Okay, okay. We'll be there."

"Great. I'll put in your order."

Eden, her sagging spirits lifted a little by Heather's invitation, ate a leisurely lunch and returned to The Hole in the Wall much refreshed.

She didn't get a chance to tell Jared about the invitation until three the next morning, after he'd appeared at her doorstep as he always did, materializing out of the trees once he'd left his pickup at Oggie's place.

She opened the door to him and he came into her waiting arms. For a time, as always when he touched her, she forgot the rest of the world in the beauty of his kiss.

At last, he pulled back enough to look at her. "What a night, huh?" It had been just as busy as they'd anticipated. From seven o'clock on, Eden had felt like she'd never stopped moving.

"Yes. I'm beat." She sighed. "I want a bath and then I want to fall into bed. With you."

"Well, let's get to it." He took her hand and started to tug her toward the bedroom.

She hung back. "Wait. I have to tell you before I forget."

"Yeah?"

"Monday, the fourteenth. We're going to dinner at Heather's house."

"We're what?" His voice was perfectly level. Yet for some reason, the sound of it had her wanting to cry again.

She pasted on a cheerful smile. "Your daughter invited us to dinner, Monday the fourteenth. It's okay, isn't it?" She loathed the slightly pleading note she could hear in her voice.

He rubbed the back of his neck. "Eden..."

"What?"

He looked so sad and strained. She *hated* to see him looking like that. He seemed to choose his next words with great care. "That's more than a week away."

"So?"

"Who knows what could be happening in a week."

"What are you getting at, Jared?"

He looked at her. His whole lean body seemed full of tension. And weariness, too. If she could have read minds, she would have cried in earnest at his thoughts right then.

Right then, the longing in Jared was very bad.

He wanted what he'd wanted since the night he first made love with her. He wanted to make her his true wife before the world.

But Jared knew he must not forget all the things that would forever stand between them. He was forty years old. Eden was only five years older than his own daughter. He was virtually unemployed. He'd been divorced and he had a rotten disposition.

Hell, he could hardly imagine a worse prospect for a husband than himself. Even if Eden said yes, he would never let her marry someone like him.

That was why he had to set her free of him. And the only way he was going to be able to do that was to get away from her, to go somewhere where he wouldn't have to see her anymore.

The morning just past, when they lay in bed together and he found himself longing to hear her tell him she loved him, he had finally realized that he had to put a stop to this. He had to end this sweet torture and get out of her life, once and for all.

The hiring of Nick Santino was a step toward that aim. Nick was smart and quick. Jared's plan was to have the young man trained and ready to fill his own shoes within a week, two at the most. And then he would leave town, not to return for a long, long time. He would get away and he would get over her.

Eventually, when she found a more suitable man, she would remember him with fondness. Hell, she'd probably even be grateful to him for keeping her from wasting her life.

"Jared, I asked you a question. Are you going to answer me or not?"

"What question?" His grim thoughts had made him lose completely the thread of their conversation.

"What are you getting at when you say 'Who knows what could be happening in a week'?"

He knew he should probably tell her now. But that would only make the remaining days they had together all the sadder. No, the best way was to keep quiet until the end, and then cut it clean.

"Forget that," he said.

"But, Jared—"

"We'll go to dinner at Heather's, okay?"

"But Jared, I think—"

"Stop thinking." He pulled her against him. "Kiss me."

"But—"

He covered her sweet lips with his own and there was no more discussion that night, or the rest of the weekend for that matter. By the time they got home Saturday, Sunday and Monday nights, they had little energy for anything but a quick bath and bed.

Nick Santino began work, as agreed, on the day after Labor Day.

From the first, he proved to be everything Jared and Eden had hoped he might be. When it came to any task, he only had to have it explained to him once and he was ready to perform it on a regular basis. And there was no job too menial for him. He bused tables and scrubbed floors with the same meticulous care he brought to mixing a fancy drink. He did what he was told to do, and he never sat around on the job.

By his third day of work, the Thursday after Labor Day, Eden decided Nick was ready to open up the bar on his own. She told him that tomorrow, Friday, she wouldn't be coming in until two or three in the afternoon.

Nick gave her a proud smile and an enthusiastic "Yes, ma'am" in response.

So the next morning, Eden and Jared slept late. They shared a leisurely brunch at around eleven and then found their way back to the bedroom to make use of the bed one more time. At a little after one Eden decided she probably ought to get ready to put in her appearance at work.

Jared had a different idea. "Let me go in early, why don't you? You can take the whole day off."

Eden tried to protest. "It's Friday, and it'll probably be busy. I can't—"

"Yes, you can. I have a hunch things won't be too heavy tonight, anyway. The summer's over. It's been quieter all week, you've said so yourself."

"But I—"

"Come on. Nick and I will do fine. Give yourself a break." He reached for his pants, which were on the floor by his side of the bed and pulled some money from a pocket. He rolled back to face her and held out the bills. "Go down to Grass Valley and buy yourself a new dress or something."

"Jared, I don't think—"

"Right." He wrapped her hands around the money. "Don't think. Just have a good day. And be waiting in this bed for me tonight."

Eden considered. The idea was tempting. She hadn't had a break from work in ten days, after all. She might as well enjoy the benefits of having a dependable employee. And Jared could take some time off, too. This Sunday, if all went as expected, she'd insist that he skip a whole day's work as well.

"All right. I'll do it." She waved his money under his nose and grinned at him.

"Good."

An hour later, he left her to enjoy her day off.

Eden took Jared's suggestion and drove to Grass Valley. After a trip to the bank, she stopped at Brunswick Plaza, where there just happened to be a bridal shop. She only went in the bridal shop to look around. But once she was there, she found she wanted to try on some of the gowns. The saleslady was very helpful.

Before she knew what was happening, Eden did the craziest thing. She took the money Jared had given her, plus quite a bit of money of her own, and she bought a floor-length ivory wedding dress.

It was just nuts of her to do such a thing, she knew, but she couldn't resist that dress. She loved the old-fashioned basque waistline, which dipped to a point in front. The portrait collar framed her smooth shoulders and long neck and the skirt was a filmy wonder, chiffon over satin. Venise lace and tiny seed pearls decorated the fitted point sleeves and adorned the hem.

After choosing an ivory-colored fingertip-length veil, Eden walked out of the bridal shop with the dream of a dress laid carefully across her outstretched arms. She wondered how she would explain to Jared what she'd done.

She decided she wouldn't tell him, at least not right away. She'd give him back the amount of money he'd given her and say she hadn't found a dress she liked after all.

Fantasizing shamelessly about the day she would wear the beautiful dress, Eden shopped for groceries. She stocked up on the brand of cola that Jared liked, and she stacked the cart high with steaks, pot roasts, and racks of country-style ribs. Jared, after all, was a meat-and-potatoes kind of man. Last, she stopped at a bar and restaurant supply house to order some new beer mugs and a case of champagne flutes.

She returned to North Magdalene and drove straight to the cabin to put all her purchases away. She was already feeling a little foolish about the wedding dress, so she stuck it in the back of her closet, thinking she'd surprise Jared when he asked her to become his wife by telling him how she'd found it in Grass Valley that day he'd told her to buy herself a dress.

Eden fixed herself a light dinner, and then she went to see Oggie at Delilah's house. She found the old man alone. He was sitting in the living room watching a game show on TV.

"Come in, come in, gal. I been wantin' a word with you anyway." He pointed the remote at the television, and the big box went silent. "What the hell are you doing out and about at this time of the evening? Shouldn't you be over at The Hole in the Wall makin' us rich?"

"Well, Oggie, I—"

"Say no more. I know the answer already. It's that Santino kid you hired, am I right?"

"Yes, he's turned out to be quite a find."

"All the Santinos are a find. Those kids were well brought up. Julio and Maria had 'em all workin' from the time they were knee-high to a gnat's behind." He felt in his shirt pocket, and didn't find what he was looking for. "Damn. I could use me a good cigar. But Delilah's after me night and day not to smoke in the house."

"Well, I suppose it won't be long until you're back at your own house again, anyway."

Oggie shrugged. "Who knows? Even if I'm dyin' half the time for a smoke, it ain't so bad to have my breakfast and dinner cooked up for me, not to mention my clothes kept clean. And Sam and Delilah swear I can stay as long as I want to. So we'll see, we'll just see...." He shot her an oblique glance, and Eden realized he was working up to saying what was really on his mind.

She prompted, "Oggie, is something wrong?"

"Well, I gotta tell you, I been wonderin'..."

"What? Say it."

"Hell. The truth is, I been wonderin' how come you went and hired you a helper without consultin' your partner?"

Eden felt instantly contrite. The hiring of Nick Santino had come about so swiftly, she'd hardly had a moment to stop and think. And she should have consulted Oggie, she knew, though she was also sure he would have told her to go ahead and do what needed to be done.

"I'm sorry," Eden said. "I really am. It all happened kind of quickly. Jared felt we had to get right on it, or we'd miss out on the chance to hire him. I hope it's all right with you. But if for some reason, it's not—"

"So it was Jared's idea, eh?"

"Well, yes. He said that we really needed a relief person. And it's true, we do."

Oggie looked at her sideways. "Now really ain't the time of year to be hiring someone new."

"Business has just been great, Oggie. You know that. There's plenty of work for another pair of hands."

"Yeah." Oggie grunted. "I guess so. Especially if one pair of hands is walkin' out the door."

Eden frowned. "What does that mean?"

"Nothin' much. Just that it looks like Jared's gone and hired his replacement."

Eden, who'd perched on the end of the couch, found she was too anxious, suddenly, to sit still. She stood up. "No, that can't be."

"Why not?"

"Well, he promised you he'd stay until you could work again, didn't he?"

"He's stayed to find someone to *do* the work. He knows damn well no one would fault him for that."

"But... but *you* would, wouldn't you?"

Oggie's beady brown eyes were infinitely patient. "Eden, honey. If he wants to be a damn fool, who am I to roll my wheelchair in his path?"

Behind the couch, a big window looked out on a group of white-barked birch trees. Eden stared at those trees, thinking that their leaves were noticeably turning to gold.

Autumn. Autumn was in the air. Everything was changing. And Jared *was* setting things up so that he could leave her.

"Eden, you okay?" Oggie's voice came through to her as if from a long way away.

"Yes, fine. Just fine."

"You don't sound so fine. Matter of fact, you look kind of green around the gills."

He was right, of course. She was not fine. It took her a moment before she realized exactly what she felt right then.

Anger.

It was moving through her in a slow, expanding, engulfing wave.

Her six half sisters and four half brothers and myriad stepsiblings had known the truth about Eden. They all said, "It's almost impossible to make Edie mad. But when it happens, watch out!"

It was happening now.

She was simmering now, and in a few minutes, her rage would reach a rolling boil.

She seethed.

How could she have been so blind? Jared had not only coaxed her into hiring his own replacement, he hadn't even had the consideration to tell her honestly what he was doing.

Nick was already good enough at his new job that he and Eden could manage alone if they had to. If Nick worked this whole weekend, he would no doubt be capable of either opening the place *or* closing it up come the slower midweek days. Jared could head out of town Monday and now that The Hole in the Wall would get along just fine without him.

How Eden was going to get along without him clearly didn't concern him.

Oh, she knew what he had told himself. That he was doing the right thing. So what if he was breaking her heart? After all, he was leaving her for her own good.

She'd given him everything, all that was in her. Her love. Her body. And every ounce of patience she possessed. She'd agreed to keep their passion a secret and to take things one day at a time. Though their deceit had chafed her sorely, she had kept their love a shadowed thing. For him.

And he was leaving anyway, without warning, as soon as Nick was ready to take his place at The Hole in the Wall.

Well, he had another think coming if he thought he was going to get away so easily. She was going to have a word with him on the subject.

And she was going to do it now, at The Hole in the Wall. She was through sneaking around. She was going to tell him what she thought of him, and she didn't care who heard what she said.

Eden turned from the view of the changing birch trees and pointed herself at the front door.

She was stopped halfway there by Oggie, who had moved with surprising swiftness, spinning his wheelchair right into her path.

She looked down at him. "Get out of my way."

"Er, Eden? Eden, maybe you oughtta sit down."

"No, Oggie. I ought not. I have to go now."

"Eden, I gotta tell you. You got that look. That rageful woman look. It's a dangerous look to be wearin' on the street. Stay here for a bit."

"No."

"Eden—"

She darted around him and flew out the door.

Chapter Sixteen

Eden descended on The Hole in the Wall about five minutes later. She found a free space on the street, so she entered from the front.

She shoved back the double doors and stepped inside.

That small hush happened, as it always does whenever someone new arrives at a bar. Everyone turned to look at her, and then turned back to what they'd been doing before.

Rocky waved. "Hey, there, Eden. We been askin' where you were."

Eden nodded at Rocky and spared a moment to look around the room. There was a game of pool in progress, and several of the tables were full. There was only one free stool at the bar itself.

Nick was behind the bar, in Jared's place.

If Eden had cherished the slightest doubt that Jared planned to leave her within days, it vanished the moment she saw Nick standing at the little rubber mat where Jared always stood. Tonight, since it was Nick's first night, he should have been doing the footwork while Jared took the money and mixed the drinks. But Jared had put the younger man right into the main job. He was training him as fast as he could.

Eden perceived one of the finer points of Jared's deceit. He'd pushed her to take the day off so that he could speed up Nick's training without her witnessing what he did. And she, fool that she was, had gone out and bought a wedding dress. It was hanging in her closet even now, proof positive that she was a blind, hopeless idiot who refused to see the truth until Oggie laid it out for her in so many words.

Eden clenched her hands at her sides. If she didn't watch herself, she was going to grab the one free bar stool in the place and send it hurtling into the big mirror above the bar. She didn't want to destroy the mirror. She'd paid for it herself, after all. The one before it had been shattered in a brawl.

Oh, yes, Eden most definitely was going to have a word or two with Jared Jones.

Just as she savagely imagined the grim satisfaction she'd feel when she told him exactly what was in her mind, he appeared through the split in the curtain that led to the card room, carrying her service tray stacked high with empties. He saw her at once and froze where he stood.

They confronted each other across the length of the room.

His face was utterly expressionless, his eyes like twin pieces of slate. Yet she knew that *he* knew exactly why she had come.

A hush fell over the crowded room. Every eye in the place looked from Jared to Eden and back again.

Someone muttered, "Woo-ee, this don't look good, boys. She's gonna murder him for sure."

"What's he done?"

"Hell if I know, but you can bet your mama's britches that whatever it was, he's gonna pay in spades."

Eden ignored the whispers. She held her chin high and demanded of the man across the room from her, "When?"

He drug in a breath. "Eden, I—"

"*When* are you leaving? Tell me. Tell me now."

"This isn't the place to talk about this."

"Oh, isn't it?"

"No."

She threw back her head and laughed.

Every man in the room shivered at the sound.

She said, "*You* think it isn't the place. But I can see no reason in the world that *I* should be ruled by what *you* think."

"Eden—"

"*I* think it's time we got everything out in the open. That's what *I* think. *I* think everyone in this bar should know exactly what's been going on between you and me."

"Damn it, Eden..." He dropped the full tray on the nearest table. The bottles and glasses on it rocked and clinked.

"I want them all to know what you are to me, what we are to each other, that we've been—"

He didn't let her finish. She'd never seen even *him* move that fast before. It was spectacular. He literally leapt across the room.

A unified gasp went up.

And then Jared had his hand over her mouth and was dragging her backward out the door, shouting, "Take care of business, will you, Nick?"

"No problem, Mr. Jones."

Eden kicked and struggled. She wiggled and flailed her arms. She even tried to bite the hand that was clamped over her mouth. But it did no good. Jared held her in a grip of steel. He hauled her outside, then dragged her around to the driver's side of her car. He flung open the door and pushed her in ahead of him, not letting up until she scrambled over the console. Then he thrust her down in the passenger seat.

She had made the mistake of leaving the key in the ignition. He held her in the seat with one hand and started the car with the other. She made it as hard for him as she could, squirming and punching him and calling him terrible things.

He pulled away from the curb and swung immediately into a U-turn, which he barely made. He missed a light pole and Sheriff Pangborn's big four-by-four by mere inches. He also left half of the rubber of her tires on the pavement. But somehow, he avoided an actual collision.

He sped off up the street and burned more rubber at the corner, where he turned onto Middle Fork Lane.

By the time he pulled up in front of the cabin, Eden had stopped struggling. She sat there, absolutely rigid, her arms crossed tightly over her breasts, staring straight ahead.

He stopped the engine and then turned to look at her.

She said nothing. She flung open her door, swung her feet to the ground and marched up the steps to the kitchen door. She went in and strode straight to the big living area. She sat on the couch, which faced a stone mantel that served as a mounting place for a large black wood stove.

Jared followed her inside, but stopped in the kitchen to make a phone call. She heard him talking to his brother Patrick, asking Patrick to go over to The Hole in the Wall and give Nick a hand.

"Something's come up," Jared said. "So see that the place gets closed up right tonight, will you?"

Apparently Patrick agreed, because Eden heard Jared say, "Thanks, brother," and that was all.

Soon enough, Jared came and stood in the doorway between the main room where she sat and the kitchen. His eyes found her. They looked at each other.

At last, Eden quietly demanded, "When are you leaving?"

He said nothing.

"*When?*"

He let out a long breath. "As soon as possible. In the morning, I think."

As she heard him say what she already knew in her heart, she realized that the hot wave of her anger had peaked and receded. She felt drained. But at least she could think clearly now.

She wanted some answers. And she intended to have them.

"Why didn't you tell me the truth?"

"It's better this way."

"Is it?" She stared at him. "Then why do I feel like you've cheated me?"

"Someday you'll thank me."

She shook her head. "You have me all figured out, don't you? You have *everything* all figured out. It's all . . . for my own good, right?"

"You can sneer all you want. But yes, that's exactly what it is."

"You're doing me one gigantic favor by forcing me to live without you for the rest of my life."

"Yes, I am."

She stood up. "Well, it doesn't feel like a favor. And I don't want to live without you."

"You'll feel differently. Someday."

"I will not."

"I'm too old for you."

"Only in your own mind."

"I don't even have a damn job."

"Yes, you do. You know you do. Oggie would step aside for you in a minute, and be glad to do it." She walked slowly toward him. "And we could be happy together, our life could be good and full together, if you'd only—"

He put up a hand. She stopped where she was.

"My mind's made up, Eden. I'm leaving. Let it be."

"Just like that?" Eden felt the pressure of tears again, thickening her throat, pushing to get free behind her eyes. Oh, how she wished for the wave of anger to come back. Anger was so much better than this sadness, this soul-deep despair.

"Yes. Just like that," he said flatly.

"Oh, Jared..." She took another step. And another.

His body tightened in defense against her approach. "Don't..." The single word was a plea.

She ignored it. She reached out and wrapped her arms around him and brought her body against him with one long, yearning sigh. She laid her head against his hard chest.

"I love you, Jared," she said against his heart. "Now. Tomorrow. For the rest of my life."

He stood rigid for endless, excruciating seconds. Then he grabbed her against him with a hollow groan. She lifted her face, wet now with unashamed tears, and he took her mouth in a kiss that seared her to the bottom of her soul.

And then he swung her up against his chest. He went on kissing her as he carried her across the space she'd covered to reach him, to the couch. He laid her down and knelt on the floor next to her.

He waited, there on his knees, until she opened her eyes and looked at him. Then he wiped the shining tracks of her tears with a tender thumb and combed his fingers, soothingly, through her hair.

"Make love with me." The whispered words had trouble finding their way through the tightness of her throat. "One more time. And don't leave until I'm asleep. I think it might kill me, if I had to watch you go."

"Eden..."

"Shh. Don't say we shouldn't. It was one of our agreements, remember? That you'd stop saying we shouldn't."

"Eden..."

She touched his lips with a tender hand. "Please."

That did it. His mouth descended. With an eager, grateful sigh, Eden raised her arms and wrapped them around his neck.

He kissed her for a long time. Then he lifted his mouth, swollen from loving hers, and slanted it the other way. Eden idly stroked his shoulders at first, reveling in the bliss he could bring her, accepting the drugging wonder of his kiss.

But then an urgency came on her, to touch him, to feel his body, naked, against hers.

Still kissing him, she sat up and struggled quickly out of her blouse and bra. And then she slid the black vest off his shoulders. She unbuttoned his shirt, pushing it free of his hard chest as she kissed a trail down his throat.

She planted a thousand hungry kisses on his chest and shoulders and she stroked his skin as she kissed him. She wanted to touch him everywhere, with all of herself. She had to memorize him, after all, because tonight was the end of all that they shared.

Her lips moved, soft, tender, insistent like her love for him, down the trail of hair at his belly. She laid her hand on him, through his black jeans. He threw back his head and moaned.

Swiftly she slipped off his belt and parted the placket of his jeans. He sprung free into her hand.

She kissed him then, as he had kissed her that first night, a kiss shattering in its utter intimacy. She took him into her mouth, stroking him, finding the rhythm that his body sought, until he cried out and clutched her bare shoulders.

He tried to hold back, she knew it. But she didn't allow him to hold back. At last, he surrendered. His body tightened in that final ecstatic agony. He found his release.

When it was done, he dropped back, his knees folded beneath him, his head bowed. She lay down once more and languorously reached out to comb his hair with her hand.

For a long time they remained that way, Jared on his folded knees before her, Eden stretched out on the couch.

And then, without a word, he lifted his head and looked at her. His eyes branded her. He stood, not even bothering to button his jeans, and he scooped her up in his strong arms.

He carried her to the bedroom, put her on the bed and quickly got rid of the rest of his clothes. Then he removed what was left of hers as well.

He stood looking down at her. She knew what he was doing, because she did the same. They were memorizing each other. Every line, every curve, every last splendid inch.

She lifted her arms to him. He went down to her. He felt so strong and good, all along the length of her.

The kisses began again.

It all began again.

Eden gave herself up to it utterly. It was their last time.

At three-thirty the next morning, Jared rose from the bed.

Silently he dressed and gathered up his things. When he was ready to go, he couldn't resist one last look at her, dreaming there, in the bed where he'd loved her once, and then again, not wanting to leave her though he knew that he must.

She was so beautiful, her hair tangled and soft all around her sweet face, her skin pale and lustrous.

Oh, how I wish . . . he caught himself thinking.

But then he made himself turn from her. She had a whole life to live. And the best thing he could do for her was what he was doing now.

Jared left the bedroom and went through the quiet house on silent feet. He let himself out into the night and disappeared into the shadowed trees.

Chapter Seventeen

Eden woke at dawn. The blue jays and squirrels were chattering away outside the window, but the thought of pausing to watch their silly escapades held no appeal at all.

She felt infinitely weary, yet she forced herself to rise and strip the sheets from the bed and carry them out to the ancient washing machine in the garage. She washed the sheets and changed the bed. She knew it was the right thing to do, to erase the scent of their lovemaking from the sheets, to help her forget.

Once the bed was made she took a long, hot shower, because her body, too, carried the scent of passion on it. When she was done, she smelled like soap and bath powder and her own perfume.

Next, she went through the cabin, looking for the slightest sign of Jared. She found very little. It saddened her all the more to find how little he had left of himself for her to clear away. There was a disposable razor to toss out, and a nearly empty tube of toothpaste. She took the case of cola she'd bought for him yesterday out to her car. She'd take it to work with her. They always needed cola at the bar.

She remembered the wedding dress, but decided not to deal with it today. Someday soon, on a day off, she'd take it back down to Grass Valley and try to get her money back. That decided, she went out to the garage and put the newly washed sheets into the dryer.

She went in and had her breakfast. Then she called Nick Santino and asked him how he'd managed the night before.

"Patrick Jones came in and helped me. It all went just fine," Nick told her.

"Good. Nick, I know it's asking a lot, since you worked late last night, but do you think you could handle opening up today? The closing shift is always tougher on weekends, so I think I should take that one."

"Er... what about Jared?"

Eden swallowed the knot that had suddenly formed in her throat. "He won't be helping out anymore. He was only... filling in until we could find someone like you, anyway."

"Well, okay. I'd be glad to go in early. I'm happy to get the hours, I've gotta say."

"Great. And next week we can talk about raising your pay. Your training time is over, from the way it looks now."

"Hey. Terrific." Before he hung up, he asked cautiously, "Er, everything all right then, Miss Parker?"

"Everything is just fine," she lied. "And for heaven's sake, call me Eden, okay?"

"Sure. Well, okay then. Eden. I'll see you at—"

"I'll be in by five, just to make sure you're doing all right. And call me if it gets too busy. I'll be right over."

"No problem. See you at five, then."

Eden hung up. And then she realized that she had eight hours ahead of her with nothing to do. It might be better to keep busy.

Maybe she ought to call Nick back and tell him she'd decided to work both shifts, have him come in around seven to help at the busiest time.

But then she reconsidered. Just the thought of getting ready for work right away made her feel totally exhausted. It was strange, really, because Eden usually felt energized at the idea of work.

But not today. Today, she was tired to the bone. She'd go in at five as she'd promised Nick, and that would be good enough.

She called Patrick next and thanked him for helping out the night before. He asked her cautiously about Jared.

She told him the truth. "He's gone."

Patrick was silent for a moment. Then he muttered, "The damn fool. Look, Eden. If there's anything I can do—"

"There's not. But thanks."

After she told Patrick goodbye, she got up with a sigh and wandered back to the bedroom. She lay down on the bed and closed her eyes and took a long nap.

Strangely, when she woke, she didn't feel at all refreshed.

Laurie called about three.

"Hey, pal. It seems we never get together anymore. I was just thinking, maybe I could take a few days off and—"

"Laurie, didn't your new semester just start?"

"Look. I can manage it, don't worry."

It didn't take a genius to figure out what Laurie was up to. Eden cut through the well-meaning subterfuge. "All right. Come clean. Did Patrick call you?"

"No. Honestly, I haven't spoken with him."

"Then who *have* you spoken with?"

"What do you mean?"

"Laurie. Don't lie to me, please."

"Oh, all right. Evidently Patrick called Oggie and Oggie called just about everyone, including Heather. It was Heather who called me."

"And told you what?"

"Oh, Eden..."

"Just say it."

Laurie sighed. "Heather says that Jared has left town again."

"So." Eden dragged in a deep breath. "Everyone in the family knows, right?"

"Well, I guess, more or less."

"It sounds like more, not less, to me."

"Eden, I know you need a friend right now."

"I'm fine. Really. I'll survive. I'm just...a little tired, you know?"

"Oh, Eden. It's bad, isn't it?"

"Please. I will call you. When I'm ready to...have a good cry. Okay?"

"Or if you don't want to be alone. Whatever. I'll come."

"I know you will. And thanks. But listen, I have to go..."

"But, Eden—"

Eden gently hung up the phone.

Oggie called at four.

"I'm gonna find out where that damned idiot went and bust his head in for him."

"Oh, Oggie. Please just let it go."

"Good God, gal. I'm a Jones. I ain't never let nothin' go."

"Oggie, I have to hang up now. I'll call you, I will..."

She could hear him huffing and puffing his outrage into the phone even as she laid it back in its cradle.

It was time to get ready for work. She put on her black slacks and her white shirt and trim little vest and then drove over to The Hole in the Wall.

The sly winks and knowing grins started as soon as she walked in the door. Eden got right to work and tried to ignore the veiled questions concerning herself and Jared and if they'd "worked things out yet."

If she hadn't felt so numb and listless, she would have been pleased at the way Nick reacted to the ribbing she received. He stepped in consistently whenever the teasing comments got too extreme, either redirecting the jibes, or else quietly suggesting that he and Eden had heard about enough.

At six, Patrick came in, and the teasing mysteriously stopped. He sat at the bar the rest of the night, nursing watered-down drinks and giving measuring looks to anyone who spoke to Eden.

It was a good night, in terms of business, but not near as busy as those last hectic Saturday nights of the summer had been. Eden was glad when it was through and she could go home and go to bed at last.

She decided to open the tavern on Sunday, Tuesday and Wednesday, because those nights were generally slower nights and she thought Nick could handle taking the closing shift.

Sunday, when she opened the doors, Delilah's husband, Sam, was waiting there with Rocky to get himself a stool. Sam stayed until Eden left at 11:00 p.m. Not a soul that whole day or evening mentioned the name Jared Jones. By then, Eden had figured out that the Jones men were intent on protecting her from gossip and verbal abuse.

She told Sam it wasn't necessary. "It's not a big deal to me, Sam. I can take it, I really can."

Sam just shrugged. "There's no damn reason why you should have to take it, and that's the plain truth." Sam had beautiful pale blue eyes, infinitely gentle eyes, Eden thought. She could see, looking into those eyes, why Delilah seemed to be such a happy woman.

Eden glanced away from Sam. When she looked at him, she kept thinking about the contentment he and Delilah obviously shared. Some couples had all the luck. They found each other, and they both accepted that what was between them was meant to be. Everyone in town said that

Sam and Delilah had once been archenemies. Eden just knew that had to be pure bunk.

"Let us stand by you, Eden." Sam went on. "If not for your sake, then for ours. It'll make us feel better to know you're not getting a rough time from any of the hooligans around here."

"But—"

"Please?"

How could she resist the appeal in those kind eyes? She agreed that they could all waste their time if they wanted to.

Monday, she didn't have to work. The first thing she thought of in the morning was that she and Jared were supposed to have gone to Heather's for dinner that night. But now that wasn't going to happen. She thought, to be polite, that maybe she should call Heather and formally express her regrets. But somehow, she just couldn't go through with it. And Heather knew what was going on anyway.

Eden wandered out to the kitchen, considered making coffee, and then returned to bed instead. She slept most of the day. Laurie called, waking her, about two in the afternoon. Eden's friend suggested that they meet in Grass Valley for a girls' night out. Eden said that she was very tired, some other time maybe. Laurie asked if Eden was sick.

"No, really. I'm fine. Listen, I have to go now."

She hung up and went back to sleep. She was sleeping a lot; she knew it. But somehow, her tiredness just wouldn't go away.

Tuesday, Brendan sat at the bar through Eden's whole shift. And Wednesday, it was Patrick once again.

Thursday morning, Eden had to drag herself out of bed. She really was just terribly tired.

Everything seemed so very...dull lately. As if there were a dirty window between herself and the rest of the world. Her wonderful life in North Magdalene seemed to have lost all of its luster. Somehow, with Jared's leaving, her whole existence had become tedious and drab.

Far back in her mind somewhere, she felt that her real, vital self was an unwilling captive to this deadness, this numbness that had completely claimed her life. She could almost hear a faint voice inside her soul calling her, chiding her to put away her sorrow and get on with living once again.

She understood that she'd have to pull herself together sooner or later. She'd have to spend more time at work. Also, she really should clean up the cabin, which had somehow become a real mess. Her dirty clothes seemed to be everywhere, and the kitchen was a disaster area.

But just thinking about tackling the dishes that seemed to have piled up so high in the sink made her so tired she could hardly stand up. If she couldn't even face the dishes, how was she going to face getting on with her life?

Really, all she wanted was to be allowed to climb back into bed. Come to think of it, she was too tired to work today at all.

She thought of Patrick. Maybe he'd be willing to help out if she called him.

She did call him. When she asked if he'd cover for her, he acted surprised and apprehensive.

"Eden, are you sick or something?"

"No, no. I'm fine. I just . . . I need a little rest, that's all. And since Nick will be taking the opening shift, if you would just help me out by closing up tonight, well, I'd really appreciate it. I just don't feel like working today."

Patrick didn't answer for a moment. Then he said, "Eden, I'd be glad to close up for you."

"Great. Thanks."

"But maybe you ought to—"

"Look, Patrick. I have to go now."

"Eden, I—"

"Thanks again. I mean it."

Eden hung up and dragged herself back to bed. She lay down and pulled the sheet over herself and closed her eyes.

The phone rang. She ignored it. She just wanted to be left alone to sleep. At last, the ringing stopped. Eden let out a long breath of relief and settled deeper into her bed.

She wasn't sure how much later the pounding started. She groaned a little in her sleep and wrapped her pillow around her head.

"Eden! Eden, gal, you answer this damn door!"

Eden gritted her teeth and tuned out the shouting. If she refused to get up and answer the door, the racket would stop eventually, she was sure.

She sighed in relief and relaxed a little when the pounding and shouting finally did stop. She even put her pillow back *under* her head where it belonged.

And then she heard the kitchen door slam. And someone stumping—there was no other word for it—through the kitchen.

She felt no fear. She knew who it was by the way he was moving, and the shouting voice had been quite familiar. All she wished was that she'd had sense enough to lock the door before going back to bed.

But it was too late now. Oggie was in her house, and he was going to find her.

"Eden! Where the hell are you, gal?"

Eden moaned and pulled the blankets over her head.

"Eden? I ain't foolin' around here. If you ain't decent, you better make it known now, 'cause I ain't leavin' until we've had us a talk." Oggie paused, listening, no doubt, for her response. When he got none, he announced, "All right, then. Have it your way. I'm comin' in."

The stumping started again, slow, loud and determined. She heard every last thump of his laborious approach. Finally he halted with a hard thud of his crutches in the open

doorway to her room. She could hear him panting from his
exertion and settling himself a little against the door frame.

She stayed burrowed under the covers. Though she knew
her behavior was thoroughly childish, she still hoped that
if she refused to even push the blanket off her head and
look at him, he might just go away.

No such luck. He had caught his breath and he was ready
to tell her exactly what was on his mind.

"Pitiful," he said with utter disgust. "Purely pathetic,
that's what you are."

She resolutely did not respond.

"This place looks like *my* place, for godsakes, gal. It's a
disgraceful mess. And look at you, hidin' like some silly,
wimpy little twit under them covers. What the hell's wrong
with you?"

Through her numb exhaustion, she felt a twinge of irritation at him. He'd always been a pushy old goat. Who did
he think he was to come bursting into her house like this?
Hadn't she made it perfectly clear to him—and to everyone—that all she wanted was to be left alone?

"You answer me, gal!"

Oh, why wouldn't he just leave?

"I mean it. Answer, or by God, I'll—"

She didn't want to hear what. "Go away," she whined,
though she had told herself she wasn't going to say a single
word.

"Not on your life," Oggie intoned. "Now, get out from
under those covers, and face me like the real, strong, gutsy
woman you used to be!" He struck the wall with something, probably a crutch.

"Leave me alone." Eden pulled the blanket tighter over
her head.

Oggie grunted and mumbled. Then she heard the thud of
his crutches as he started walking again.

She heard him approach the bed and then stop right beside her head. There was a nerve-racking silence and then

a bunch of clattering, then silence again. Eden, still cowering beneath the blanket, surmised that Oggie had just thrown his crutches to the floor.

Eden clutched the covers tighter and gritted her teeth and refused to peek out and make sure that the old fool was okay. He could just pick up those crutches himself and toddle on out of here, whenever he got tired of standing there staring at the lump her body made under the covers. She was not going to talk to him. She was not going to talk to anyone, and that was that.

But then, out of nowhere, she felt the blanket yanked away, ripped free of her hands.

Eden let out a yelp of pure outrage, closed her eyes and turned away. "Go away, Oggie. I mean it. I don't want to talk to you."

He grabbed her shoulder and forced her to turn back to him. "Look at me, Eden Parker. Look at me now."

His voice was so compelling that her eyes popped open. "What?"

"Hear what I have to say."

"I don't feel like it."

"Do you think I give a damn whether you feel like it or not? I ain't leavin' till you've heard me out."

Eden groaned. There was just no escaping Oggie Jones once he had his mind made up about something.

"You listenin'?"

"Oggie, you've got no right..."

"Just answer. Are you listenin'?"

"This is not fair."

"What part of *'Are you listenin'?'* didn't you understand?"

She glared at him. "Oh, all right."

"All right, what?"

"All right, I'm listening."

"Good."

Grumbling to herself, Eden sat up and pushed her tangled hair out of her eyes. "Okay. Get it over with. Say what you came to say."

"I will." He was holding on to her night table, trying to brace himself there while he hopped a little to keep his balance on his good foot.

Eden found it hard to watch his struggle to stay upright. It had to be painful. As exasperated as she was with Oggie right that moment, there was no denying the facts: the man was seventy-five years old, and still barely able to get around without a wheelchair. It would be cruel to make him totter there in front of her much longer.

"Oh, wait a minute," she said sourly. She reached for her robe that was thrown across the foot of the bed, pulled it over her sleep shirt and then slid off the bed on the other side.

Then she went to him, picked up his fallen crutches and took him out to the big main room. She led him to the most comfortable chair and helped him get seated, propping up his bad foot on a hassock.

"That's better," he said when he was settled back. "Now. You got coffee?"

She put her hands on her hips and cast her gaze toward the beamed ceiling. "Honestly, Oggie."

"Well, I ain't had but one cup this morning," he said with a mildly affronted snort. "I got up a little late, and got me one cup, and then Patrick calls and tells me you don't *feel* like working today. I mean, what the hell's the world coming to when Eden Parker don't *feel* like goin' to work?"

"I've been . . . very tired."

"Tired, my rosy-red behind," Oggie muttered. "Anyway, I started callin' and you wouldn't answer, so I got Sam to drop me off on his way over to the store. I towed these old bones all the way up those damn stone steps out there. I deserve a second cup of coffee if any man ever did. I'll say what I came here to say only after I have been sufficiently fortified with caffeine." He pulled a cigar from his pocket. "Mind if I smoke?"

"Would it make any difference if I did?"

His beady eyes gleamed. "Hell, no." He struck a match.

She grabbed an ashtray from the mantel and put it at his elbow. "All right. I'll make the coffee," she grudgingly agreed.

"Three sugars," he instructed, as she went through the door to the kitchen.

Fifteen minutes later, Eden returned carrying a tray with the coffee and sugar, spoons and cups on it. She'd had to wash the cups and spoons, since almost every eating utensil she owned was dirty. She set down the tray on the coffee table and served Oggie his coffee while he sat there, thoroughly pleased with himself, puffing on his smelly cigar.

At last, having served herself, too, she took the seat across from him. "Okay, Oggie. What do you want to say?" She realized with some surprise that she actually wanted to know.

It also occurred to her that bickering with her partner had done her a world of good. She felt more lively than she had since the morning she woke to find Jared gone.

Oggie said, "You are actin' like a quitter, Eden Parker. And that has got to stop."

Eden looked down at her coffee cup. "I know," she said softly, and realized that the dirty window between herself and the world seemed to have been wiped clean. She felt sad, still, it was true. And just the thought of Jared's name caused an aching in her heart. But the numbness was fading.

Her partner was right. She *was* acting like a quitter, and she did have to stop.

Oggie hadn't finished yet. "I didn't partner up with no quitter."

"I know."

"And I'm sorry that my fool son left you. When I find him, I'll break his face. But even if it really was over between the two of you—"

"It *is* over, Oggie."

"We'll get to that." Oggie shifted his cigar to the other side of his mouth. "Where was I? Oh, yeah. Even if the two of you never work things out, you got to pick yourself up and go on."

"I know, I—"

Oggie's eyes grew moist. "Believe me, I know what it is. That dead-numb feelin' when your love is gone. When my beautiful Bathsheba passed on, I thought more than once about takin' the shortcut to her side. But I held on. And I learned to live again, though a part of me will grieve for her for all my born days." A single tear trickled down Oggie's wrinkled cheek.

Eden, feeling as if she intruded on something very private, looked away. And then she heard Oggie's quick sniff and saw in her peripheral vision that he wiped the tear away.

"Well, I do digress," he said, and puffed some more on his cigar. "The point is, you got to get on with your life. You of all people oughtta know that, 'cause like I said before, you are not a quitter. That's why I picked you out for my Jared in the first place. 'Cause you got real stamina, gal. Not to mention one great pair of legs."

Eden gaped at him. "Excuse me?"

Oggie actually blushed. "Well, now, gal. It ain't no secret about them legs of yours."

Eden wasn't asking about her legs. "No. I mean what you said about *choosing* me. For Jared."

"What about it?"

"I could have sworn you said that you *picked me out* for Jared."

"You got it."

"You mean ... when I first came to town with Laurie, when Jared was nowhere around, when I didn't even *know* him? You're saying you *selected* me for him *then*?"

"You're damn straight I did. You think I would have given away half my boy's inheritance to anyone but the woman destined by fate to become his wife?"

In spite of her shock at what Oggie seemed to be saying, Eden felt it only fair to point out, "You hardly *gave* it away to me, Oggie."

"Hell. You know what I mean. And you *are* just right for my Jared. You got the patience and the good sense and, until lately, you never took things too serious. Besides that, you're nice to look at. My boys all deserve pretty women, 'cause my boys stay true until death. A true man deserves someone nice to look at for the rest of his life, don't you think?"

"Well, I—"

"Yessiree, I knew you was the one for Jared the first night Laurie brought you into The Hole in the Wall."

"Oggie, you can't really be serious."

"Oh, but I am. Just look at me, gal. Look at me good. I'm an old man. And an old man *knows* things. Otherwise, what's the point of gettin' slow and stooped and all wrinkled up?"

"But, Oggie, I—"

"You purely talk too much, gal. Anybody ever tell you that?"

"Well, I—"

"But that ain't the end of the world. My beautiful Bathsheba, she never could shut her yap, either."

"She couldn't?"

"Hell, no. And still, she was and always will be the empress of my heart."

"Yes, I think you've mentioned that before." Actually, Oggie had rhapsodized about his dead wife more than once since Eden had met him. And he never failed to refer to the woman at least once each time as *the empress of his heart.*

"But enough about an old man's memories," Oggie decided. "We've got some serious plannin' to do. If you're through hidin' in your bedroom, that is."

"What do you mean, planning?"

"Are you through bein' *tired?*"

"Well, yes, I—"

"Listen. You put some clothes on and drive me back to Delilah's now. And then you clean up this place. And then, when you're sure you don't want to crawl back in bed and hide some more, you and me will have a talk."

"But, Oggie—"

"Nope. I am firm. You gotta be strong in your heart to do what I'm thinkin' of. I gotta be sure you're ready to face the world alone again, before we even *consider* how we're gonna get that troublesome man of yours back home where he belongs."

"Oggie—"

"Go. Get some clothes on."

Though she coaxed him for several minutes more, the old man would not tell her what he was thinking of.

At last, Eden got dressed and drove him to Delilah's.

"You call Patrick and tell him you'll be goin' in tonight after all," Oggie said, when she helped him out of the car and got him propped up on his crutches.

"Oggie, you are pushing it," Eden told him tartly.

He cackled. "That's what I like to see. A little fire and indignation. What good is any woman without fire and indignation? Anyway, you work your shift tonight, and you and me will talk after you close up."

"You want me to visit you here at Delilah's?"

"Hell, no. I told you I can't smoke in her house. And I got a feelin' I'm gonna need a good cigar between my teeth in order to explain this to you right."

"Is it bad, is that it?"

He only winked at her. "I'll be waitin' at your place when you come home tonight. Someone will drive me."

"But—"

"Just leave the door unlocked."

Chapter Eighteen

Oggie took his cigar from his mouth, looked at it and stuck it back in. "So whaddaya say? You think you're up for it?"

Eden rose from her chair and went to the big window that looked out on the deck. It was a little after three in the morning, so she saw nothing in the glass but a shadowed reflection of herself and the main room of the cabin behind her. Outside, it was pitch-black.

"Well?" Oggie prompted.

Eden was thinking. His plan was a crazy one. She doubted it would work. But even though she realized now that she *could* go on without Jared, she didn't want to live her life without him if there was any possible way she could draw him to her side.

And even if Oggie's plan was crazy, what else was there? Nothing that she could think of. While Jared was with her, she'd tried everything she could imagine to get him to give their love a chance. She'd slowly coaxed him into telling her about himself. After they'd become lovers, she'd shown him what they might share. At the end, she'd pleaded and even fought with him outright to try to get him to see the light. None of it had worked. She was fresh out of ways to convince Jared to return to her.

Oggie's plan, on the other hand, was a totally different approach than any of the ones Eden had used. It was clever and outrageous—not to mention devious and manipulative.

As a general rule, Eden despised deviousness and manipulation. But Oggie seemed so certain that what he had in mind would work. His confidence, as always, was contagious.

And besides, at the very least, the plan might draw Jared out, bring him to her. Then she'd have a chance to try once more to make him see that she wanted nothing so much as to spend her life at his side.

"But how will he find out what we're doing?" She turned from the window to face the old man. "We don't even know where he is."

Oggie was ready for that. "The other boys'll find him. You wait and see. If you got the style to pull this off so it looks real, they're all gonna be purely outraged. Every one of them believes you and Jared are a match made in God's heaven. They're practically as brokenhearted as you are at the problems you're havin'. But they're not beatin' the bushes for Jared, because they think there's no big rush for him to get back here. All we're gonna do is provide that big rush." Oggie puffed on his cigar and then sighed in contentment. He went on. "They'll all be howlin' mad when they get an earful of what you and me are gonna do. They'll be sure I took advantage of you on the rebound. Hell, when my girl Delilah hears what we're plannin', she'll be breathin' fire. After she tells the two of us off good and proper, she'll go lookin' for Jared, too. And nobody hides from Delilah when she's riled."

"You think she'll be able to find him?"

"I ain't got a doubt in my mind about it."

"Well, if you're sure..."

Oggie chortled. "Trust me, gal. I know what I'm doin'." He granted himself a generous sip of the whiskey Eden had poured for him. Then he cautioned, "We have to make it look real, though. First, we get a license, and then I'll have me a little talk with Reverend Johnson...."

Oggie's black-haired daughter knocked on Eden's door at eight Saturday morning.

Eden, still in her robe, had just finished making coffee.

"Um, good morning Delilah. Won't you...come in?" Eden held open the door and Delilah stepped in inside. "Would you like some coffee?"

"No, thank you." Delilah folded her slim arms over her rather magnificent breasts. "Eden, last night I spoke with my friend Nellie Anderson. Nellie works as a volunteer secretary over at the Community Church."

"I see," Eden replied. She didn't really know what else to say. She had a pretty good idea where this was leading, but there wasn't much to do but let it play itself out. Delilah continued with some delicacy, "Nellie had some interesting news for me concerning a *wedding*."

Eden swallowed. "Oh," she heard herself say.

"After hearing this news, I said several very rude things to my father. And then I decided that it was time you and I had a talk."

"Yes. All right." Eden gestured toward the living room. "Why don't we sit in there?"

In the living room, Delilah sat on one end of the couch. She wasted no time getting to the point. "All of us in the family are certain that you're in love with Jared. Is that true?"

Eden, who felt unable right then to sit down, responded with an evasion. "Why do you want to know?"

Delilah's black eyes bored through her. "That's an absurd question if I ever heard one. But, for the sake of form, I'll answer it. I want to know if you love my brother, because if you *do* love him, then you really should *not* be marrying my father in a week."

I'm not marrying your father, Eden thought. *It's only a trick, to get Jared to come back to me.*

But she couldn't say that, of course. Part of the plan was that the rest of the family must believe she really intended to marry Oggie.

What could she say? She bravely threw herself into the deception. "Oggie and I get along well. We're quite fond of each other. And I believe we'll have a good marriage."

When Eden finished speaking Delilah gaped at her for a moment. And then Oggie's daughter tossed back her head and laughed, a wild laugh that made Eden think of what a strange woman Delilah was, a prim schoolteacher one moment, a wild gypsy creature the next.

"What is so funny?" Eden asked tightly, when Delilah was through laughing.

"Nothing." Delilah wiped away a few mirthful tears. "I just figured this out, that's all."

"What do you mean?"

"This is one of my father's brilliant schemes, right?"

"I don't know what you're talking about."

"You are an appallingly bad liar."

"Honestly, I—"

Delilah waved away Eden's protests. "Are you sure you know what you're doing?"

Eden felt lost. "About what?"

"Listen, all I'm saying is that my father's schemes can be dangerous. And more often than not, he has some hidden agenda. As his partner, you ought to have learned by now that you've got to watch all the angles when Oggie Jones is around. Because you can be sure *he'll* be watching them. You must be very careful, or you could end up doing what *he* wants, rather than what you thought he'd agreed you *both* wanted.''

"What are you saying?"

"My father has a crush on you, did you know that?"

Eden frowned. "He does?"

"Yes, I'm sure of it. But he's also downright fanatic about seeing all his children married and settled down. So, in addition to having a crush on you, I believe he really does want to see you and Jared work things out. The question is, what is my father's underlying objective here? Luring Jared back into town? Or is it actually that my father wants to marry you himself, and he thinks he can trick you into it by arranging this wedding and convincing you it isn't really going to happen?"

Eden could hardly believe what she was hearing. "Oggie wouldn't—"

"You'd be surprised what my father would do. But tell me. What will *you* do, if Jared still refuses to come back, even after he learns that you plan to marry his father?"

"Well, I—"

"Never mind. Don't tell me. It doesn't matter if I know, so long as *you* know what you'll do." Delilah's smooth brow furrowed. "You do know what you'll do, don't you?"

Eden's head was spinning. "Truly, Delilah, right this minute, I haven't the faintest idea."

"Then think about it."

"Yes. I certainly will."

"And I suppose you should go and talk to Jared. It's going to be pretty hard for him to stop you from marrying my father if he doesn't even know you're doing it."

"Well yes, exactly. And I'd love to go talk with him. If I only knew where he went. As a matter of fact, Oggie said he thought that *you* might be able to find him."

Delilah let out an exasperated groan. "I *do* have a life, you know? And I probably shouldn't even have come to talk to you about this. I always end up in trouble myself whenever I get involved in my brothers' problems. I could tell you stories...." She sighed. "But never mind. Yes, I do have an idea where he is."

"You do?" Eden's heart picked up a faster rhythm. "Where?"

"Look. This is just a hunch. I'm not guaranteeing he'll be there. And I'm only going to show you the way. You can go after him yourself. After all, he's your man, not mine."

Chapter Nineteen

Though anticipation kept her nerves on a razor's edge,
Eden waited until Monday to use the map Delilah had
drawn for her. She worked both Saturday night and the
early shift Sunday. She wanted an entire free day in which
to seek Jared out. And she didn't want to ask anyone to
cover for her at work. For one thing, she didn't want to explain where she was going. Also, she'd slighted her business enough during those grim days right after Jared left
her. Whenever possible, she wasn't going to do that anymore.

Thus, on Monday morning, she got in the Bronco four-
by-four that Delilah had told her she might borrow, and
headed out of town. She turned off the highway at the place
Delilah had described to her.

She drove what seemed to her like forever. Most of the
ride was through shady forest of oak and evergreen. The
road clung to the side of the mountain, winding upward.

At last, soon after the road grew rutted, and she was forced to switch over to four-wheel-drive, she came out onto an open place of manzanita and close-growing buckbrush. There the sky was a splendid expanse of blue and the sun beat down, friendly and warm with just a hint of autumn's chilly bite in it.

A mile or two later, she came to the turnoff and the crude gate Delilah had described to her: a thick cablelike wire strung between two pine trees and secured with a heavy padlock. She got out of the Bronco and used the key Delilah had lent her.

She crested the mountain soon after that and began driving down into a small valley. The hillsides of manzanita and brush were left behind and she was back among the trees again. Sunlight came down through the branches in ribbons and shafts, creating natural spotlights that pointed out the iridescent green of a mossy rock, or the sparkle of natural crystal within a quartz boulder.

Eden took in the wild beauty around her. Concentrating on the scenery helped her to ignore the tension that kept coiling tighter in her stomach. Very soon, she might be coming face-to-face once again with the man she loved.

She reached the valley floor, crossed a pair of narrow streams and found herself on a plain of baked-dry red dirt, within a sea of willow bushes on which clung leaves that had already turned gold. To her left, red dirt hills rose, steep and absolutely naked of all greenery until the very top, where the forest started again, ragged at the edges like a torn carpet. Eden knew what the blasted hills signified. Once, hydraulic mining had been done here.

Eden stared at the stripped hills and marveled at what she saw. She'd heard that they called the huge hoses that had done this thing "water cannons." Now she understood why. For almost a century, mining for gold by ripping through to ancient riverbeds with powerful jets of water had been illegal. And yet still the blasted hills remained flayed bare, even after decade upon decade had come and gone. The damage was long-lasting. And spectacular to see.

Eden turned her gaze ahead once more and saw the cabin.

As Delilah had warned her, the place was very crude, a tar-paper shack where Jared's Uncle Cleve and his partners used to stay while they worked the hard-rock mine across the ravine for gold. The shack sat on the edge of the valley of willows, with the ravine at its back. The red hills loomed over all. Opposite the hills, the faraway mountains seemed to go on forever beneath their verdant blanket of evergreen.

The shack had a door with two wooden steps leading up to it and what looked like a deck on one side. The deck had long ago collapsed and was slowly in the process of tumbling piecemeal down the ravine.

A tin chimney stuck out of the cabin's roof. From it, smoke drifted lazily toward the pristine sky. In front of the cabin there was a small ring of stones with a rusted grate over it: a barbecue pit. Jared's truck was parked on the far side of the barbecue pit, right below the rise that led up to the outhouse.

Eden stopped the engine. She got out of the Bronco. She shut the door firmly. The sound was like the crack of a rifle in the stillness. Ordering her suddenly racing heart to slow down, she marched up to the shack and pounded on the door.

Nothing happened.

So she took the cracked porcelain knob in her trembling hand and turned it. The door opened toward her with a long slow groan. She peered beyond the threshold into a rough room with one small window, plank shelves lining the walls, an ancient wood stove and a sink with a pump faucet. There was a rickety table and two chairs. And an old brass bed against one wall.

Jared was sitting on the bed, his feet stretched out in front of him, using the wall for a backrest. He was fully dressed. In fact, it looked as if he might have stayed fully dressed in the same clothes for the past couple of days at least. He hadn't bothered to shave for a while either, and his dark beard was rough and random on his scowling face.

He held a half-empty bottle of whiskey in one hand.

For a moment, he blinked and stared at Eden. She knew he was wondering if what he saw was real.

And then he must have decided he wasn't quite drunk enough to be seeing things.

"Get the hell out," he said.

Eden didn't move. She wanted to cry. She wanted to rant and rail at him. But most of all, she ached for him.

The sink was full of dishes, the table displayed the remains of a number of meals. There were clothes strewn on the chairs and thrown across the foot of the bed. The place was a mess. He was going through exactly what she'd gone through in trying to forget what they'd shared. But it was worse for him, because he'd hidden himself away where it took a four-by-four to get to him. And because he'd embraced his old demon, alcohol, to try to drive her from his heart.

"Oh, Jared . . ."

"Get out."

"Jared, I—"

He turned his head toward the wall.

"Please come back to me," she pleaded softly. "I miss you so."

He said nothing.

"Jared—"

"You heard me. I said get out."

"Once you told me that you always tried to do the right thing, remember?"

"I said—"

"But the right thing always backfired."

"—Get out."

"Well, look at you now, Jared. Is sitting here drunk in this filthy shack the answer to anything? Why can't you believe I know my own mind, Jared? Why can't you believe that when I say you're the man for me, I mean what I'm saying? Why can't you trust just one more time, Jared? Reach out your hand to love just one more time?"

He raised the bottle of whiskey, put it to his mouth and swallowed deeply. Then he grimaced as it burned its way down his throat. "Give it up, Eden," he said. "Give it up and go."

She stepped beyond the threshold and pulled the door closed behind her.

He turned away again, muttering under his breath.

She could think of nothing more to say to him, no new way to tell him of her love. She had hoped, yearned really, for a tender reunion. But she'd known Jared's stubbornness well enough that she hadn't actually expected one.

And he'd armed himself doubly against her with alcohol, she knew. She'd worked in bars long enough to have learned that it never did a bit of good to reason with a drunk. It was pointless to try to get through to him now.

Eden realized there was nothing left to do but hit him with the news of what she and Oggie planned and then go. Either he'd take it from there, or he wouldn't.

She went and stood beside him, though he resolutely refused to look at her again. "All right. I'll go. But I wanted you to know that your father's made me an offer. And I've accepted. I came here hoping that you'd ask me to change my mind, but it appears I was living in a fool's dream on that score."

She had his attention now. He rolled his head and pinned her to the spot with his bloodshot gaze. "What offer?"

She didn't waver. "He's asked me to marry him. I said yes. We'll be married in the North Magdalene Community

Church in five days' time, this coming Saturday at 2:00 p.m."

Jared went on glaring at her. Then he muttered an obscenity and turned away again. "I don't believe you."

"Fine. That's up to you." She started to turn away.

He demanded, "Why the hell would you want to wreck your life? What for?"

Eden felt a tiny surge of hope. Maybe they were getting somewhere after all.

But before she could answer, he waved his own outburst away. "Forget it. Never mind. What you do with your life is your own damned business. If you want to ruin it to get even with me, you can go ahead and be a fool. I'm not involved. Now go away."

Eden, wounded to the core and also truly disgusted with him, felt tears of total frustration rising to her eyes. She looked away from him. She didn't want to give him the satisfaction of seeing her cry. That was when she noticed the rifle, on a wall rack by the door.

It took her five giant steps to get to it. She reached up and ripped it from the wall. Then she checked to see if it was loaded; it was.

Jared commanded, "Put that damn thing back where it belongs."

Eden looked at him. She was not crying now. She marched back to his side and held the gun out to him. "Here. It's loaded. Why don't you go ahead and shoot yourself, Jared Jones, instead of killing yourself slowly with whiskey this way? Because I know and you know that you love me. As long as you're breathing, you'll love me. And if you don't reach out and take me, you'll have to stay drunk the rest of your life to stand the pain of what you threw away yourself. That's how the men in your family are when they find the right woman for them. And if that's not *involved*, I don't know what is!"

Jared, whose mouth was hanging open, carefully accepted the rifle from her hands and set it on his other side, where she would be unlikely to be able to reach it again.

Eden wasn't finished. "You think about it, Jared. You consider carefully if you can afford to just sit out here in the woods with a whiskey bottle for company and let everything you ever wanted slip right out of your hands. Because I'm not in love with your father, but I do care for him. And I believe he and I could have a good life together. I truly do. You see, I'm not obsessed with how old a man is the way you are, Jared. It's the heart and the mind that matter. And as long as two people are both adults, how may years lie between them doesn't make too much difference to me." She bent down to him and put her face right up to his. "On the day you left me, I took the money you gave me and I bought a wedding dress. I dreamed then that I would wear it when I became your wife. But whether you're there or not, Jared, I'll be wearing it next Saturday. Do you hear me in there? Have I made myself clear?"

Slowly Jared nodded.

Eden drew herself up. "Good."

Without another word, she strode to the door, flung it open and walked out into the fall sunshine. She never looked back.

Jared stared at the door for a long time after Eden went through it. Then he blinked and lifted the bottle of whiskey slowly to his thirsty lips.

But, as luck would have it, just before he tipped back his head and drank, he had a vision.

He saw Eden in a wedding dress. And he saw his father slipping a ring onto her slender hand and then gathering her into his gnarled old arms and pulling her close for a vow-sealing kiss.

With a curse so foul it was a good thing no one else heard it, Jared threw the bottle across the room. It shattered, splattering whiskey all over the wall.

Chapter Twenty

"It's certainly a beautiful day for a wedding, Edie."
Eden's mother, Julia, lowered the bridal veil over Eden's
face and smoothed it on her shoulders so that it didn't
bunch or gather.

Eden smiled through the veil. Julia and Eden's stepfa-
ther had come from Bakersfield for the ceremony. And
Eden's father and stepmother were here from Fresno. Also,
two of her half brothers and three half sisters, one stepsis-
ter and two stepbrothers, plus a number of spouses and
children had all seen fit to drive to Eden's new home on
very short notice to watch her walk down the aisle.

There was one motel in North Magdalene. It was full to
capacity with the members of Eden's family. Some of them
were also staying at the cabin and some with Laurie's parents. It did Eden's heart good to see them all. She had cried
happy tears when so many of them called and said they
wouldn't miss her wedding for the world. All her life, she
had felt a little like an outsider in her own family. But now,

on her wedding day, she knew she was loved and included by them all.

"Yes, it is a good day for a wedding, Mom," Eden said. "And I'm glad you all came."

They stood in a small room right off the narthex of the North Magdalene Community Church. Through the tall, double-hung window, the sky was clear blue. The flame-leaf maple right beyond the glass displayed the brilliant red fall leaves for which it was named.

From the chapel, Eden could hear piano music. The sound was lovely, lyrical and tender, though Eden didn't know the name of the song. She'd spoken only briefly with Regina Black, who was the church's volunteer pianist. Eden had asked Regina to use her own judgment about the music, and she was glad she had.

Julia went on, "And this is a charming little town. I can see why you'd want to make your life here."

"Yes, I do love it."

"And your fiancé is... quite a character."

The catch in her mother's voice was not lost on Eden. "Yes. There's no one quite like him. Everyone in town says so."

"Are you sure—" Julia coughed delicately into her hand "—that this is what you want, Edie?"

Eden kept her smile. "Yes, Mom. I'm sure."

"Because, you know, it isn't too late to—"

"Mom. I know what I'm doing. I'm going to marry the man I love. Be happy for me, please?"

"I will." Her mother smoothed the lace of Eden's sleeve. "But there hasn't been much time for us to talk. And I would never forgive myself if I didn't tell you what's in my heart."

"Oh, Mom." Eden took Julia's hands. "I know. You think he's not right for me."

Julia nodded. Eden saw there were tears in her eyes. "Yes. That's what I think."

"Just trust me, Mom." Eden gave the hands she held a squeeze. "Everything will work out all right." Someone had thoughtfully set a box of tissues on a small credenza beneath the window. Eden took one and gave it to her mother.

Julia delicately dabbed at her eyes. "Well. It's your life, of course."

"Yes, Mom. It is."

"And at least I've told you about my doubts."

"Yes. And thank you. For being honest."

"I just wish—"

Eden raised a hand. "Please. No more."

"Yes, of course. I understand."

The door opened and Laurie, the maid of honor, came in. She wore the tea-length autumn-gold dress she and Eden had chosen together at the bridal shop in Grass Valley only a few days before. Her honey-brown hair had been swept up into a smooth French twist. Laurie's smile was determinedly bright. "All ready?"

Eden nodded. "How long until we start?"

"Soon."

The door opened once more and Nellie Anderson, Delilah's friend and the church secretary, appeared. Nellie had a rather pinched face, but she was doing her best, like everyone else, to keep a smile on it.

"The pastor has asked me to find out when you'd like to sign the license," Nellie said.

"Would after the ceremony be all right?"

"It's your wedding," Nellie said, in much the tone one might say, *It's your funeral*. And then she seemed to realize that her attitude was slipping. She hastened to add in a too-solicitous voice, "And I believe that signing the papers after the ceremony is traditional, now I think of it. A wise decision."

"Great, then, we'll sign them after," Eden said.

"Fine." Nellie resolutely kept smiling. "I'll be back in a few moments to give you the signal to start."

"Thank you," Eden said.

And then Nellie was gone.

Laurie came close. "Oh, Eden. Are you sure that you—"

Eden didn't let her finish. "Shh. Not a word. This is exactly what I want." She lifted her veil and gave her friend a reassuring peck on the cheek.

Laurie looked as if she might burst into tears any moment.

To distract her friend, Eden asked brightly, "How many people came?"

"The church is packed," Laurie answered. "There are as many folks out there as when Sam and Delilah got married."

Eden was surprised. Since the word had gotten out about the wedding, she'd had nothing but dire warnings. Everyone she talked to begged her to change her mind. She'd felt sure the people in town would demonstrate their concern by failing to attend.

"I wonder why the crowd," she mused.

Laurie had found the box of tissues and was making use of it. She blew her nose. "Nobody's happy about this, Eden. But no one would miss it for the world, either. You haven't lived here long enough to understand that yet, but someday you will."

Eden just shook her head.

Julia handed Eden her bouquet. Then for a few moments, the three women stood silently, sharing an occasional reassuring smile or a quick squeeze of a hand.

And then Nellie stuck her head into the room. "All right. Mrs. Lumley," she said to Julia, "it's time for Brendan to escort you to your seat. And Laurie, you'll follow on Sam's arm shortly after. The bride—" Nellie nodded at Eden "—will wait here until her father comes for her."

Within seconds, Eden found herself alone in the room. The lovely, unknown music ended. The wedding march began.

Eden clutched her bouquet and stared out at the burning brilliance of the flame-leaf maple. As she stared, her lips moved in a litany, a chant so softly spoken, that she couldn't even hear the words herself. "It will be all right. It will be fine. I'm doing the right thing. It's not too late. He could still come. He *will* come. I know it. I believe it. He will . . ."

"Eden?"

Eden turned and forced a wide smile for her father.

"You look beautiful, Edie."

"Oh, Dad. Thanks."

"It's time. Are you ready?"

Eden nodded. He backed out of the doorway and she walked toward him, into the narthex. The wedding march seemed to swell in her ears as she moved closer to the sound. Her father held out his arm. Eden took it. They stood in the inner door to the chapel. Eden saw how full the small church was. There was not a single empty space in any of the pews. People sat in folding chairs along the sides and at the front. They stood by the windows, too.

Regina Black caught sight of the bride. She played even louder. Heads turned and everyone gaped. No one liked it, but no one wanted to miss it, either. It was a moment that would be whispered about in the lore of North Magdalene for years and years to come, the moment Eden Parker walked down the aisle to marry the father of the man she loved.

Reverend Johnson was at the altar. The maid of honor and the best man stood to the side. The groom, propped up on his crutches and dressed in an ill-fitting outdated suit, waited, grinning slyly, for his young bride.

Eden and her father began the long walk up the aisle. With every step, Eden felt her heart breaking, shattering like her hope.

But she didn't falter. She maintained her smile. And in her mind, she didn't give up. She kept up the chant.

He will come. He does love me. This will work out. It will....

Eden reached Oggie's side. Her father stepped away.

Pastor Johnson intoned, "If the bride and the groom will please join hands, we will begin."

Oggie grunted a little as he readjusted himself on his crutches so he could stick out a hand. Eden took it.

"Dearly beloved," Reverend Johnson began.

And all hell broke loose.

The big doors at the back of the church were suddenly flung wide.

The guests begun murmuring.

"What the—"

"Who is it?"

"It can't be—"

"It is!"

Eden turned, hope, fear and finally blazing joy searing their way through every inch of her body.

Oggie tossed back his head and crowed with glee, then announced, "You had me a little worried there, boy!"

But Jared didn't hear him. He was looking at Eden. He marched up the aisle and stepped between the bride and groom.

With slow, careful fingers, he lifted Eden's veil. She saw that his eyes were clear. His breath was sweet on her up-turned face.

"You're the most beautiful thing I've ever seen in my life," he said softly. "And I spent way too much money on this damn suit."

She glanced down and saw that he was, indeed, dressed like a man might dress on his wedding day. She opened her mouth to tell him she thought it was a fine suit and that he looked splendid in it. But somehow, no sound would come out.

It was okay, though, because he had more to say.

"I thought about what you told me, when you found me at my uncle's cabin. And I decided every last word was true." His voice was grim, but his gray eyes were shining. "You're the woman I've been looking for all my life. And if you're so damned sure it's not too late for us, then who am I to say different? I love you. And I suppose I'll have to marry you, to save you from my dad."

Eden opened her mouth again. But for once in her life she found she really was totally speechless. She stared up at him, still not fully daring to believe that he had really come, that he was truly here.

She *had* known it would happen. She had not allowed herself to even imagine that he would not come for her. But still, it overwhelmed her, that he was actually here. That he was smiling at her with all the love she'd always known was in him gleaming in his silver eyes.

Jared looked worried. "Honey? Are you okay?"

She nodded.

"And will you marry me?"

She nodded once more.

He glanced at his father. "Step aside, old man."

"You betcha." Oggie braced his crutches up under him and stomped to the first row on the groom's side, where Patrick got up and gave him his seat.

Jared turned to Pastor Johnson. "Okay, Reverend, get on with it."

Pastor Johnson coughed and clutched his bible against his chest. "Er, Mr. Jones, this is highly irregular."

"Do it anyway, Reverend!" Rocky Collins shouted from a middle pew.

"Yeah, for Pete's sake, yer worship," someone else said, "don't mess things up now."

The ripple of agreement rolled over the packed church.

"Yeah, marry them!"

"It's how it's supposed to be!"

"Do it!"

"Yeah, do it now!"

The reverend cast a nervous glance around the room and came to the decision that a volatile crowd like this should probably be appeased.

He opened his bible.

A prayerful hush swept the chapel into instant silence. Jared tenderly smoothed down Eden's veil and took her hand in his. They turned to the minister and the ceremony began.

At the end, Eden barely managed to whisper, "I do."

Jared's voice, however, was firm and clear as he promised to love, honor and cherish Eden Parker for the rest of their lives.

Epilogue

It was remarked in later years that there was never a man so changed as Jared Jones, after the day he stole Eden Parker from his own father. From that day, Jared went through life with a smile on his rugged face and a good word for everyone on his lips.

Oggie Jones smiled a lot, too. He'd gone to great lengths to see Jared hooked up with Eden. After all, for a man to point a 30-30 at his own foot and pull the trigger on purpose takes more than a little grit. Not to mention the fact that he'd nearly had to marry Jared's bride himself.

But even though Oggie's old flesh healed slowly and there were some in town who smirked that he'd been jilted at the altar, Oggie was content. At last, he could retire. And he knew that in heaven, his beautiful Bathsheba was smiling.

Hell, the real truth was, he'd do it all again in a New York minute if it meant another one of his children would find true love at last.

*　*　*　*　*

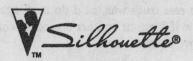

WILD RIVER

by
Laurie Paige

Maddening men...winsome women...and the untamed land they live in—
all add up to love! Meet them in these books from Silhouette Special Edition
and Silhouette Romance:

WILD IS THE WIND (Silhouette Special Edition #887, May)
Rafe Barrett retreated to his mountain resort to escape his dangerous feelings
for Genny McBride...but when she returned, ready to pick up where they
left off, would Rafe throw caution to the wind?

A ROGUE'S HEART (Silhouette Romance #1013, June)
Returning to his boyhood home brought Gabe Deveraux face-to-face
with ghosts of the past—and directly into the arms of sweet and loving
Whitney Campbell....

A RIVER TO CROSS (Silhouette Special Edition #910, September)
Sheriff Shane Macklin knew there was more to "town outsider"
Tina Henderson than met the eye. He saw a generous and selfless woman
whose true colors held the promise of love....

Don't miss these latest Wild River tales from Silhouette Special Edition
and Silhouette Romance!

MILLION DOLLAR SWEEPSTAKES (III)

No purchase necessary. To enter, follow the directions published. Method of entry may vary. For eligibility, entries must be received no later than March 31, 1996. No liability is assumed for printing errors, lost, late or misdirected entries. Odds of winning are determined by the number of eligible entries distributed and received. Prizewinners will be determined no later than June 30, 1996.

Sweepstakes open to residents of the U.S. (except Puerto Rico), Canada, Europe and Taiwan who are 18 years of age or older. All applicable laws and regulations apply. Sweepstakes offer void wherever prohibited by law. Values of all prizes are in U.S. currency. This sweepstakes is presented by Torstar Corp., its subsidiaries and affiliates, in conjunction with book, merchandise and/or product offerings. For a copy of the Official Rules send a self-addressed, stamped envelope (WA residents need not affix return postage) to: MILLION DOLLAR SWEEPSTAKES (III) Rules, P.O. Box 4573, Blair, NE 68009, USA.

EXTRA BONUS PRIZE DRAWING

No purchase necessary. The Extra Bonus Prize will be awarded in a random drawing to be conducted no later than 5/30/96 from among all entries received. To qualify, entries must be received by 3/31/96 and comply with published directions. Drawing open to residents of the U.S. (except Puerto Rico), Canada, Europe and Taiwan who are 18 years of age or older. All applicable laws and regulations apply; offer void wherever prohibited by law. Odds of winning are dependent upon number of eligible entries received. Prize is valued in U.S. currency. The offer is presented by Torstar Corp., its subsidiaries and affiliates in conjunction with book, merchandise and/or product offering. For a copy of the Official Rules governing this sweepstakes, send a self-addressed, stamped envelope (WA residents need not affix return postage) to: Extra Bonus Prize Drawing Rules, P.O. Box 4590, Blair, NE 68009, USA.

SWP-S594

Silhouette
SPECIAL EDITION
TM

MEN OF COURAGE

COUNTDOWN
Lindsay McKenna

Sergeant Joe Donnally knew being a marine meant putting lives on the line—and after a tragic loss, he vowed never to love again. Yet here was Annie Yellow Horse, the passionate, determined woman who challenged him to feel long-dormant emotions. But Joe had to conquer past demons before declaring his love....

MEN OF COURAGE

It's a special breed of men who defy death and fight for right! Salute their bravery while sharing their lives and loves!

These are courageous men you'll love and tender stories you'll cherish...available in June, only from Silhouette Special Edition!

IT'S OUR 1000TH SILHOUETTE ROMANCE, AND WE'RE CELEBRATING!

JOIN US FOR A SPECIAL COLLECTION OF LOVE STORIES BY AUTHORS YOU'VE LOVED FOR YEARS, AND NEW FAVORITES YOU'VE JUST DISCOVERED. JOIN THE CELEBRATION...

April
REGAN'S PRIDE by **Diana Palmer**
MARRY ME AGAIN by **Suzanne Carey**

May
THE BEST IS YET TO BE by **Tracy Sinclair**
CAUTION: BABY AHEAD by **Marie Ferrarella**

June
THE BACHELOR PRINCE by **Debbie Macomber**
A ROGUE'S HEART by **Laurie Paige**

July
IMPROMPTU BRIDE by **Annette Broadrick**
THE FORGOTTEN HUSBAND by **Elizabeth August**

SILHOUETTE ROMANCE...VIBRANT, FUN AND EMOTIONALLY RICH! TAKE ANOTHER LOOK AT US! AND AS PART OF THE CELEBRATION, READERS CAN RECEIVE A FREE GIFT!

YOU'LL FALL IN LOVE ALL OVER AGAIN WITH SILHOUETTE ROMANCE!

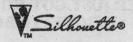

CEL1000